Out on the Wild Frontier

Frontier

Gary Jon Anderson

Many people equate courage to a lack of fear, which is not the case. Courage, *true courage* is when you are so afraid that every fiber of your being wants to turn and run away. The fear is almost palpable, your tongue clings to the roof of your mouth and there is nothing for you to swallow. But instead of giving into your fears, you face your enemy and do the job that is set before you. Others are depending upon you and you *choose* not to let them down. You fight the good fight in spite of your fears. *You fight the good fight.*

CHAPTER ONE

"Would you marry me?"

Eli Exeter was holding his breath and he didn't even realize it as he waited to see what her response would be.

"I am very flattered, thank you, but I can't marry you. I don't love you, so I could not possibly marry you." She smiled sweetly at the man who was on one knee in front of her. Many of these western men spent their time herding cows or mining and as a result had not seen a single woman in a long, long time and though she didn't really recognized the fact, Elizabeth Franco was an extremely pretty woman. The scar that was left on her face from a stray bullet only succeeded in giving her a mysterious look and drew men's attention to her large, beautiful brown eyes. Coupled with the ability to make the finest donuts, pastries and cakes around, it was no wonder that she was getting so many proposals.

Eli released his breath with a large sigh of relief.

Elizabeth Franco looked down at the young man. The bakery was full of men, who were watching in amusement as the scene unfolded. Elizabeth received two or three proposals a month and she was becoming an old hand at handling them.

The man, still on one knee, reached into his pocket and produced a ring with a diamond sparkling on top of it. Elizabeth's hand flew up to cover her mouth as she gasped at the sight of it.

"Ma'am, I struck it rich and I promise you that I will take good care of you. I'll build you the biggest, nicest house in town and buy you the most purtyest dresses you ever saw."

This one was more persistent than most. Elizabeth tore her eyes away from the diamond and beckoned him to his feet.

"Please understand, when I marry again, there are only two things that I require. First, I will only marry a man that I truly love. Second, and most importantly, he has to love Jesus more than life itself." She continued on, "money is only good for a season, and I have seen men make money and lose money. If you live your life chasing after money, you are only living a shell of a life. If you live your life chasing after Jesus, then you have a fulfilled life. I will always choose the fulfilled life."

She watched as the man walked out the door, momentarily dejected by her rebuff, but she was confident that he would have no trouble finding a woman who would be willing to wear that diamond ring on her finger.

The rest of the men in the Café returned to their conversations, coffee and food. Elizabeth returned back behind the counter, giving herself a buffer between her and the customers.

Eli Exeter and Steven Bosco were seated at one of the tables in the farthest corner of the room where they could have some semblance of privacy. Steven had watched Eli's face during the exchange and was amused yet at the same time, he felt sorry for his friend. Emotions of jealousy, fear and desire had all played across Eli's countenance, but he did not even realize they were there.

Steven looked across the table at his friend and mentor. "You know that if you don't make your move soon, one of these days she's going to accept one of these proposals and you'll have lost her forever."

Eli looked at Steven like he had lost his mind. "I don't have a clue what you are talking about."

Steven shook his head. "All you would have to do is say the word and that woman would drop everything for you. She would marry you in a heartbeat."

Eli leaned closer and dropped his voice. "Steven, you're loco. I'm sure she doesn't give a hoot about me."

Steven shook his head. "For a man who is wise about so many things, you're down right stupid when it comes to love. You mark my words".

Eli chose not to respond, but his mind was a whirl. He did have feelings for Elizabeth, but he felt so confused. After his wife died several years ago, the thought of remarrying was out of the question. But now…

Steven stood up. "I have to get back to work." He paused as he placed his hand on Eli's shoulder, "don't let her get away." He walked back behind the counter into the store room of the bakery where he worked.

Eli stayed where he was seated, nursing the cup of coffee and pondering what Steven had said. He was lost in thought and did not even hear the rustle of a skirt behind him. "Can I refill your coffee for you?" Elizabeth asked.

Startled out of his reverie, Eli nearly dumped the remaining coffee in his cup down the front of his shirt. "Yes, please." He set the cup down and she filled it with steaming hot coffee from the pot that she was holding.

"There you are, is there anything else that I can get you?" She asked.

"Do you have time to sit down for a moment?" He asked then started to feel panic well up inside of him. What if she said yes, what then?

Elizabeth turned and looked around the room to make sure her other clientele was taken care of before answering. "Thank you. I would love to spend a moment with you." She took a clean cup from a nearby shelf and poured herself a cup of coffee then sat down across the table from him.

She continued, "I am so thankful to get off my feet for a few minutes, but enough about me, how are you doing?" She turned her full attention to him and it made him tingle when she looked at him with those large brown doe eyes. He felt like he could stare into them all day.

Suddenly he realized that he was staring and he could feel the color creeping up his neck. He cleared his throat, "Well, um, I, um..."

Elizabeth looked at him curiously. "Is everything alright?"

Before he could answer, the report of a pistol shattered the peaceful afternoon as well as the window of the café. Even as they were showered with broken glass, Eli dove out of his chair and swept Elizabeth out of hers, dragging her to the ground and shielding her with his body. Everyone else in the café hit the floor as well. In a society raised around firearms, no one was foolish enough to stand up and look.

Eli had instinctively drawn his pistol while he sheltered Elizabeth from harm. Now he raised himself up off the floor and moved cautiously to one side of the broken window. Looking out, he did not see any sign of the shooter. He dropped his head below the level of the window sill and moved around the table to the other side of the window where he could peer down the street in the opposite direction. Still there was nothing out there he could see. Puzzled as to why someone would shoot out the window of the bakery, but satisfied that the danger had passed, he turned his attention back to Elizabeth.

"Are you alright? I am so sorry, I hope I didn't hurt you."

Eli gave her his hand and Elizabeth let him help her to her feet. She let go of his hand and shook the glass from her skirt. In a shaky voice she answered, "I think I'm alright, but what a mess." She removed the pin that held her hair in place and bent over to shake more glass from her hair. When she straightened up a cascade of raven black hair fell down over her shoulders. Eli was shocked by the transformation that had occurred. The pretty woman before him had just morphed into a stunning beauty.

Everyone else was getting up and dusting off. It appeared that the only damage was a shattered coffee cup on the floor and the broken window above the table. All at once, Elizabeth grabbed Eli's hand and stifled a cry of dismay. "You're hurt."

Eli looked down at the back of his hand and broke into a big grin. Across the back of his hand was a small cut with a trickle of blood running out of it and dripping on the floor.

"You sit down right there while I take care of it," she ordered. Sheepishly he complied, picking up the chair that he knocked over and sitting in it. He held his hand in such a way as to keep the blood from dripping on the floor, but he also cupped his other hand underneath to catch any that was determined to fall.

Elizabeth hustled to the back room, returning with some supplies, trailed by Steven who was carrying a broom. Eli caught a glimpse of his friend and watched as the look of concern turned to a smirk when he saw the injury, or lack thereof that Elizabeth was fussing over. Once again, Eli could feel the blush climbing up his neck, but the look that he gave Steven over the top of Elizabeth's head made it clear that he was not pleased with his friend's amusement.

Elizabeth washed the blood off the back of his hand and covered the scratch with a piece of cloth. "You keep this on for a couple of days. You don't want this to get infected." She tied another piece around his hand to hold the first one in place.

Steven was doing his best to hold the laughter in and the harder he tried the redder Eli felt his face getting. When it finally appeared that Steven was going to bust out laughing, he spun on his heel and nearly ran into the back room. Eli heard the sound of his loud laughter just as the door slammed shut.

Elizabeth looked up. "I wonder what has gotten into him?" She queried. She looked at Eli's red face and asked, "are you alright? What's wrong?"

Eli looked down at the floor, trying to figure out how to explain the issue without making her feel bad. Finally he took a deep breath and dove in, "Ma'am, I'm just not accustomed to someone fussing over me like you've done. I really appreciate your concern but I," he lowered his voice even more so Elizabeth was the only one who would hear, "haven't had a woman show this much compassion to me since my wife died."

The smile she gave him made him feel giddy like a school boy with a crush. "Mr. Exeter, I care very much about you. Please don't be embarrassed." Now it was her turn to feel the color rise into her cheeks and quickly she changed the subject. "Well, I need to tend to my other clients." She turned away so he could not see the blush in her face.

With the sound of laughing still coming from the other side of the closed door, Eli made his exit before anything else that was embarrassing could happen.

Eli removed the bandage as soon as he got outside, stuffing it into his pocket. His face had returned to its normal shade of brown as he took stock of the street. He should have been out here trying to find the culprit who shot out the window instead of sitting in there like a love sick fool. He should have never let Steven put those silly notions into his head. He shook his head as if to remove the feelings, but he remembered those eyes and the long shiny hair. The touch of her hand and the concern in her voice made him feel something he had not felt in a long time.

Eli considered what he had to offer a woman, and it was not much. He had a couple of horses, a mule, and several guns to his name, but aside from that he had nothing in the way of worldly goods. His residence was a church parsonage and he was a part time preacher, in the business of saving souls and a part time bar keep in order to make a dollar or two. It's just not the kind of life that you ask someone to share with you.

* * *

As soon as her customers were taken care of, Elizabeth went into the kitchen to collect herself and gather her thoughts. She put her hair up in a bun once again and smoothed out her blouse and skirt. Mentally she chastised herself for being so forward with Eli. She was sure that she had chased him off with that little display. She didn't understand it. How is it that she could get multiple proposals from strangers, but the one man whom she really cared about didn't even seem to want to talk to her? She felt the tears welling up and she bit her lip to keep them from flowing over. She had made a complete fool of herself once today and she didn't want to go back out into the café looking foolish again. But she had customers to take care of, so she dabbed the tears from her eyes with the corner of her apron and took a couple of deep breaths. With a forced smile, she returned to the main room and the remaining patrons.

* * *

Eli walked along the boardwalk in the shadows. After years of being a lawman old habits die hard and he was always cognizant of everyone and everything around him. Being in the shadows allowed him to see without sun glare in his eyes and he was much closer to cover if things went awry. Every person he passed along the street was noted and cataloged. They were either a friend, a foe, a potential danger or they posed no risk, though that category tended to be very small. Eli fully subscribed to the biblical thought that the hearts of all men are evil, evidenced by the amount of wicked people he had dealt with in his years as a sheriff. Yet he still was encouraged by what he saw in those who changed their lives as they turned them over to Jesus.

He arrived at the Sheriff's Office, and knocked on the door, still watching things around him. When he was bid to enter, he slipped through the door and at the same time allowed his guard to ease up. Seated behind the desk was his friend and Sheriff of the town, Matt Wheaton. Matt's face lit up as soon as he recognized his friend. The front legs of the chair he was leaning back in hit the floor as he stood up to greet one of his only confidants. He stood and grasped Eli's hand before motioning him to a chair.

"How are you doing?" he asked of Eli.

Eli gave him a lopsided grin. "Oh, I've had better days, but I can't complain."

Matt looked at him curiously. "What's going on?"

"Well, I made a fool of myself with Elizabeth Franco just now." He would not have shared this with anyone aside from Matt and Steven, but since Steven was already aware…and had laughed at him…he needed to unload his burden on someone who was already married, who might understand.

"What happened?"

Eli related the events of the last few minutes but quickly realized that he might not get any sympathy from Matt when a smirk began to spread across the sheriff's face. Realizing the futility of sharing with the younger man, he switched tactics. "So you now have the crime of someone shooting out the window of the café. You might get over there to investigate."

Matt wiped the grin off his face. "Yeah, I will do that as soon as I can. Right now, I have a more pressing matter. In fact, I'm glad you're here. I have a missing person that was reported to me and I would love to get your advice."

It was Eli's turn to smirk. "I thought you were afraid that I would try to steal your job?"

Matt nodded in concession. "Once again, I deserve that." During one of their first meetings nearly a year ago, Matt had accused Eli of that very thing. "But I'm stumped and would love your perspective on this matter."

Eli could never hold his friend's feet over the fire for very long and he dropped the act of indignation. "How can I help?"

"A message from Inga Swensen came in today reporting that her husband never came home last night. She told me that he came to town yesterday morning for supplies and never returned. Eli, Norris Swensen is a hard working farmer with a small dairy herd. He's probably the most reliable person I know. I've asked around town, but no one seems to know anything."

Eli asked, "I assume he went to one of the general stores for supplies?"

Matt nodded, "Yeah, the Mercantile nearest the office here."

"Did the clerk see where he went after that?"

This time Matt shook his head. "No, he started waiting on another customer right after he helped Norris load his wagon, so as far as I can tell, he's the last one to see Swensen."

"What about tracks? Did you check for wagon tracks?"

"There are too many," Matt replied. "The road out of town towards the Swensen place is too well traveled."

"Did you go out to the cutoff toward his farm? There can't be that many people traveling that road. In fact, if I remember correctly, their farm is the only one out there after you leave the main road. There should only be two sets of tracks, one coming and one going."

"Thanks." Matt shook his head. "That's so simple, I can't believe I overlooked it."

"Sometimes, that's the benefit of running things by someone else." Eli grinned, "but if you keep this up, I may have to run against you next election."

"There are days that I would be glad to let you have this job." Matt shot back at him. Over the last year or so that he had gotten to know Eli and his respect for the man and his mission had grown by leaps and bounds. The light hearted ribbing that they gave each other masked the intense bond between the two men, who had gone through much hardship together in that short time.

"Is there anything that I can do to help you?" Eli was now very sincere in his offer.

"Can you look into the shooting of Widow Franco's café window for me?" Matt ventured.

Eli smiled. "I'll look into it as long as you never repeat what I told you earlier."

Matt grinned back. "It's a deal."

CHAPTER TWO

It did not take long for Matt to reach the fork in the road that lead to the Swensen's spread. When he took the turn off, he rode off to the side of the road to keep from disturbing any evidence. He looked for tracks of the returning wagon, but it did not take long to realize that there were none. He rode out to the farm house and was able to ascertain that the tracks he saw going to town were indeed coming from the missing man's place.

As he rode up to the house, the front door swung open and an attractive woman with a trim figure and ivory skin was framed in the opening. Matt wasn't sure but he estimated her age around thirty five, maybe younger. As he swung down off the horse, Inga Swensen asked, "Sheriff, ave you found out anythin about my Norris?" Her Swedish accent made her difficult to understand, but Matt knew what she was concerned about and therefore was able to decipher the request.

"No ma'am. I rode out to see if Norris made the turn from the main trail onto your road, but it appears that he did not. I'm hoping that you might remember something…anything that might assist me in my search for him."

Inga shook her head, "Der is nothin I can remember. He vas alvays so…" she searched her mind for the intended word, "…punctual."

Matt gently prodded her, "Please, can you tell me again what happened leading up to his disappearance?"

She replied, "Yes, but der is not much to tell. Norris alvays vent into town on every other Monday to get supplies. He left at day break and vas alvays home by supper."

"Was he carrying a lot of money?" Matt queried.

"Just enough to pay vhat ve owed at the Mercantile and purchase supplies. He just sold a hog last veek." She said in way of explanation.

12

Matt made a mental note to check with the owner of the mercantile to see if he paid the bill. "Ma'am, is there anything else, anything at all? Did Norris drink or gamble?"

"No, no," came the emphatic reply, "He no longer drank, and he never played cards."

"No longer? Did he used to drink?" Matt pried.

"Before ve vere married he vould but I made him stop before I vould marry him."

Something about the reply made the next question come to mind, "Did you and Norris argue recently?"

Inga did not answer, but her body language and down cast gaze gave Matt the answer. "What did you argue about?"

Inga hesitated, but Matt persisted. "This may be important for me to help locate him. I promise I will not tell anyone else what you share with me."

"I vanted to use some of the money from the hog to buy cloth for curtains and Norris did not think that it vas necessary. I miss some of the fine things that ve no longer have now that ve live out here."

"Was Norris angry with you when he rode into town?"

"No, no. He vas fine vhen he left."

Matt pondered that for a moment, wondering if the man was truly fine as he began his journey.

"Tell me about the wagon and horses. What kind of horses were they?"

Inga replied, "I don't know."

Matt prodded her, "Were they quarter horses, draft horses or mustangs?"

She shook her head. "I don't know," she insisted, "they vere brown."

"And the wagon?"

"It vas a buckboard. Just a vooden buckboard."

Matt was disappointed. Many of these western women knew as much about their horses and the equipment as the men. Unfortunately, Inga did not appear to be one of these.

"What is your brand?" He was going to get something. At least something more than 'brown horses.'

"Ve have the Slash Bar S, but these horse, Norris just bought. I don't know vhat brand they had."

Matt sighed. He didn't have any more questions, but he wondered if he was missing something. Anything. He thanked Inga for her time and threw his leg up over his horse. He tipped his hat to the woman before he rode away.

On the ride back into town, he considered what he had gleaned from Mrs. Swensen. She had made Norris stop drinking before they were married. He questioned if she was the kind of woman who was bossy and overbearing. He did not know them well and he wondered how long they had been married. He knew that they did not have any children, whether that was by design or circumstance, he had no idea. Norris was at least forty years old but was well built and muscular, a result of all of the heavy work that he did. Norris and Inga were a striking couple, both of them with blond hair and blue eyes. Matt was not really a good judge of how handsome other men were, but he supposed that Norris would be considered good looking, at least by the women.

Matt wondered about the timing of his trips to town. It was about an hour and a half wagon ride in, so that was three hours of travel time. If you gave him an hour or two to buy and load supplies, that was a total of five hours. That gave Norris several hours to kill, several unexplained hours and he wondered if Inga had ever calculated it out? What else was Norris up to?

* * *

True to his word, Eli went back to the neighborhood of Widow Franco's bakery. He wanted to go back inside and figure out where the bullet ended up, but the memory of Steven's laughter caused him to hesitate. He decided that it could wait for now. Instead he began to canvas the neighborhood, looking for any witnesses.

It was at the seventh and last business that he struck pay dirt.

Joe Tubbs ran a small lumber yard and hardware store several doors down and across the street from the bakery. Eli stepped through the door to a cheerful greeting.

"Well, if it ain't the gun-totin preacher," he roared, "What can I do you for today?"

"You didn't come to church Sunday, so I came by to see what your excuse was again Joe."

That brought a hearty laugh from the merchant.

It was almost a weekly ritual. Joe was the town atheist, denying the existence of God and willing to let everyone know it. He had taken a liking to Eli though, probably because he did not look and act like any other preacher he'd ever known. Eli dressed like a cowboy and wore his gun around town. He tended bar during the week and the saloon was his church building on Sunday, though he had expanded his congregation last year and now preached twice every Sunday.

His earlier service was now held at the local church building and was for families and the women and men of the town who were not comfortable with going to a church in the saloon. His later service was more of an outreach to the men and women on the other side of the tracks. He would serve drinks then close down the bar for fifteen or twenty minutes while he spoke to the men and women out of God's word. When he was done, he returned to serving drinks until Sam came in for the afternoon shift.

Eli changed tack, "I'm trying to get to the bottom of a shooting this morning. Someone shot out the window of the bakery and nearly struck the proprietor." He left out the information on his scratch and the ensuing debacle.

Joe nodded, "Yeah I heard the shot and at first I ducked. When I did look out, I saw Jeff Simpson running down the road like someone lit his tail on fire. I didn't see no gun, but he was the only one out on the street. I'll let you put two and two together."

Eli grinned. "Thanks Joe. If that boy wasn't involved, maybe he saw who did it." Eli pointed a finger at Joe, "I expect to see you in church on Sunday."

Once again, Joe burst out with his grand laugh. "I'll tell you what, you get Kelly Guiness to go to your church and I promise you, I'll come too."

Still smiling, Eli nodded. "Okay, you better be planning on coming soon then."

* * *

Eli found Jeff on the front stoop of the house that he shared with his parents. At eleven years old, the boy was a fixture about town. His pa was a part time handy man and a full time drunk. A mighty mean drunk. His ma was a mousy little woman who worked hard at mending clothes and doing tailoring projects for people. The couple barely squeaked by after the liquor was bought.

Left much of the time to his own devices the boy was always underfoot of someone or other in town whether it be for better or for worse. He tended to get into mischief and even though Eli had never had dealing with him, his reputation had preceded him.

The boy was whittling a stick, looking rather subdued, which in and of itself was a clue.

Eli stepped through the front gate which had a broken lower hinge and had to be lifted up to swing in so it was left in the permanently open position. He stood in front of the boy who continued his whittling without looking up.

"May I sit down?"

The boy did not look up. "Don't care. Do whatever you want."

Eli reached down, picked up another stick off the ground and sat down on the opposite side of the dilapidated staircase from Jeff. He lifted his pant leg and removed a hunting knife from his boot and began to whittle the stick that he had picked up.

After a few moments, he broke the silence. "Do you know who I am?"

Without stopping his destruction of the stick the kid replied, "yup."

"Oh?" Eli was quite surprised.

"You the preacher who shot up them there outlaws a while back," the boy responded.

Eli silently whittled away at his stick for a minute or two. "Do you know what I did before I was a preacher?"

"Yup, you'zz a lawman."

Once again the two lapsed into a long period of silence, carving away at their respective sticks. Eli broke the silence.

"Once when I was a young boy, oh maybe a little younger than you are now, I had my pa's rifle." He paused before continuing, watching the boy's reaction out of the corner of his eye. "I wasn't supposed to touch that gun unless my pa was with me. Well, I accidently shot this young pig that we had bought from a neighbor. I was walking with my finger on the trigger and well…" He saw Jeff stop whittling, even though he would not look his way. "My dad wasn't home, but I knew that he would find that pig was dead when he returned. So I carefully cleaned the rifle and reloaded the round I had fired. I worked hard on a story to tell my pa when he got home. All day long, I mulled over what I was going to tell him, working on the perfect lie so that I would not get into trouble."

He stopped the story and continued to work on his stick. Finally the boy turned his attention to Eli. "What happened?"

"My pa came home that night and asked if I had slopped the hog. I started to tell him my story, the story that I made up, but I couldn't. Instead, I told him what really happened."

"What did he do?"

"He didn't say a word, he just lit a lantern and went out to check on the pig. He discovered that the bullet had only caused a cut across the top of the pig's head. He washed it off and was able to nurse that pig back to health. We eventually butchered that hog and ate the meat from him for what seemed like a whole year."

"What happened to you?"

"Oh, I got into trouble for messing with my dad's rifle, but he explained to me that he would have made my punishment far greater had I tried to lie to him. It was a lesson that I never forgot."

"My pa would kill me if'n I ever did anything like that." The look on Jeff's face confirmed that he really believed what he was saying.

"A man, a real man, has to take responsibility for what they've done." Eli carefully considered his next words, "Even if it means going to the person that they have wronged and making amends for their actions…maybe working off the damage they have done. Only a kid or a coward would try to shirk their responsibility."

"I ain't no coward!" Jeff replied defensively.

"I never figured you were," Eli responded.

Jeff paused a moment. "If it were you, what would you do?"

"I'd go to the Widow Franco and ask her if there are any chores that you can do to work off the damage to her window." Eli replied. He stood up and walked toward the gate. He stopped when the boy called out.

"You ain't going to tell my pa?"

"Don't seem necessary if you take care of your responsibility. Does it?"

"No sir." Jeff answered while his face brightened considerably. "Thanks."

Eli winked at him, paused to shove the knife down into its sheath and covered it with his pant leg. He would check with the Widow Franco later to see if the boy followed through.

CHAPTER THREE

Becky Wheaton glanced out the window when she heard the horse. She turned back to the stove when she saw that it was Joshua returning from school. She estimated that it would take about twenty minutes before he came inside as he always took care of his horse. She stirred the supper then moved over to the side board. She put out some milk and a piece of fresh apple pie on the table.

Joshua had come to live with them last year, after a notorious gunman had left him fatherless and his mother had died. The transition had been rough, but Becky had come to love the young man like her own son. With her husband being the sheriff and often called to work long and odd hours, having someone around to take care of was a blessing. She relished the role of being a mother, even if he wasn't her real son and it gave her a feeling of worth that was unexplainable.

The door opened and Becky turned toward it, "how was your day?"

"Okay." Joshua spied the snack and made a beeline toward the table.

"Well tell me about it." Every day she had to pry the story of his day out of him but she had the patience of Job.

"Not much to tell." Joshua spoke between bites of pie.

"What subjects did you cover in class today?"

"Readin, writin and 'rithmatic."

Becky reached over and pull the plate with the unfinished pie out from under his poised fork. "If you want to finish this, you better start talking."

With a deep sigh, the teen set the fork down. "I had to read out loud today and I couldn't 'cipher some of the words and I got a "D" on my spelling test. I ain't never gonna to do no good in readin' and writin'," he announced.

Becky raised her eyebrow at this proclamation.

"And I got a hundred percent on my math test."

"Joshua, that's wonderful." Her delight was apparent.

"Can I finish my pie now?" he asked.

"Yes you may." Becky pushed the plate back across the table.

He plowed into it quickly, before she could take it away again. She always fussed over his day at school, and though he would never admit it out loud, he liked the fact that she actually cared.

Becky walked over to the stove and poured herself a cup of coffee, then returned to the table.

"I think that we need to prove your self-prophecy wrong," she proclaimed.

"Ma'am?"

"I think that you can improve your spelling skill quite quickly."

"How?" Joshua was wary. This sounded like work, not that he was lazy. He never minded doing his chores and even was willing to do extra. Since he had come to live with the Wheaton's he made sure to earn his keep. But this sounded like doing more school work, even more than the teacher had already assigned for him to do at home.

Becky suppressed her smile for she could almost see the wheels turning in his head. "One of the best ways to learn to spell words is to read." She went on to explain, "The easiest way to figure out how a word is spelled is to see it written out on a page and to say it out loud." She added, "it's a lot easier than having you spell out a word one hundred times on the black board at school."

He shuddered at the thought of doing that again.

"Well if you are done with your pie, why don't you head out and do your chores." Becky reached over and picked up the dishes from in front of him.

Joshua wiped his mouth with the sleeve of his shirt. "Yes ma'am."

Becky sighed in exasperation. With hands resting on her hips she exclaimed, "how many times have I told you not to wipe your mouth on your shirt?"

"Too many, ma'am." Joshua was already headed toward the front door.

Becky just shook her head as she watched him go.

* * *

Matt headed toward The Saloon. Several times he had suggested to Sam that he change the name, but the same old sign still hung over the door. He stepped into the front alcove and let his eyes adjust before stepping through the batwing doors.

Inside, the sheriff made careful study of everyone inside the bar before he walked across the floor. The only thing out of place was the stranger at the table in the corner. He was seated so he could watch the door and still have a view of the entire room. Matt also noted that the man had on a single pistol, strapped down on his right thigh. His left hand held a glass of whiskey while his right hand nonchalantly rested in his lap, inches from the handle of his pistol.

He stepped up to the bar, standing at the end so he could keep the man in his vision. Sam carried a beer over and set it down in front of him.

"Thanks." He fished a nickel out of his vest pocket and tossed it on the bar. "So who is the wannabe gunslinger over there?" He did not gesture but Sam knew exactly who he was talking about.

Sam slid the nickel toward himself and dropped it into the palm of his other hand which was under the edge of the bar. "No idea. He paid for his bottle and hasn't said a word since."

Matt nodded, "well that will have to wait. The reason I came in is because I am trying to find information on Norris Swensen. Do you know who he is?"

"I've met him a time or two, why? Did he do something?"

"He didn't show up at home last night. Was he in here yesterday?"

"No sir. He has never been in The Saloon when I've been working here and I worked yesterday cuz it was Eli's day off."

"Thanks, Sam." Out of the corner of his eye, he saw the gunman stand up. "Sam, are these barrels holding up the bar empty?" He slipped the thong off the hammer of his gun.

"No, they're filled to the top with sand so they don't move around, why?"

The gunslinger was slowly coming his way. "I just wanted to know if they would stop a bullet."

The young man sidled up to the bar near Matt. His clothes were dirty with more than just trail dust and no sooner did he lean on bar beside him and Matt could smell the stench of body odor. He stepped back slightly, hoping for a whiff of fresh air.

"Sheriff," Matt estimated him to be no more than eighteen, "I understand that the man who killed Rob Handy lives in this here town."

Matt looked at the younger man with a steady gaze. "Well, you understand wrong."

The youngster grinned at him with crooked, yellow teeth. "Really 'cause that ain't what I heared. I think yur trying to protect this man. Why?"

"I do believe you just called me a liar. Words like that can get you killed around here." Matt's steely gaze remained steady, unwavering.

"Is he here or ain't he?" The smile had been replaced by an angry snarl and his hand lifted slightly so it was poised near the handle of his six shooter.

The slap started from the thigh. As Matt swung his hand he pivoted at the waist so the entire weight of his body was behind it when the open palm struck the man's face. The blow spun the gunman half way around. Stunned and angry, it took him a second to realize what happen. With a roar he started to grab for his gun when a bullet hit the top of the barrel next to him, spilling out sand on the floor.

Elijah Exeter stood in the doorway of the saloon, his gun poised for a second shot if necessary, but the gunman let his hand drop when he realized he was flanked and out gunned. Matt reached over with his left hand, removed the man's pistol from its holster and slid it down the bar to Sam. While Eli covered him across the room, Matt searched and located a second gun tucked into his waistband behind his coat and a bowie knife on his belt. Both were delivered to Sam in the same way as the first one. Once he had been disarmed, Matt pushed him back into a nearby chair.

The gunslinger ear was still ringing from the blow and the left side of his face had turned beet red. He was going to have quite a bruise in the near future.

Matt locked eyes with him until the young man dropped his gaze. "You ride out of town. Don't ever come back because if you do, I'm going to assume it is for the purpose of shooting me and I will shoot you on sight. Do I make myself clear?"

"What about my guns?" the man demanded.

A smile played around the corner of Matt's lips. "I'm going to ship them to the Sheriff in San Francisco. You can pick them up there. Now," He paused and then yelled, "*GET OUT OF HERE!*"

Startled, the man scrambled to his feet and knocked over a chair as he sprinted for the door.

Chuckling, Matt and Eli stepped to the bar together.

Sam walked down the bar to them but before he handed the weapons to Matt he asked, "you hit him because he called you a liar, right?"

Matt immediately knew where this was going. "That and I didn't want him to have a chance to draw his gun."

"But you know where the killer of Handy is, so didn't you actually lie to him?" Sam wasn't trying to play the devil's advocate. He was truly curious.

This time the sheriff did smile. "Nope. He asked where the man was. Joshua is still just a boy and I plan on giving him the chance to be a boy and not have the course of his life dictated by some snot nosed punk out to make a reputation for himself." He turned to Eli, "by the way, how could you have missed him?"

Eli smirked, "I wasn't aiming for him. I was aiming for the barrel." The smirk was wiped off his face as he glanced into the mirror behind the bar.

* * *

Joshua finished his chores and headed back into the house, wondering what Mrs. Wheaton had up her sleeve. It had been about a year ago when the Wheaton's had taken him in. Mrs. Wheaton cared for him like he was her own son. Matt treated him almost like he was an equal, although he could come down like a ton of bricks when he had too. Joshua tried to make sure that rarely happened, but he really liked them both and more than that, he respected them. Neither of them ever made an issue out of the outlaw that he had killed, for the man had shot and killed his own father. After his mother died, he hunted the man down and killed him. He still had nightmares about the shooting, waking up in a cold sweat. Mrs. Wheaton was always there to comfort him when that happened.

He walked through the front door and there on the table were two Bibles. One was positioned at his place at the table and they both were laying open.

"I figured that each day we are going to read a chapter of the Bible together," Becky spoke before he had a chance to ask. "You are a very smart young man and I have every confidence in you."

Joshua felt a bit of pride at the praise but still looked at the books with anxiety. "Yes ma'am." He did not want to let Becky down.

As he sat down, he looked to see his name at the top of the page. He glanced up at his new tutor and saw her smile.

"We will start with the story of Joshua." She continued, "it is very exciting, but it also has a lot of God's truth in it."

"Yes ma'am."

"You start reading aloud and I will follow along silently. If you have any difficulties, I will be here to help you out." Becky instructed.

Joshua sighed, but he knew better than to argue. For all of her sweetness, Mrs. Wheaton was about the most stubborn woman he'd ever known. He had discovered that it was useless to fight with her because she would always get her way. Not that it did not stop him from trying every once in a while, but today, he did not have the wherewithal in him to resist, so he began reading.

True to her word, Becky would let him sound out the words, but when he got stuck she would help him out. When he finished the chapter, Mrs. Wheaton explained, "Joshua in the Bible was a great military leader and was the man that God used to bring the Israelites into the Promised Land." She went onto explain the story of Israel's captivity in Egypt and Moses leading them out into the wilderness. The people's refusal to go into the Promised Land the first time and how they wandered for forty years.

Joshua listened patiently and when she finished, he looked at her.

"Can we read the next chapter too?"

* * *

The gunslinger ran out of the bar, fuming with anger. How dare that sheriff kick him out! He did nothing wrong! He stormed over to his horse tied in front of the saloon and swung himself up into the saddle but as he started to turn the horse, he spied his Winchester. He slid the rifle out of the scabbard and dropped out of the saddle, allowing the reins to fall, ground tying the horse. He stormed back into the bar. He used the barrel of the rifle to push the bat wing doors open but coming directly from the bright sunlight into the dim bar, he was temporarily blinded and could not see his intended target.

Eli drew even as he turned and the flames blossomed out of the barrel of his gun. A split second later, he heard the roar of Matt's gun to his right and then the boom of Sam's shotgun to his left. Eli kept fanning the hammer on his pistol and the thundering of the gun did not cease until the last round had been fired.

The gunman stumbled back, firing his one chambered bullet, but with the amount of lead that he was taking into his midsection, he was unable to work the lever on the rifle to get another round in.

He tried to run, but his legs wouldn't work. He fell backward through the doors he'd just come through. Even as he tried to stand up, he came to the realization that he could not feel his legs...or his arms. A coldness moved through him, starting at the outer extremities and moving inward. He wanted to speak, but the words would not come out. He wanted to cry out, to curse the men who had just killed him, but he could produce no sound. He was a shootist! How could they have gotten him?

His life blood ebbed out of him there on the boardwalk in front of the saloon.

Eli stepped to the doors, his second gun poised for more action, but one look told him that the gun was not necessary. He turned to Matt, only to realize that neither Matt nor Sam were standing! Rushing to the plank that made up the bar, he saw Matt kneeling over the prostrate form of Sam.

Matt looked up at Eli, "Get Doc and hurry!"

Eli was already moving for the door at a full run, jumping over the body of the outlaw. Meanwhile the few bar patrons moved to assist the sheriff with the injured man. They had him moved onto a table out on the main floor by the time Eli returned with the Doctor.

"Get me rags and clean water," Doc demanded. *"Now!"*

Eli sprinted for the back room and the requested provisions.

The doctor ripped the shirt open and used a scalpel from his black bag to cut the red Union Suit open. The bullet hole from the single shot the gunman got off was gushing blood. He shoved his finger into the wound and as soon as Eli returned with the clean cotton rags, he barked out orders, "Cut me some strips, *quickly!"*

The boot knife appeared and soon several pieces were ready. Doc took the first one and removed his finger, only to begin shoving strips of cloth into the hole. He poked cloth down into the hole until he could not get anymore in. Only then did he instruct the men to roll Sam onto his side. While they held him there, he checked for an exit wound. He found a bump against the skin of Sam's back. Using the scalpel he sliced the skin of the unconscious man and popped the lead ball out onto the table. More rags were inserted into the new opening until no more could go in.

Once the feverish work was completed, the Doctor slowed his pace and began cleaning the blood from the body of the injured man. Eli broke the silence.

"What else can we do to help?" he asked.

Doc stopped his work and looked up at the men who circled the table. "Right now the only thing you can do is pray." With that he resumed his work on his patient.

Eli moved back to do as instructed and to his surprise, all the men did as well.

One of the men addressed the preacher, "I don't rightly know how to pray, but if you'll speak out for us, we all are behind you."

Eli looked at each of the men and realized they were serious. "I'd be glad to."

He removed his hat and the others followed suit as he began to pray. He earnestly spoke to God, asking for divine intervention for Sam, and wisdom for the doctor. Suddenly he stopped praying mid-sentence when someone interrupted him. The voice that he heard was audible, or so he believed at first. He finally realized that he was hearing the voice inside of him and he silently began to argue with God, "I can't do that. They'll think I'm insane." The men around him looked up because of the sudden silence, and watched him, not sure what they should do next.

Eli finally stopped his inner struggling and stepped over to the man on the table. The words that came next were not his own, but words that the Holy Ghost told him to speak. With trepidation, but in obedience, Eli placed his hand on Sam's sweating forehead, "In the name of Jesus, Sam, be healed."

Doc looked up from his work like he thought Eli was crazy. Maybe he was. Even Matt looked skeptical. Surprisingly the other men did not seem to react at all. This was all new to them and they just figured this was the way it was supposed to go.

Almost imperceptibly, Sam's ragged breathing began to even out. It was the only noticeable change in the man, yet it was a change.

Doc finished cleaning around the wound and bandaging it. "I've done all I can do for him here. I need to get him to my office so I can perform surgery and cauterize that wound. Can a couple of you run to my office and get the litter that is leaned up behind the door?"

Two of the men ran off to perform the request. Matt grabbed a couple of the others that were present.

"We need to get the body of the outlaw out of here."

Eli was left alone with Sam and the Doctor. Doc looked up into the concerned eyes of the preacher. "It doesn't look good. Where that bullet went and the amount of blood…I'm afraid that the bullet nicked an artery. I have them rags stuffed in there, but he probably is still pumping a lot of blood inside of him." He sighed. "Eli, he's not the healthiest of men and my skills…" his voice trailed off.

"Doc, he's in God's hands. You do the best you can and let the Lord   perform   the   miracles."

CHAPTER FOUR

Steven finished his chores at the stable and he moved to the back room and stripped down for a bath. Once he'd finished bathing out of a bucket, he toweled off and carefully dressed for his job at the bakery.

He contemplated his past as he got ready. Less than a year ago he had been the town drunk but after a series of miracles he had been freed from the bondage of alcohol. He was holding down two jobs and with the help of Eli, was teaching the men who were new believers in Jesus how to follow after Him. Eli would coach him in a subject and then help Steven to formulate a lesson to teach to the other men.

Tonight was the night of his class and he ran through the lesson in his mind for the umpteenth time. In spite of the fact that he had been teaching now for the better part of three months, he still got butterflies in his stomach at the thought of presenting this information to the men. The nice thing, he thought, was the fact that he was speaking on the authority of God's word and not on his own authority. Because of that, he could speak with boldness. He just wished he could read better so that he did not have to rely upon his memory.

He checked his reflection in a broken looking glass and slicked down his hair one more time and grabbed his hat before heading out the door.

The walk to the bakery was a pleasant one and as he passed by people, he would nod and say, "Hi" or he would tip his hat to the ladies. It was a blessing that now a day's people smiled and returned his greeting. In the past many of these same people just looked down their noses at him. Not that he blamed them. He did not care for the man that he had once been either.

Steven stepped through the door and removed his hat. Mrs. Franco looked up from her work, harried by the frantic pace she had been keeping all morning, "Mr. Bosco, I'm so glad you're here." She smiled sweetly. Even in the chaos, she made it a point to make everyone feel comfortable, including her subordinate. She pointed to a paper on the counter. "I've made a list of goods that I need from the store. Would you please do that right away?"

"Yes ma'am." Steven was amazed at his good fortune to have her for a boss. Most men didn't like the idea of working for a woman, but he could not think of anyone he would rather work for. He worked hard and in turn, she was constantly telling him what a good job he did.

A quick glance at the list confirmed that he would need the wagon, so he went out back to hitch up the team. He was threading the reins through the harness ring when the sound of gunfire erupted in the distance. His curiosity nearly got the best of him, but he had a job to do. He wasn't getting paid to go running around town checking out every time some young rowdies decided to shoot up a saloon. He climbed up in the wagon and started toward the Mercantile.

* * *

Doc had the man on the table in his surgery. He rolled up his sleeves once again and dipped his hands and forearms into a bucket of water, scrubbing vigorously before rinsing off and drying them on a clean towel. When he finished his prep, he looked over at Eli.

"You better get yourself washed up as well."

Eli obediently followed suit and when he was ready, Doc explained the next step.

"I'm going to remove all that cloth that I stuffed down inside the wound. It"s going to start gushing again as soon as I do that, so I need you to be ready to hand me them hot pokers that I got in the coals there. I'm going to need to cauterize the wound, fast. Are you up for this?"

Eli nodded, "yup." His many years as a lawman had allowed him to witness some pretty gruesome stuff and he was confident that he could handle this as well.

Doc uncovered the wound and tossed the old bandage into a barrel. He picked up a pair of forceps from a tray that he had set next to the table and grasped the cloth that was sticking out of the hole. He pulled it out and then reached in and pinched the end of the next one. Each piece was removed and tossed into the trash barrel.

"Okay, if I counted right this should be the last one in the front hole. Get ready to hand me that poker."

Eli grabbed the wooden handle and removed the glowing instrument from the fire, poised to hand it to the doctor. The concern for his friend was etched on his face.

Sweat beaded the brow of the doctor as he poised the tool over the unconscious form. He carefully inserted the tip of the forceps into the wound and grasped the final cloth strip. He looked up at Eli. "Ready?" he asked.

At Eli's nod, he pulled the cloth out, tossed the forceps aside and reached for the poker. Even as he handed the instrument over, the Preacher noticed there was no blood spewing out of the hole. Doc noticed as well but insisted on putting the red hot iron into the wound, cauterizing the hole.

They did the same for the hole where the bullet had been removed.

When that was finished, while he was bandaging the wound, Doc Mercer turned toward Eli.

"I have done all that is humanly possible. It's going to be a wait and see situation, but like I said, he is not the healthiest of men. If he were younger and in better shape, I would give him much better odds. The fact is that he's not a spring chicken and I don't think he's ever taken care of himself, so…"

As he was speaking to Eli, Sam's eyes opened. He looked up into the face of the doctor. "Oh," he moaned, "I must be in hell."

"What the…" the astonishment showed on the Doctor's face.

Eli's countenance lit up with excitement.

"Sam, you're awake," he exclaimed. "How do you feel?"

"I'm hurtin' real bad," he groaned. "I feel like someone just stabbed me with a hot brandin' iron." He sucked his breath in from the pain.

Doc Mercer turned to the cabinet, grabbed a bottle and quickly dosed his patient with laudanum. He was mumbling under his breath while he worked, but his expression revealed his disbelief.

After swallowing the medicine Sam moaned. "I feel like I just finished wrassling a bear? What am I doing here and what is that old codger sniveling about?"

"Oh shut up you old coot," the doctor nearly spit out the words, still unable to wrap his head around what had just occurred. "You just lay there and get better."

* * *

Joshua finished reading for the day and sat at the table, a look of consternation on his face.

"What's the matter?" Becky asked. "You did really well."

"Thank you ma'am," Joshua replied. "It's not that. I was just thinking about school."

Becky was surprised as he had never opened up to her before. She seized upon the moment. "What's happening at school? The other kids aren't picking on you, are they?"

"No ma'am," Becky could not get him to stop addressing her in this way. "It's more like they're afraid of me."

Becky didn't know what to say, so she just waited.

Joshua continued, "they all know that I killed Rob Handy and they all just kinda keep their distance from me. I ain't got no friends there."

Becky picked her words carefully, "Joshua, a reputation is a hard thing to fight. Sometimes people take one thing that they know about a person and develop a whole persona around that."

"What's a persona?" the boy asked.

"In this case it is deciding what they think you are like, based upon the one thing that they know about you. Do you ever talk to any of them?" She asked.

"No ma'am, not much anyhow."

"What are you doing to try to make friends?" Becky probed.

"I dunno. I just ain't good at making friends."

Becky moved over so she was seated next to the boy and took his hand. "Let's pray about it."

* * *

Matt sat at his desk undecided. He needed to continue his search for Norris but he was also deeply worried for his friend Sam. *Well*, he decided, *he wasn't getting anything done sitting here*. He grabbed his hat off the peg and pushed it down on his head. When he opened the door, he did not step out onto the boardwalk until his eyes adjusted to the Nevada sun. He made a careful survey of the street to make sure there was no one out there who might be an enemy. Only when he was satisfied that no danger lurked out there did he step onto the boardwalk.

The body of the gunman was over at the undertaker's and one of the men had covered the blood stains with sand. He reflected that this was the second time within a year that a man had bled out on the steps of that Saloon.

He made his way to the doctor's place first. Norris had been missing for a day, a few more minutes wasn't going to make a difference at this point.

He was shocked to see Sam sitting up drinking a cup of coffee!

"Wait a minute. Last time I saw you, you were knocking at death's door. What happened?" Matt was staring at him in utter amazement.

"Well," Sam took his time, savoring the attention that he was getting, "it seems that Eli done healed me."

Matt shook his head. *Again*? A second miracle in this town now as well! "I thought he was crazy when he stepped over and put his hands on your head, but obviously, he know's more than I do. I need to find out more about what he has. This is amazing."

Matt left the doctor's house with a feeling that things were unreal, yet he had been there for the shooting. Now he had seen what had happened with Sam. It was unbelievable still, he had seen it with his own eyes! The first miracle he had only heard about, which was Steven being delivered from the clutches of alcohol, but this time he was standing right there when Eli prayed over Sam. Even if he didn't know it at the time, he had actually been part of the second miracle!

Shaking his head, he turned his attention back to his investigation. He still had a job to do, so he'd better get on with it, though the sight of Sam sitting up still kept returning to his mind.

There were still several more saloon's in town, so Matt began his rounds, checking in with the barkeep on each of them. Norris was not a man who apparently frequented saloons. There was not a single saloon keeper who was familiar with Swensen, other than just knowing him in passing. Matt sighed as he pushed his way through the doors of the River Saloon. This time though, the story was different.

"Yeah, he comes in here. Every other Monday he comes in, has one beer and leaves."

Matt pressed the issue, "Just one beer? He never had more than that?"

"One time, he drank enough to get tatered, but that was a long time ago. He ended up getting into a fight and the two of them busted up the place pretty good."

"How come I never heard about this?" Matt demanded.

"Sheriff, if I ran to you every time someone busted up the place, I wouldn't have any customers. Besides, the man he fought paid his half and Swensen comes in every other Monday and pays a couple bucks on his bill and buys one beer."

"You let him buy beer when he still owes you money for damages?" Matt was amazed.

"Sure, why not? I could let him just pay what he owes, but then he'll go to another saloon to drink. This way, I make money on the beer and he is still paying what he owes." The barkeep redirected the conversation. "What's this about any way? Why all the questions about Swensen?"

Matt chose to be vague. "I just need to talk to him. Do you know which way he would go when he left the place?" He knew it was a long shot, since the bartender was probably busy, but still…

"Naw, I don't have any idea. You might ask Peggy," he replied.

"Peggy?" Matt wondered if it was the Peggy he was already familiar with.

"Yeah, one of the working girls."

Matt nodded. It was the same Peggy. "Thanks. Last time I was in here the barkeep wasn't as friendly or as wise as you are. Thank you for talking to me."

"Not a problem. I ain't one to stand in the way of the law." The man walked down the bar to a waiting customer.

Matt turned and looked around the room for Peggy, but did not see her. He waited for the bar tender to come back and tossed a nickel on the bar. "I'll have a cup of coffee please."

The man returned with a mug of thick black coffee that had steam rolling off of it. Matt took the cup and walked over to a corner table where he could wait in the shadows. The coffee was strong enough to float a horseshoe in it, but Matt drank it anyhow. It was nearly gone when he saw Peggy coming down the stairs laughing and playing it up to the customer that she had just finished with. The sheriff waited until she was on the floor and looking the other direction before getting up and approaching her.

"Peggy, it's been a long time." He had walked up behind her so she did not have a chance to slip away.

She turned and the smile on her face quickly disappeared. "What do you want?" The smile was replaced with a look of disdain.

"We need to talk." Matt continued to have an even, pleasant tone with her.

"I only talk to paying customers," Peggy's voice dripped with venom.

Matt's face became hard. "I didn't arrest you for your complicity in the kidnapping and beating of Elijah Exeter last year, but that can change, so unless you want to spend some time in my jail, I suggest you lose the attitude and begin to cooperate."

Peggy's face did not change, but she grudgingly move to the table that Matt motioned to.

"What do you want?" she demanded.

"What can you tell me about Norris Swensen?" Matt kept his tone soft as he seated himself across from the prostitute.

"Nothing." she replied tersely.

"I understand that he's one of your clients. When is the last time that you saw him?" Matt's patience was already wearing thin. It had been a long, hard, emotional day and he was not in a mood to take much garbage.

"I don't know." Peggy did not like the Sheriff and her tone of voice reflected that dislike.

"Was he in here yesterday?" Matt's tone hardened.

"I don't remember." She sneered at him.

Matt's chair fell backward as he stood up suddenly. All heads in the room swiveled to see what the commotion was. He grabbed her right bicep in an iron like grip and bodily lifted her out of the chair.

"Ow. You're hurting me." She cried out.

"You're under arrest as an accomplice in the attempted murder of Elijah Exeter." The Sheriff dragged her toward the front door.

When he realized what was happening the bartender yelled and started around the bar toward the pair, but he stopped in his tracks when he realized he was staring down the barrel of a .45 Colt. He never even saw it come out of the holster, yet there it was, pointed right between his eyes!

"Son, I can close this place down quicker than you can spit, if that is what you'd like. Otherwise, I suggest you return to the other side of that bar." Matt was angry and almost to the point where he hoped the man would choose to fight.

But the bartender had looked into the dark eye of death and decided he wanted to live another day. He quietly moved back behind the bar.

With his gun still trained on the man, Matt continued. "Keep your hands on top of the bar, because if they go under the bar, I might think you were trying for that shotgun and I'd have to shoot you."

The bartender raised his hands to shoulder height, "I wouldn't want you to get the wrong idea," he volunteered.

Every other set of eyes in the bar were trained upon the two men, but no one else felt the need to toss their hat into the ring.

Matt dragged the saloon girl out through the batwing doors and marched her down the main street in the late evening dusk. The entire trip, she whined about how he was hurting her, but he wasn't going to give her a chance to slip out of his grasp, or worse yet get her hands on his gun!

Once inside the jail, he pushed her into the cell. He checked the folds of her dress and found a two shot derringer. Matt shivered when he thought of what might have happened if he had not found it so he did a thorough search of her person, throughout which she made a litany of suggestive comments. He also found and removed the dagger that she had strapped to a sheath on her leg. He slammed the door shut and removed the key once the door was locked. Without a word, he walked out to his office and slammed the solid wooden door shut that separated the two areas.

Wearily, he sat down behind the desk and put his head into his hands. He hated it when he let his emotions control his actions. It was not the way he wanted to be and he realized it was a good way to make bad decision.

Fortunately, he had enough to hold her on the charge, though the judge probably would not find her guilty, since the man who had paid for the whole debacle was dead and he did not even have her two partners.

He made sure everything was locked up and then went outside into the night. It was time to head home, he would let Peggy cool her heels for the night.

CHAPTER FIVE

Tuesday dawned a bright new day. Eli rose early to spend time in the Word as he did every morning. He didn't rush his time with God, but he recognized that he was going to have to do Sam's work while the man was recuperating and wondered when he would have time to prepare for Sunday's sermons. While he was praying for guidance, a thought struck him and the more he contemplated it the more he felt it was from the Lord.

He cleaned up the saloon and then put on a large pot of chili. He could not even begin to cook like Sam could. For cryin' out loud, who had ever heard of dill weed, much less used it in cooking, but there it was in Sam's pantry. Regardless, Eli stuck mainly to salt and pepper for most of his cooking.

He opened the doors right before noon and soon a trickle of people turned into a rush and he was running around like a chicken with its head cut off. He good naturedly accepted the jokes about his cooking skills, or lack thereof.

As the lunch rush dwindled and Eli had a chance to catch his breath, the door open again. Glancing up, he saw Steven coming in, which surprised him as Steven never came in during business hours. He simply did not want to be around the temptation of alcohol. Eli turned to the stove and poured Steven a steaming cup of coffee.

He slid the mug across the bar over to his friend. Steven smiled wide and accepted the cup. "We missed you this morning over at the bakery," he said.

"After yesterday, I'm pretty sure Mrs. Franco doesn't want me around there anymore." Eli grimaced at the embarrassment he'd experienced.

Once again, Steven gave him that look like he was out of his head. "You two are the most..." He fought to find the right word. "...dense people that I know. You are so worried about what she thinks and she is so worried about what you think and everyone around you two can see that you are meant for each other. You remind me of a couple of school kids." Steven sighed in exasperation.

"That's easy for you to say, but what have I got to offer a woman like that?" Eli countered. "I live in the church parsonage, I work in a saloon, I preach twice on Sunday and my savings are dwindling down to nothing. For me to court a woman, especially at my age, I need some sort of home, if nothing else."

Eli came around the bar and they walked over to a table and sat down together.

"That's your pride talking now." Steven interjected. "She has a home, she has a business and if you was to start courtin' her and it went somewhere you might actually be able to be a full time Parson. You're just too proud to allow a woman to take care of you. Well, Mr. Preacher man, if I recall my Bible correctly, and I believe I do, Jesus had woman followers who supported Him in His ministry."

Eli looked at his friend in disbelief. Steven had just taken what he had taught him and had thrown it back in his face! He was ashamed to admit, but his protégé was right. He looked down at the table and it was his turn to sigh. "I know you're right, but it is something I have to work through myself."

He switched the subject, "I really need a favor from you."

Steven looked over the cup of coffee at his mentor, "You name it. If I can you know that I will."

Eli smiled at the solid commitment of his friend. "I have to take care of this place for Sam, and I don't have time to put together a sermon for Sunday. I was hoping that you would be willing to stand in for me. I already have the message ready for the Saloon service, but I don't see how I could ever put together a second sermon."

Steven's face turned pale at the thought. "I don't know…"

"I'll be honest with you, while I was praying about it, it was you who came to mind. I really believe that God is calling you to do this, or I would not even have asked." Eli earnestly entreated his friend.

Steven struggled with the whole idea. He wasn't a preacher, he struggled just being a teacher of a small group of men. Men that he had come to look upon as really good friends.

"If you don't do this, I will have to pull one of my old sermons out and dust it off."

"That would probably be better than having them listen to me," Steven replied hopefully.

It was Eli's turn to look at his friend as if he were the crazy one. "Let me remind you," he interjected, "the last time you spoke, a huge number of men and women came forward and accepted Christ. That is why I think you need to do this. God used you in a tremendous way before and I think that he will do the same this Sunday."

Steven thought back to that day on the bank of the river when he had simply told his story, how he had been saved from drinking and had accepted Jesus as his Lord and Savior. Over a dozen people had come forward and accepted Jesus and were baptized with him. He looked up at his friend across the bar.

"Okay, I'll do it. What should I speak on?" Steven asked.

"I'll leave that up to you. Pray on it. You do what the Holy Ghost leads you to do. I know you will do it with excellence."

Steven nodded and stood up. "Just make sure you show up tomorrow at the Bakery." Then he added, "we need a good laugh." He stepped away from the table quickly so his friend couldn't smack him and then headed for the door.

Eli just shook his head and rolled his eyes. He called out across the room to his friend's back, "Mañana."

* * *

Sam looked up at the doctor, "Would you quit hoverin' like an old biddy hen?" He felt really good considering what he had just gone through, but the doctor could not accept that he had been healed. Sam couldn't believe it either, but there was no denying that here he was sitting up, eating soup a few hours after being shot.

"I'm afraid that there is bleeding inside you and that you might keel over. I'm keeping you here at least until the end of the week." The doc stood firm in his resolution.

"What about my place. It won't run itself you know." Sam was anxious to get back. If he wasn't working, he wasn't making money.

"Have you ever even taken a day off since you opened that place," the Doc countered. "It's time you take a break, just a few days off."

Sam realized that to argue was fruitless. "Alright, but just a few days."

* * *

The following morning Matt sat at his desk, frustrated that he had made no progress on the Swensen case. Though he learned that the man had secrets that he kept from his wife, he still had no idea how deep or dark those secrets were.

He pondered what he knew. Swensen came into town every other Monday. He had a beer before going home, though he had only gotten drunk once. Matt paused. If he had gotten into a fight and busted up the bar, what did he tell his wife to explain the cuts and bruises that the fight would have caused? How come Mrs. Swensen had not mentioned this when he spoke to her?

Swensen also appeared to have some kind of relationship with the prostitute that he currently had here at the jail. It was time to see if her tongue had loosened up any.

He opened the door between the office and the cell. Peggy was sitting up on the bed and judging by the smeared grease paint on her face, she had been crying. She looked up as the door opened and the attitude was totally different today.

"What do you think is going to happen to me?" she whined.

"That's going to be up to a judge, but I can tell you that if you want to help yourself out, you better start talking." Matt was at least hopeful of garnering some information now.

"What do you want to know?" Peggy sniffed.

"Who were the two men that helped you grab Eli Exeter?" Matt started there, since that was why he had arrested her in the first place.

"I'm not in the habit of asking men their names." Peggy was starting to get her attitude back.

"Listen Peggy, I will make a deal with you. You help me catch the men that you worked with and I can let you out of here on your own recognizance, provided you agree to testify at the trial."

"My own what?" she asked, entirely baffled.

"I will let you out of jail on your promise that y'all show up in court when you're supposed to," Matt explained.

"Will I be charged with a crime?" Peggy was all ears now.

"I can talk to the judge and see if he will let you go with time served. But, if I find out that you lied or didn't tell me the whole truth, all bets are off." Matt's hopes soared.

Peggy sat there staring at the floor for what seemed like eternity then finally looked up into the face of the sheriff. "Okay. You got a deal."

Matt held his hand up to stop her as she started to stand. "You also have to tell me everything you know about Norris Swensen as well."

"Okay, but there's not much to tell." Peggy did not want to spend another night in that cell.

Matt led her out to his office, got a chair for her and poured her a cup of coffee. He sat down behind the desk, pulled a piece of paper out of the drawer and searched for a pencil. Peggy sipped her coffee while he pulled out a knife and sharpened the writing instrument he'd located.

Matt looked up, "Okay, tell me about the men."

Peggy responded, "I only got first names from them, Bill and Danny, but I can tell you what they look like."

"Okay, shoot."

Matt wrote furiously as she provided a very detailed description of the two men, right down to the birthmark on the back of one of their hands. As he wrote he thought to himself, *"She would have made a great detective with that kind of eye for detail."* When she finished, she gave him a statement of how she had lured Eli into the alley, how Bill was laying on the ground to draw attention so Danny could hit him over the head. How both men kicked the unconscious man and then carried him away. She even told of her effort to extort money from Brother Smith when she discovered that Eli was back in town. Matt raised an eyebrow over that information, but he did not comment, he just kept writing.

When she finished, he looked up from the paper. "Okay, what can you tell me about Norris Swensen? I understand he was a client of yours."

"That's the funny thing, he really wasn't," she replied.

"He wasn't?" It was Matt's turn to be puzzled.

"No. He would buy me a drink so that I would sit down and talk with him. I kind of liked him, he was always polite and respectful, which most the other men in that saloon are not. That's the main reason why I even took time to talk to him." She smiled, the first time Matt had ever seen her do so and it surprised him, because she suddenly seemed like the sweet young girl next door, not the painted lady that she was.

"What would you talk about?" was his next query.

"He would tell me about his dreams, wanting to own thousands of acres and run and grow corn and wheat. He wanted to be the biggest rancher around. I used to tell him that when he got that ranch, I'd run away with him."

"I don't think his wife would be too keen on that idea," Matt interjected.

"Oh, I saw the wedding ring, but never thought much of it. He always left it on though, unlike many of the men who take them off and try to hide the fact that they are married. You can't hide that white circle on a sun weathered hand," she laughed. "A lot of my clients don't talk about their wives, if you know what I mean." She said with a smirk. "It doesn't surprise me though, he is a good looking man." Peggy paused and then asked a question of her own. "Why all this interest in Norris? What did he do anyway?"

"He never showed up at home on Monday and I'm trying to find out why. Do you have any ideas on that?"

Peggy was thoughtful as she responded, "No…he came in, bought me a drink, had his beer and we talked. I didn't notice anything different, except…"

"Except what?" Matt prodded.

"He seemed to have…" she searched for the right word, "more resolve. Like he had finally made up his mind about something. He just never told me what."

"Did you happen to notice which direction he went after he left the saloon?"

"No, I was with another client by then."

Matt was running out of questions. "Alright. If I have any more questions for you, I'll come over to the saloon. You're free to go for now." Matt stood up. "You might want to wash your face before you go out there."

She checked her reflection in the window. "Oh no," She gasped. Matt directed her to the washbasin and gave her a towel.

When she finished scrubbing the smeared rouge off her face and had dried it, Matt handed her the derringer minus the bullets. "I'll drop your knife and these off at the saloon later."

Peggy looked at him like she was seeing him for the first time. "You know, you can be really nice when you want to be." With that, she turned and hurried out of the Sheriff's Office.

CHAPTER SIX

Elizabeth Franco finished pouring coffee to the last of the patrons in her bakery and no one was needing anything at the moment. With some time to breath, she poured a cup for herself and moved around behind the counter to replace the pot on the stove. She sat down at the kitchen table and sipped the steaming hot liquid.

She thought of Eli and sighed. He had not been back in since the day she had embarrassed herself so badly and she realized how much she missed him. She so enjoyed the short conversations they would have. He was quiet and shy around her, but that just endeared him more to her. Eli was always a gentleman, never loud or obnoxious. She had really hoped to get to know him better, yet it appeared that she had chased him off. Mentally she kicked herself.

Steven came out of the back room. "I finished putting the supplies away. What would you like me to do now?" he asked.

"Sit down." The way she said was more of an invitation than a demand. She got up, poured him a cup of coffee and handed it to him.

"Thank you." Steven took the cup and sat down across from her. "Ma'am, are you alright?" he asked.

"Yes, thank you. I'm just reflecting, wishing I had done something a little differently." She replied.

"Something to do with the bakery?"

"No, this is more personal." Elizabeth changed the subject. "How are things going for you?"

"Ma'am, the honest truth is, I'm quite a nervous wreck right now."

"Steven, what's the matter? Is there something I can help you with?" Deep concern shown in her eyes.

"Eli asked me to preach for him on Sunday and I am plumb scared to death. Ma'am, I can barely read and it makes it all the more difficult."

Elizabeth smiled broadly, "I think that is incredible, you preaching on Sunday. What are you going to speak on?"

"I have no idea," he replied.

Mrs. Franco reached across the table and put her hand over Steven's. "Let's pray about it." With that, she bowed her head and he did the same. Elizabeth simply talked to God like he was seated at the table with them. She asked for wisdom and spiritual guidance for Steven and asked for wisdom in picking a topic to preach on. When she finished he simply replied, "Amen."

"As far as the reading issue, I can help you with that," Elizabeth continued. "I taught my children to read before they…"

Her voice trailed off as the memory of the children she had lost washed over her in a wave of grief. She had never been one to wallow in self-pity though and she was not going to start now. She stood up and walked over to a nearby table leaving her reveries behind. She retrieved an old newspaper and brought it over to the table, this time sitting down next to Steven.

"A traveler left this behind." She said as she laid it down in front of him. At the top of the front page the title, "ST. LOUIS TIMES" jumped out at him in large type.

"We will work our way through this, a little each day. You can catch up on the news and learn to read at the same time."

He reflected upon the time that Eli had done the same thing with him out in the desert. Steven had rescued Eli after he had been attacked and left for dead out there. In return Eli got him to read the Bible out loud during his recuperation.

The article spoke to the problem of vagrancy around the city and how the town council was trying to address the problem with the hobos that were riding the trains. The reporter blamed much of the crime in the area on the transients coming into town and the difficulty that the town's police department was having catching them because they did not have roots in the area and would come and go at will.

Steven and Mrs. Franco discussed the article and in the end Steven questioned the validity of the argument that the reporter used. Yet he honestly had no idea if he were right or wrong. When he had ridden the rails in his early years, he never stole from anyone, but he was only one man.

He thanked Mrs. Franco for her assistance and decided it was time to head home. He still needed to figure out what he was going to preach on come Sunday.

He lit the lamp in his small room off the livery and opened his Bible. The page fell open to the book of John and as he read, he suddenly realized the message he was going to teach.

* * *

Eli hurried through his chores this bright and sunny Thursday morning. He felt as if a great weight had been lifted from his shoulders now that Steven agreed to take his spot at the church on Sunday morning. He had already prepared his message for the Saloon crowd and was optimistic that he could make it to the bakery this morning. He glanced around the Saloon to make sure he had missed nothing then headed down the street.

He opened the door to the mingled aroma of many delicious baked goods and a friendly nod or "Howdy do" from many of the occupants. He sat down at an empty table and Mrs. Franco headed his way with a cup and the pot of coffee fresh off the stove. When she finished pouring, before he even had time to thank her, she addressed him in a very soft voice.

"Mr. Exeter, I know this is extremely unusual," she began, "but may I have a seat?"

In answer, Eli stood up and quickly pulled out a chair for her. Once she was seated and he had pushed the chair in, he sat down again.

"Mr. Exeter," she was still speaking softly and he had to strain to hear her words. "I just wanted to apologize to you for that display the other day. I hope you will also forgive me being so forward."

The color was beginning to creep into her cheeks as she spoke.

Eli spoke softly but earnestly to her.

"You have no reason to apologize. It is I who needs to ask your forgiveness. I made a complete idiot of myself. You on the other hand did nothing to be ashamed of."

He could see the curiosity of the men and women around them, but none of the other customers were able to hear the exchange between the two.

"Mr. Exeter, you don't need to…"

Eli held up his hand to cut her off. "This is foolishness. Now we're both starting to act like a couple of school children. Why don't we try to forget about the other day and start fresh?"

A beautiful smile crossed her face.

"Alright then. The other day you were going to ask me something before we were interrupted. Would you like to pick it up from there?"

It was Eli's turn to begin to turn red but to his credit he did not hesitate.

"Yes ma'am." He felt like his collar was way too tight, but he pushed on. "I was wondering, well hoping ma'am that…well…I…"

"Mr. Exeter, are you alright?"

"No ma'am." He paused for several moments. "Right now I am in uncharted waters."

"Whatever do you mean?" She had a puzzled look on her face.

"Ma'am, I assume that you know that I am a widower, correct?"

She nodded in the affirmative.

Eli took a deep breath, "Well, my wife and I grew up together. We were really best friends even as young children and it was just natural that we would grow up and marry when we were old enough. There was no formal courtship or any of the ritual that goes along with that, we just grew up into our life together. I really don't know or understand the rituals of courtship."

Elizabeth nodded her understanding.

He wet his dry lips and continued. "What I have been trying to say… to ask you, is would you allow me to see you socially?"

CHAPTER SEVEN

Joshua looked down at Mrs. Wheaton.

"Are you sure ma'am?" he asked.

"I'm absolutely positive. You let all the children at the school know that we are going to have a party here on Saturday and they are all invited. You tell them to come at four in the afternoon. We'll have a huge picnic and some cake and there will be games and dancing".

"Are you sure?" the boy repeated himself emphatically, desperately seeking a way out.

Joshua was not at all convinced that this was going to work. In fact he was certain that it was going to blow up in his face. Mrs. Wheaton on the other hand was all excited.

"Joshua, you just do it, okay?"

Still not convinced, he just nodded and turned his horse toward town and the one room school house. Nobody was going to come to a party, at least not one that he was throwing. He contemplated not even inviting anyone then telling Mrs. Wheaton that no one wanted to come, but as soon as that idea entered his mind he discarded it. He was brought up with the notion that a man's word is his bond and he could not lie, especially to Mrs. Wheaton. The Wheaton's had done so much for him that he could never betray them even in the smallest of matters. And so, Joshua rode his horse toward school with a cold ball of fear growing in the pit of his stomach.

The ride to school was the longest he could ever remember. He dreaded every foot fall of the horse for each one brought him closer to his moment of reckoning. He spent far too much time fussing over the animal after he arrived, just to give himself a few extra moments to remain outside. When he could no longer justify being with his only friend, he and that horse had been through a lot together, he drug his feet in the dirt raising small clouds of dust around his boots.

Miss Elliot stood at the doorway watching the young man approach. It was very obvious that Joshua did not want to be here today. She reflected upon this strange young man who had been thrust into adulthood through a series of life circumstances only to try and resume his childhood in the last year. Unfortunately he could not just return to where he had left off because the experiences of his young life could not be erased. Inevitably they had shaped the boy for better or for worse and the result was a reticent youngster who was neither a boy nor a man. Her heart went out to him but he remained withdrawn and aloof with all the kids his own age.

She waited until he was almost to the steps and went down to meet him.

"Joshua, may I talk to you for a moment?"

He lifted his gaze from the dirt that he had been so focused upon.

"Yes ma'am."

"You stay right here," she instructed.

Miss Elliot disappeared inside of the classroom where she gave the rest of the class instruction on the lesson they were to get started on then returned to the anxious boy waiting outside. She began to walk toward the horses and away from prying ears inside the school house. Joshua followed one step behind her. She glanced back toward the school house as they walked and saw a number of curious faces at the window.

When they had walked far enough, she turned toward the boy. "Joshua, you appear to have something very heavy weighing on your mind this morning. What's wrong?"

The boy looked down at his teacher whom he had an enormous crush on, though he would never admit it to anyone. At nineteen years old, she was just a few years older than he was but when you are thirteen, six years might as well be a hundred. She was not even as tall as he and she had beautiful red hair that shined in the sun light. Entranced with the fact that he was standing here alone with her, he paused for what seemed like eternity before answering.

"Mrs. Wheaton wants me to invite the school kids to a party on Saturday."

Miss Elliot's face lit up with a huge smile.

"I think that's wonderful," she replied.

Joshua shook his head.

"What if no one comes?" he asked.

His issues came into crystal clear focus for her now. He was afraid of putting himself out there in front of the class and being rejected. She recognized that he was scared and she could not blame him, but she was sure that he had nothing to worry about.

"Joshua, I know you are," she searched for the right word, "reluctant to take risks but I am going to tell you a secret. If you never take risks you will never accomplish anything. What is the worst thing that can happen if you ask people to a party?"

"No one will come." His face reflected the tragedy that such an outcome would be.

"Correct. Now what is the best thing that could happen if you invite the class?"

"Everyone comes."

"Now let us consider the first scenario. If nobody came, would it be the end of life as you know it?"

He allowed a smile to flicker around his lips.

"No ma'am."

"Right. Your feelings might be hurt for a little while but the other side of the coin is that you might make some real friends. You'll never know unless you put yourself out there and *take the risk*."

Joshua nodded. Just talking it out with Miss Elliot made him feel a little better.

"When we get to the school house I will have you come up front with me and you can invite everyone in the class."

Joshua's stomach knotted back up at the thought of standing in front of a group of people but he swallowed his fear.

"Thank you, ma'am."

Once he was in front of the room Joshua's mouth went dry and the sweat began to bead on his forehead. His legs felt weak and his knees were nearly knocking against one another.

"I, I, I, I jus, jus, just, wa, wa, wanted to," Joshua stuttered. He had never stuttered before and the realization that he was now caused his face to turn bright red.

Miss Elliot rescued him.

"Class, what Joshua is trying to say is that he is having a party at his house on Saturday and would like to invite the entire school to attend."

The excited chatter that erupted from the other students let Joshua know that he had nothing to worry about. One of the older boys turned his attention toward the front.

"Ma'am, what time?"

Joshua answered this time, "four o'clock," he announced. "We will be having a pig roast and cake and some games."

Once again there was spontaneous noise as the students began discussing the prospect of a party.

"Alright, time to settle down." Miss Elliot tried to staunch the flow of the discussion, but the excitement was evident. She turned to Joshua with a smile on her face.

"Why don't you take your seat while I try to get these ruffians under control?"

Joshua's face glowed as he headed to his desk.

* * *

Matt sat down and looked at his notes. Norris had big plans for ranching, but this was a hard area to make a go of ranching on a large scale. The dry arid climate did not lend itself to large ranches. You had to have graze and you need water, two things that were not readily available in the desert. Most of the available water and range had been laid claim to years ago. So if he was dreaming big, where did he plan on making these dreams happen? More importantly, would he leave his wife behind to go pursue his dreams? Matt sighed. Every time he found out more information it seemed to raise more questions.

Outside on the boardwalk, he heard footsteps approaching his door. Matt turned the chair slightly to better face the door if someone did come in. As the door swung open, the Sheriff had his hand on the butt of the pistol that was concealed under the desk, pointed at the door.

The man standing in the doorway was about his age and there was something familiar about him. Matt couldn't put a finger on it, but he knew this person or had dealings with him or maybe he had seen his picture on a wanted poster. Matt racked his brain, but wasn't coming up with anything useful.

"Can I help you?" Matt started the ball rolling.

"I hope so Sheriff," his mannerisms were familiar as well. "I'm looking for a man and I'm hoping you can point me in the right direction."

Matt smiled at the man even as he desperately tried to place him. "I'll do what I can. Who are you looking for?"

"Elijah Exeter."

"And what is your business with Mr. Exeter?" Matt inquired, suddenly suspicious.

"Personal," the stranger replied.

"I'm sorry, I can't help you." Matt was none too friendly at this point. Until he knew whether this man was friend or foe, he wasn't about to give away the location of his closest friend.

The man tipped his hat, "Thank you anyway." He turned to walk out the door and stopped, as if he were going to say something more, thought better of it and headed on out.

Matt gave the man a couple of minutes and then he himself left the office, only he was doubly cautious as he did so, not wanting this man to ambush him. He suddenly wished he'd gotten a name.

Matt took a circuitous route to get to The Saloon, making sure he was not followed. He slipped in the back door and waited for his eyes to adjust to the dim room before he continued in.

Eli was busy with his customers so Matt made his way to the bar, standing at the end where he was able to keep an eye on both doors. Eli was just coming his way when the batwing doors at the front of the business opened. Matt's head pivoted and immediately he recognized the man standing there. The same one who had been in his office ten minutes ago! He slipped the thong off the hammer of his gun, ready for what may come.

CHAPTER EIGHT

The stranger was half way to the bar when Eli finally looked up. A huge smile lit up his face and he hurried around the bar.

Matt's concern suddenly turned to laughter as he saw the two men together. It was no wonder the stranger looked familiar. He was taller with a husky build and even though he was sporting a beard, there was no doubt in Matt's mind that he was looking at Eli's son.

Eli clasped his son's hand and then clapped him on both shoulders. "Ben, what are you doing here? I didn't know you were going to come! Where is Naomi?" his excitement bubbled over.

"Dad, dad." Ben was laughing at his father's enthusiasm. "Naomi is at the hotel with the baby. They're resting after the stage ride."

"The baby?" Eli grabbed Ben by the forearm. "Is it a boy or a girl?"

"You have a grandson, dad. His name is Elijah." Ben was watching his father's face to gauge the reaction.

"You named him after me?" Eli had to pause as emotion overwhelmed him. "When do I get to meet him?"

"We were hoping to have supper with you tonight." Ben ventured.

"Of course, of course." Eli was having trouble containing himself but he pulled it together. "Sit down, son."

He pulled out a chair at an empty table and as Ben seated himself, he asked, "can I get you anything?"

"Is the beer cold?" Ben asked.

"It is. There is a man in town who cuts ice up in the mountain lakes and he stores it in a warehouse a couple buildings down from here. He is quite the entrepreneur. Let me get you a glass."

Eli turn toward the bar but noticed Matt, who was still at the end of the bar. He beckoned him over to the table and introduced the two younger men to each other.

Ben grinned. "Yes, the sheriff and I met earlier."

Eli face revealed his surprise.

Matt returned a wry smile. "Sorry about that. I was trying to be careful." He turned to Eli. "Ben came in and asked about you. I brushed him off then hurried over here to warn you, only you were busy and Ben was too quick in figuring out where you were."

Ben nodded, "I know. My father has made many enemies over the years."

Eli's former career as a sheriff had left him with a cautious streak. Years of ingrained habit were hard to shed because you never know when you might run into one of your old nemeses.

Eli left the table only to return a few moments later with three frothy mugs of draught beer. The three men engaged in conversation until Matt finished his beer at which time he excused himself.

Ben turned toward his father. "Didn't you get any of my letters?" he asked.

"The last one was nearly a year ago. You shared that you were going to be a father but after that I never heard from you. Tell me what is going on in your life."

"Naomi and I have been called to be missionaries."

Eli's jaw dropped. "What? Where? By whom?"

"We are headed to Oregon." Ben answered.

"What about your medical practice? I thought you were very successful back east." Eli was trying to wrap his head around the whole idea.

"Dad, I did have an extremely successful practice, but as you know, success is not everything. Naomi and I had just about everything you could want, a nice house, plenty of money, prestige, dad we even had a pew near the front of the church, right behind the governor's family pew but something was missing. Both Naomi and I felt that there had to be something more."

"Hold that thought, I'll be right back." Eli hurried to the bar to serve a customer who was standing there impatiently. When he finished helping the man he announced to the room, "The bar will be closing early tonight, so this is last call." Several patrons hustled up to get one more before it was too late. When the last drink had been served, Eli returned to the table.

"I'm sorry about that. So you felt there had to be something more?" he prompted.

Ben nodded. "Even with little Elijah, we still felt God was calling us elsewhere. It was like we had gotten too comfortable where we were."

"How did you end up choosing Oregon?" Eli asked.

"We didn't choose it, it chose us. A man from the Bureau of Indian Affairs came to me because they need medical doctors to go to the reservations to care for the Indians. Many of them are dying because of the diseases that they are contracting from the white man. They have asked me to go up to care for the Paiute and Shoshone tribes near Fort McDermott." Ben was starting to let his enthusiasm show. "I am going not only with the blessings of the Bureau of Indian Affairs, I have also been commissioned by our church denomination as missionaries to them as well."

Eli shook his head. "That is absolutely amazing. Ben, I am so glad to see you and Naomi being obedient to God's calling."

Ben simply smiled. "Dad, I had a good example."

"Maybe," Eli replied, "but I waited pretty late in life to head down that road."

"Did you go when you knew God was calling you?" Ben queried.

"Soon. I had to get used to the idea first, but I hadn't had the calling for long."

"Then you set the example that was needed. I just know that you raised me with the knowledge that I needed to follow God, no matter what. I also know that as I was growing up, you were constantly sharing your love of the Lord with anyone you had a chance to." Ben continued earnestly, "You were ready in season and out of season, it did not matter. So yes, you did set a good example. You set a great example in fact."

"Thank you son, I needed to know that." Eli's eyes were moist "I am so proud of you."

"I've been doing all of the talking. How are you doing?"

Eli paused for several moments and collected his thoughts, thinking back on those people that had come to Christ as a result of his ministry. He thought of the opposition he had faced and overcome through the grace of God, much of which he had already shared in his letters to Ben and Naomi.

"I have met a woman whom I am just starting to court. She loves the Lord with all of her heart and is simply a very lovely person. In fact, I would love for you and Naomi to meet her."

"That would be wonderful. Is there any chance that she could join us for supper?" Ben asked.

"I can certainly ask her. Did you want to meet at The Top Sirloin Eatery at seven o'clock? It is located right next to the Hotel."

"Sure. I hope your lady friend can make it." Ben replied.

"Me too," Eli responded. "Me too."

* * *

Elizabeth heard boot steps on the boardwalk and then the door swung open. Her heart skipped a beat as she realized who it was.

Eli removed his hat and stepped through the door. His eyes swept the empty room and finally rested on the woman who had touched his heart when he thought none would be able to. He strode across the room and stood in front of her. He desperately wanted to reach out and take her in his arms, but restrained himself. He wanted to build this relationship properly, not based upon physical desire.

"Mrs. Franco…Elizabeth, I was hoping you would accompany me tonight for supper. My son and his wife have invited us to join them. I would so love to have you meet them."

Elizabeth jumped at the chance. "Of course, what time are we meeting them?"

Eli pulled his pocket watch out of his vest. "In about an hour. Is that enough time?"

She looked about her, assessing the chores left to finish. "I'll do my best," she replied.

Eli desperately wanted to go get himself cleaned up, but instead he put aside his own interests. "What can I do to help?" he smiled.

Together they got the bakery into some semblance of order and Elizabeth locked up. She looked in the window and straightened out a stray wisp of hair before placing her hand in the crook of his arm. He watched her as she quickly tidied herself and marveled at the beauty she exuded even when she was weary from a long day of work.

Eli escorted her the short distance to the restaurant where they stopped outside the door and Eli removed his hat, using it to slap away the dust from his clothes. He ran his fingers through his mussed up hair, wishing he'd had time to clean up. Meanwhile, Elizabeth took the time to really look him over and it was her turn to feel blessed that this man was her beau.

Together they stepped through the doorway.

* * *

"Joshua that is wonderful." Becky was animated with the excitement. "We have a lot to do. I want you to ride to the butcher's shop and arrange for a pig. We will have Mr. Wheaton set up a spit to cook it over. I have plenty of vegetables from the garden and watermelon and if you go pick some of those berries I can make pies." She continued to list the things that needed doing before the upcoming event.

Joshua on the other hand began to realize how much work goes into a party and though he had never shirked his chores, the added work was intimidating. Still, Mrs. Wheaton's enthusiasm was contagious and as they progressed in their work, Joshua found the dread was ebbing away and he even began to get a little excited himself.

Evening found the pair nearly ready for the event. Joshua had picked two buckets full of black berries and then had fashioned some rough benches out of some scrap lumber in that Matt had in the barn for repairs around the place. He even had the fire pit dug to cook the pig.

Now, Becky hustled to prepare dinner and Joshua wearily staggered to the barn to finish off his evening chores. *These parties are a lot of work,* he thought to himself, *I hope it is all worth it.*

Matt came riding in at supper time and the puzzled look on his face when he came through the door made Becky laugh. She scooted around the table to him and stood on her tippy toes to give him a kiss.

After giving his wife a big hug, Matt stepped back, still looking a little unsettled. "What's going on around here," he asked.

Becky smiled big, "we're having a party." She replied.

"What?" You could have knocked him over with a feather. "What brought this on? Since when do we throw parties around here?" Matt was confused.

"Since this coming Saturday." Becky replied enjoying her husband's reaction.

"Why? What's the occasion?"

Joshua came through the side door in time to answer that question. "I invited the school over for a pig roast," he announced.

"Well I'll be." Matt was still trying to wrap his head around this whole deal. He wasn't sure what to think at this point. "Well I'll be dad gummed."

Excitedly, Becky shared how the whole plan was hatched and executed, with Joshua filling in many of the details. When she had dinner on the table and they had prayed, she turned to Matt. "Would you be able to cook the pig on Saturday?" she asked.

Matt gave her a big smile. "Do I have a choice?" he teased.

"Of course you do…if you want to sleep in that jail of yours." She shot back showing the spunk that Matt found so endearing and yet so frustrating.

Matt turned to Joshua with a twinkle in his eye. "It appears that you have fallen victim to the wiles of a woman."

Joshua nodded. "Yes sir, she didn't give me much choice either," he replied.

"Oh you two." Becky interjected. "Sometimes you men just don't know what is good for you."

The discussion of the impending event continued on over desert and right up until Matt had to leave for his evening rounds. As he rode back toward town, once again he marveled at the wonderful woman that he was married to.

Upon his return home, Matt and Becky lay in bed together. Becky rested her head on his chest as Matt shared his frustration with his missing person case. As the cares of the day began to fade the pair drifted off to sleep in one another's arms.

* * *

Eli's first glimpse of his grandson in his mother's arms would be forever etched in his memory. The young child was sleeping and Eli was sure that he was looking at a cherub.

The introductions were made and Eli pulled out the chair for Elizabeth. Once they were seated, Ben turned to Elizabeth, "Mrs. Franco, please tell us about yourself."

"Please call me Elizabeth." She responded. Briefly she shared about herself and then turned to Naomi. "Your baby is so lovely. How are you doing?"

"I'm exhausted after the trip, but I so love being a mother." Dark circles under her eyes evidenced her tiredness.

"Well we won't keep you up too late, but I am so honored that you allowed me to join you tonight."

They talked at length about each of their impending plans. Throughout the meal, Ben shared their vision to bring medical treatment to the Indian tribes in Oregon and his hope to use that as a springboard for sharing the gospel with them. Naomi spoke of her dream to start a school for the Indian children and Elizabeth told them of her bakery and her plans to expand because she had already outgrown the space she was in.

Eli listened to the loved ones who surrounded him and as he sat back in his chair sipping his coffee, he marveled at the blessed life that he led.

Eli finally turned to Ben. "I know that this young lady needs to sleep," he said referring to Naomi, "How long are you going to be in town?"

"They won't be ready for us for at least two months." He replied. "We came early to spend time with you."

"Fantastic!" Eli blurted out. "You can stay with me at the parsonage."

"Are you sure you have room?" Naomi asked.

Eli smiled. "For you three I will make room."

They arranged to make the move from the hotel the following day. They bid one another good night and the two pairs went their separate way. Even though he was lacking in knowledge of the courting rituals, Eli was ever the gentlemen. He walked Elizabeth back to the Bakery, hitched up her wagon and together they rode to Elizabeth's house.

During the ride, Eli was enjoying the time, seated beside this lovely woman. They spoke to one another of their dreams and desires, where they wanted to go in life and what they hoped to accomplish in the years that they had left on this earth. Elizabeth finally changed the subject.

"I had a most unusual visitor today."

Eli turned to her, "Oh. Who was that?" he asked.

"Young Jeff Simpson came by this afternoon and asked if he could do chores around the bakery to pay for a broken window. You don't know anything about that would you?"

Eli explained to her how Matt had asked him to help him investigate the shooting and how it led to Jeff. He told her of their little talk and his suggestion. He was happy to hear that Jeff had followed through.

"Are you letting him work off his debt?" Eli asked.

"I am." Elizabeth replied. "I had him nail boards over that window for now. It is going to be a couple of weeks before I can get the glass in to replace it. He is also going to come in and work helping Steven around the place for the rest of the week."

"Good." Eli was emphatic. "It is important that you not let him get away with it scott free. He needs to understand the cost of his actions. Besides, I think that Steven will be a great influence on him. I'm pretty sure that he does not have a great example at home."

Elizabeth nodded.

When they arrived at Elizabeth's house, he helped her down from the wagon and as his hands encircled her tiny waist to lift her out, a thrill ran through him at the touch. Once they were inside, he struck a match and lit the kerosene lantern. Elizabeth started to rekindle the fire in the stove to push back the chill of the night. Eli headed back outside where he led the horses to the barn and unhitched the team, tossing hay into the manger and hanging the harness from the pegs in the wall that were there for that purpose. When he had cared for the animals he walked back to the house.

His horse was hitched out front for the return trip to town, having been tied to the back of the wagon.

Eli tapped on the door to say goodbye. Elizabeth opened the door and stepped back. "Would you like to come in for a cup of tea?" she offered.

Eli hesitated. "Thank you ma'am, but I'm not sure that would be proper, considering the hour and all. I should head home and get some sleep. I know that you have an early morning ahead of you as well." He continued, "thank you so much for accompanying me tonight. You made a wonderful evening into an extraordinary one with your presence."

Elizabeth stepped out the door and gave him a light kiss on the cheek. "I'm the one who needs to thank you for including me. I feel so special to be a part of tonight."

Eli was thrilled at the kiss and it took most all of his self-control not to sweep her up into his arms, but somehow he managed. He wanted to tell her that he loved her, but he stopped himself just in time.

As he rode home he contemplated the feelings that he had for Elizabeth and began to ask himself some very hard questions. Was he simply infatuated because of her extraordinary beauty or was he willing to give himself completely over to her. He considered the different Greek words for love and was really asking himself, was he feeling Eros, a sexual attraction, the thought which made him blush slightly in the dark, or was he willing to Agape her, the love that Jesus demonstrated when he died on the cross for the sins of the world. Right then and there, he determined that he would not speak to her of love until he was sure that the love he had for her was the right kind of love. The Godly kind of love. When he was positive that he loved her like that, then he would profess his love to her but not before. If he never came to that place in his attraction to her he wanted to at least have the option of remaining friends. This was new territory for him and he wanted to proceed with great caution. He had seen men who left broken hearted women in their wake and he never, *ever* wanted to be that kind of man.

By the time he arrived at the parsonage, his emotions were in turmoil and sleep was hard to come by. He contemplated of the wonderful evening both with his family and with Elizabeth and kept thinking of the kiss on the cheek and the momentary touches. Eli began to pray for the Lord's guidance and finally sleep washed over him like a wave of darkness but his dreams were as topsy-turvey as his emotions.

* * *

Elizabeth stood out in the chill on the front porch, hugging her shawl around her shoulders as she watched Eli ride away. Only when she could no longer see him did she step in and close the door.

As she sat at the table sipping her tea, she reflected back upon the evening and a feeling of contentment flooded her heart.

A widow for the last four years, she had not yet met a man whom she was willing to walk down the aisle with again. It was not that she lacked for suitors, it was the fact that none of them were right for her...none until now.

She sighed. She so wished that Eli would have taken her in his arms and embraced her but in her heart she knew if that had happened the outcome may have been dangerous. She blushed at the thought.

She had been in love with Eli for most part of a year, patiently waiting for him to come around. Now that he was pursuing their relationship she was finally at peace. She prayed that he was discovering what she had known for the longest time. They belonged together.

* * *

Matt rolled out of bed at the first crow of the rooster. By the time he had his horse ready and hitched out front, Becky had teased the fire back into flame from the banked coals in the bottom of the stove. She had the bacon and eggs on the back of the stove, simmering and the coffee was ready. Gratefully, Matt wolfed down his meal, anxious to be moving before the sun was too high in the sky. He kissed his wife, threw his leg over the saddle and began his ride, not toward town but toward the Swensen spread.

His horse had a smooth gaited trot that ate up the ground and soon he was in the vicinity but instead of heading to her house, he began checking side roads that were not often traveled. There had been enough wind since Norris had been reported missing that any tracks were probably covered with sand. As a result Matt was hunting blind. As the town sheriff he really was not responsible for anything that happened outside of town, but his compassion for Mrs. Swensen gave him a sense of urgency to find the man. If not him, who was she going to turn to?

A morning of exploring the desert left him no closer to solving the mystery than he had been before. He had only been able to explore a few of the many possible roads but decided to return to town.

He immediately headed to the bank. He swung down off the horse and tied the gelding to the rail. As soon as he entered the building Mr. Truman, the owner of the bank, ushered him into his office.

"Good afternoon, Matt," the banker launched right in, "what can I do for you?"

"Does Norris Swensen have an account here and if so, did he withdraw any money recently?"

"Yes and no," replied Truman. "Yes, he has an account here and no, he has not taken any money out, as little as it is. Why do you ask?"

"Swensen did not return home the other day and he is missing. I haven't found hide nor hair of him," Matt replied. "I wondered if he withdrew all his money and skipped town."

They chatted pleasantly for a few more minutes, but Matt was anxious to get back to work so he cut it short.

* * *

Steven finished his stable chores quickly and changed for his bakery job. Adam, the owner of the stable had allowed him to sleep in the loft in exchange for some basic stall cleaning back when he was the town drunk. After his miraculous healing and return from the desert, Adam eventually made him his foreman and had him running the place during the mornings. He let Steven make a bedroom out of the tack room and it was an arrangement that suited Steven just fine. As a former horse wrangler, he loved caring for the animals. The smell of the leather mingled with the plethora of other odors associated with the horse were a balm for him and he reveled in his good fortune. He had a roof over his head, two jobs that paid him more than he needed to live on, in fact he was able to put money away in the bank.

He knew that he started way too late in life, but he was determined to make the most of the time he had. His goal was to find a place of his own, it didn't have to be big. He had learned to be satisfied in his circumstances, especially after his former life of alcoholism, vagrancy and never knowing when his next meal would be or where it would come from. He had come a long way from the bottom of the pit that he had dug himself into and he wanted to make the best of his time to come.

Steven also wanted to find a wife. A Godly woman who would walk by his side to be a part of him. Someone to care for and to cherish for the rest of his life. The problem was all the women in town knew of his past and even though the transformation in his life was evident, there was still a barrier he could not seem to cross. He had burned too many bridges in his past.

His introspection created a melancholy in him as he realized what seemed to be an insurmountable problem. Where was he to find a woman like that in this town? Yet he believed that God had him right here for a reason. He was having an effect in the lives of the men that he ministered to and was not going to give that up in search of a wife.

At times like these he would begin to pray, asking God to provide what he desired and allowing the peace of God to come in and wash away the hopelessness. He knew what was impossible for him to accomplish was not a problem for the God of the world, who created everything by just His word. Knowing that he could place these things into the hand of a Creator who loved him helped bring him peace and he rested in that.

* * *

Matt went to the Saloon to get lunch and while he ate he mulled over what he knew. He arrived at the end of the lunch rush and even though Eli's cooking paled in comparison to Sam's he was grateful for the meal. As he was finishing his coffee, Eli came over to the table carrying a cup of coffee.

"May I sit down?" he inquired.

"Of course," Matt replied. "By the way, you really need to brush up on your cooking skills."

"If you don't like it you don't have to eat here you know." Eli retorted, slightly annoyed. Then he gave Matt a crooked grin. "I will be glad when Sam comes back though. I'm afraid he's going to lose all of his customers if he stays away much longer."

"Oh, everyone will come back when they hear he's cooking again." Matt gave a little laugh. "By the way, where is Ben?"

"He and Naomi are moving their things over to the parsonage. They are going to stay with me for a while." Eli went on to share their future plans with Matt.

The door swung open and both heads turned to see who was coming in. You could have heard a pin drop. Eli was first to react, shoving his chair back and racing across the room to give Sam a huge hug.

"What in heavens name are you doing here?" He exclaimed as he stood back to examine his employer and friend. Sam was wearing the blood stained clothes he had on when he got shot because no one had even thought about bringing fresh clothes to him yet.

Sam couldn't wipe the grin off his face at the expression on the faces of the others. "Doc tried to keep me from leaving, but I was feeling so dang good I had to return. Besides, I couldn't get a word in edgewise with that old coot. For crying out loud, that man needs to get hisself a wife."

Eli felt like dancing for joy. "God is so good. Hallelujah!"

Matt just stood there shaking his head in disbelief.

Sam laughed at the look on Matt's face as the other patrons in the bar gathered around, slapping Sam on the shoulder and generally welcoming him back to the land of the living. Everyone was excited to see him back for he was very well liked by the men who came around. He had always run a clean saloon, no gamblers to cheat them of their money and no woman to prostitute themselves out. He provided good food and cold beer and his patrons were loyal to him.

"Boys, it's good to be back," Sam addressed the crowd, "but I really need to get changed out of these bloody clothes." He began to edge his way through the crowd toward the stairwell.

Eli followed him to the bottom of the stairs where Sam turned toward him.

"Thank you Eli. I have you to thank for so much, healing me…"

Eli lifted his hand and stopped him. "I didn't heal you. God healed you. I simply obeyed and stepped out in faith."

"Regardless, I was healed and you had a hand in it. Besides, you held down the fort for me while I was lazing around." Sam responded. "I owe you."

"No, you don't owe me a thing. I just hope you will open your heart to Jesus after what He has done for you." Eli was not going to miss the chance to lead Sam to the Lord.

"Hold your britches. I'm not saying no, I just need to get cleaned up first." Sam was smiling.

He headed up the stairs and Eli moved to the bar to take care of the guys who were clamoring for more beer.

When the crowd dwindled, Matt moved back up to the bar. "I came in to run the Swensen case by you." He explained all he had done and where he was at with it. Eli listened intently to the information and when Matt had finished he contemplated it for a while, running the angles through his mind. Matt waited patiently while Eli mulled it over.

"I guess we have to accept that a lot of people have been lost in this wilderness that surround us, never to be found. We may never know what happened to Norris, but I have to say that you have pretty well covered everything as far as I can tell." Eli knew the frustration of having an unsolved case and he could tell that Matt didn't want to leave it hanging, but this was the reality of it.

Matt sighed. "That's the same conclusion that I came to, but I wanted to have a fresh set of eyes look at it."

He took his leave a cloud hanging over him. He would have to ride out and let Mrs. Swensen know that the trail had gone cold. He felt that he had let her down, but he had no idea where he could continue to look. There was a lot of desert out there and it was impossible to cover it all, he kept telling himself and yet it did not make him feel any better. With feelings of misgivings, he turned his horse toward the Swensen spread.

CHAPTER NINE

Joshua had finished school for the day and contacted the butcher, who assured him that he would have the pig slaughtered and ready for him to pick up Friday afternoon. In spite of himself he was beginning to feel excited about the party, but there was a feeling of anxiety as well. He wanted it to go well but if it was dependent upon him…

He rode home and after caring for his horse, he went into the house. Mrs. Wheaton had fixed something for him to eat and as soon as he finished, they sat down for their daily reading lesson. He began reading aloud the third chapter of Joshua.

"And Joshua said unto the people, "Sanctify yourselves, for tomorrow the LORD will do wonders among you" and Joshua spake to the Priests, saying, "Take up the ark of the covenant and pass over before the people."

Joshua stopped reading and turned to Becky. "What is the ark of the covenant?" he asked.

"The ark was a golden box with two handles and two cherubim on top. Inside of the box it contained the Ten Commandments, the almond rods from Aaron the priest and some manna." Becky replied.

She opened her worn old Bible to Exodus 25 and read aloud.

"Thou shall put the mercy seat on top of the ark, and in the ark you shall put the testimony which I will give thee. There I will meet with thee; and from above the mercy seat, from between the two cherubim which are upon the ark of the testimony, I will speak to thee about all that I will give you in commandment for the sons of Israel."

"How do you know all of this?" Joshua asked.

"I read my Bible every day." Becky responded. "Did you know that in some places of the world, you cannot read the Bible? They have written it in a language called Latin and the common man cannot read Latin…many of them can't read their own language. They have to rely upon priests to teach them. Here, we have the privilege of reading the Bible in our own language and I take advantage." She held up her Bible. "This is the very Word of God, written for our benefit and I love to hear what He has to say to me."

"How many times have you read through it?" Joshua inquired.

Becky pursed her lips and wrinkled her forehead as she pondered the question. "I honestly don't have any idea. I have been reading and memorizing this Book since I was a little girl."

"Gee." Joshua exclaimed. "Do you think that I will ever get through it?"

A big smile lit up Becky's face. "Of course you will. Everyday your reading is getting better and better."

Joshua beamed at the praise. Ever since he had come to live with the Wheaton's, he felt like they really cared about him and Mrs. Wheaton especially made him feel like he was smart. In the back of his mind was the constant worry that he would be taken away or sent away. It was why he tried so hard to be good. He didn't want to give them any excuse to kick him out. Besides, he just like to do things that pleased the Wheaton's.

Becky brought him back to the present. "That's enough reading for now. You have chores to do while it is still daylight young man. After dinner you can read some more."

As he headed out the door, Joshua shook his head. Who would have thought that he would ever look forward to reading, yet here he was, wanting to find out what happened next to his namesake in the Bible.

* * *

Steven was also continuing his reading lessons at the bakery. Whenever time would allow he would sit down with the old newspaper that the Widow Franco had given him. Daily he would painfully work his way through another article. Today, he started the third page, a bunch of ads placed in the paper by people who were trying to sell things or buy things or advertise their wares. There was one seeking a man to go door to door selling brushes. In another one, a farmer was selling off the extra wiener pigs he had.

The ad that caught Steven's eye and made him catch his breath read:

"Christian woman seeking a husband. I am thirty two years old and skilled at cooking, sewing and all aspects of keeping a house.

The man that I marry must love the Lord more than anything else." There was an address in St. Louis to send responses.

Steven looked at the date on the front page. It was dated over three weeks ago. Surely someone had responded to this woman by now. The west was full of men who were seeking wives, yet he somehow felt hopeful. He set the paper down and went back to Widow Franco who was in the back store room.

"Ma'am," he asked hesitantly, "Do you have a paper and pen that I can use?"

She smiled sweetly. "Of course, what do you need them for?"

"I, I, I'd like to write a letter," he stuttered.

"That's wonderful. Would you like some help?"

Steven started to blush. "No ma'am. Thank you ma'am."

He took the materials and Elizabeth watched the retreating figure with a mixture of amusement and curiosity. Whomever he wanted to write to, he was obviously embarrassed about, which of course made her want to know even more what he was up to. But as a woman of integrity, she could never spy on him. If he wanted to let her know, he would do so in his own time.

Steven sat at the table and stared at the blank piece of paper. Out here, paper was a precious commodity and he did not want to make any mistakes on the one piece of paper that he had, so he just stared. His thoughts were all jumbled and there was so much that he wanted to tell her, but he didn't know where to start or even what to say.

It was over a half an hour later that the door to the back room opened and Elizabeth peeked her head in. "If you are done, I need some help moving some boxes back here."

Steven pushed back his chair and sighed. He walked back toward the door.

Elizabeth watched him come and just by the drop of his shoulders she could tell that he was discouraged. She held the door and he walked past her with a look of dejection. Once the crates had been shuffled around and stacked, she put her hand on his shoulder.

"Are you sure I can't help you out? You know that as a friend, I would do anything that I can. Whatever you need, all you have to do is ask."

Once again the color began to rise in his face but to his credit he swallowed his pride. "Thank you ma'am. I read an advertisement in that there paper for a Christian woman who is looking for a husband. I wanted to write to her, but I just don't know what to say.

Elizabeth suppressed her smile and moved her hand to his forearm. "Mr. Bosco I would be happy to help you out. Why don't you grab your paper and pen? Bring it back here and I will assist you." She hesitated then added, "I think that is very sweet."

Steven brought the requested items as well as the newspaper. He showed the Widow Franco the advertisement. She read through it and then commented, "She did not leave her name, so I guess we'd better figure out how to address her."

Steven had the answer for that. "I would just address her as "Ma'am,'" he said.

Elizabeth wrote, "Dear Ma'am." She wrote in block letters so that it did not appear that a woman was writing it.

Together, with Steven sharing and Elizabeth arranging, they finished a letter that Steven found to be very satisfactory. Elizabeth found an envelope and addressed it to "Christian Woman" at the address listed in the ad.

Steven stood up holding the finished product in his hand and turned to the Widow Franco. "Ma'am, I can't thank you enough." He hesitated then continued, "you won't tell no one about this, will you?"

Elizabeth smiled. "Of course not. Your secret is safe with me. I just appreciate the fact that you trusted me and I would never betray that trust."

Overcome with gratitude, Steven stepped forward and gave her a hug and then suddenly stepped back, blushing furiously. "I'm sorry ma'am. That was totally uncalled for"

Elizabeth laughed. "Don't be silly. You have nothing to apologize for. Now go mail that letter."

Steven started toward the door, but stopped short. "Ma'am, I have another favor to ask of you."

"Yes?"

Steven took a deep breath. "On Sunday, I'm preaching in place of Eli."

"Yes I know." She interjected. "How may I be of help?"

"Ma'am, I'm not a good reader and I...I was wondering if you would read the Bible out loud for me?" He hurried on before she could answer. "You read so well and you have such a pretty voice. People will listen to you when you read." He took another breath.

It was Elizabeth's turn to blush. "I would be happy to read. What is the passage?"

Steven told her, chapter and verse, then quickly headed out the door before his luck ran out.

* * *

Saturday dawned with dew on the ground and a gorgeous sunrise, which turned the underside of the cotton-like clouds a beautiful shade of orange. Joshua was out of bed and hustling to get his chores done at first light.

Matt came out of the house, slipping suspenders over his shoulders. He walked straight to the fire pit and struck a match. As soon as the kindling took hold, he placed more wood on it, building it up. Once the wood burned down to coals, he spread them lengthwise in the pit. Joshua showed up to help after he finished with all his regular chores.

"Let's get that pig out of the cellar and get him put onto a spit." Matt already had the poles the blacksmith had made for him pounded down into the ground, ready to hold the spit in place. The hog had been freshly butchered and thoroughly salted the day before and Matt had placed it in the root cellar to keep cool until they were ready to cook it.

Once they had it over the fire, Matt turned to Joshua. "Okay son, you're going to have to keep turning this spit. I know it is boring, but turn it slowly so that it cooks evenly, otherwise this picnic is going to be over before it gets started." He turned to go then stopped. "I'll come out every once in a while and give you a break."

Joshua nodded, but he took the warning seriously keeping the spit turning slowly over the low fire. It wasn't long before Matt returned with a four foot piece of cherry wood from a tree that he recently pruned a large branch off. He carefully laid it under the pig then turned to the boy. "That wood is really green, so it will smoke a lot. It should give that pig some good flavor."

True to his word, Matt came out and gave Joshua some breaks, letting him get some breakfast and the occasional bathroom break. By the time the first guest started to arrive the smell of salted, smoked pork was making Joshua's stomach growl and his mouth to water.

Each of the boys had brought with them a tin plate and their own silverware as was previously arranged, since the Wheaton's did not have enough of either to accommodate such a large crowd. There were fewer girls in the school and Becky served the older ones on her good dishes while the younger ones were served on the everyday dishes.

Miss Elliott had been invited by Becky and she showed up right on time in her buggy drawn by a single horse. Matt came over and cared for the animal and Miss Elliot began immediately to help, keeping the children entertained with games until food was ready to be served.

Matt relieved Joshua at the spit to allow him to join the kids. Joshua's stomach tightened up at the thought of interacting with the others, but he soon found that it was not a concern. The boys immediately incorporated him into their play and soon he was chasing the older girls with them while the girls squealed and giggled. Miss Elliott had her work cut out for her riding herd on them, but when she saw Joshua let down his guard the first time since he started at the school, she knew that it was worth the time.

The meal was a rowdy affair with the boys joking around and talking while their mouths were full. At first the girls tried to be lady like but in no time, caution was thrown to the wind. There was laughing, hooting and hollering when the slices of watermelon came out and the boys had a race to see who could finished their slice first.

Matt stood off to the side with his arm around Becky and smiled as he watched the gaggle of children having fun. He enjoyed seeing Joshua having such a great time, but he was even more impressed with Becky's orchestration of the event and was happy to see it was such a smashing success. He turned to his wife and kissed her on top of the head.

"You are quite the accomplished party maker," he commented.

Becky beamed at the praise. "He really looks like he is having fun, doesn't he?"

Once the watermelon and pie were pretty much wiped out and the dishes had been cleared, the kids began a game of tag. There was a boy and a girl who were "It" and anyone they tagged were out until the next game. Joshua soon found that he was the preferred target, because of his long legs. The pair would team up against him and soon he found himself sitting out fairly early in the game.

He was straddling the bench watching when he realized that someone had sat down next to him. He pulled his attention away from the game and looked into two liquid brown eyes.

Michelle Youngblood smiled at him in a way that made him feel silly inside. She had seated herself on the bench with her back to the table, hands folded in her lap.

"This is a wonderful party," she said. "I am so glad that you invited me." The way she said it made him feel like he had specially asked her to the party and not as a part of the group.

Without warning, Michelle leaned over and kissed him on the cheek. Before he could even comprehend what had just happened, she jumped up and ran away, heading toward a group of girls on the other side of the game.

Joshua looked around to see if anyone had noticed what had just happened, but everyone seemed to be focused on the game. What he did not see was that his foster parents were looking straight at him.

Becky turned to Matt. "It looks like you might have to have "*that*" talk to him sooner than we anticipated." She nearly laughed aloud at the look on Matt's face.

CHAPTER TEN

That same morning, Sam walked over to Eli, who was finishing cleaning up the bar.

"I told you that I would come to talk to you about..." He struggled for the right word "religion."

Eli was happy to sit and share with Sam what it meant to become a Christian and how to be a follower of Jesus. Sam, for his part, listened intently, weighing out the information carefully. When Eli finished laying it out, Sam looked at him earnestly.

"There is no doubt, after what God did for me that I want to follow Him. Would you show me how?"

There, seated at a table in The Saloon, they bowed their heads. Eli led him in a short prayer confessing his sins and then accepting salvation through Jesus while Sam repeated the words after him.

When they had finished, Sam asked, "would you show me how to be a good Christian?"

Eli nodded, "of course I will. I'll be right back."

He went to the back room and when he returned there was a Bible in his hand.

"This is for you," he began, "each new convert receives one. I want you to read this every day to start. I'm sure that you will have many questions and I would be glad to answer any of your questions. I meet with a couple groups of men throughout the week and we spend time learning and praying. You are welcome to join us any time."

He flipped open the Bible, "There are 66 books that make up the Bible and it is split up into two parts – the Old and the New Testament. The word Testament literally means covenant. So, in essence, you have the Old Covenant that God made with mankind and the New Covenant that He made with us." He continued, "I would recommend that you begin in the New Testament at Matthew and read through it first and then move onto the Old Testament."

Sam nodded, "Okay, I'll do that." He looked over at Eli and grinned. "Am I invited to the church service as well?" he asked.

Eli laughed, "it is your saloon, so I can't hardy keep you away now, can I?"

Sam sat at the table drinking coffee and reading his new Bible while Eli finished the preparation to open for business. He kept reading right up until it was time for him to begin cooking the food.

* * *

Jeff snuck out of the house early that morning. He had learned long ago to escape before his father had finished sleeping off his Friday night drunk. He pondered how it was that he could meet some of the men coming out of the saloons, half drunk, and they were so nice to him. His dad, well he was just a plain mean drunk.

He thought about going to the pig roast at Joshua's house, but it was quite a ways out of town and he did not dare get his horse out for fear of waking his dad. There were too many Saturday mornings in which he had smelled the sour odor of stale liquor from his dad's breath while he beat him with his belt for some offense, whether real or imagined. He wondered what it would be like to have a father who didn't drink. What if they lived in a nice house where the roof did not leak when it rained, where he would not be ashamed to invite friends over?

He used the stick he was carrying to smack the top off a weed that somehow had offended him. He stopped his introspection when he realized that he was standing in front of the bakery. The thought of one of the doughnuts made his mouth water, but he didn't have any money and he was still working off what he owed. He contemplated sneaking in and stealing one, but dismissed the idea immediately. Mrs. Franco had been so nice to him, even after breaking her window. She could have made the sheriff throw him into jail for shooting up her restaurant, but she didn't. The thought of doing something to hurt her was out of the question. Besides, she was being sparked by the preacher. The one who used to be a sheriff and Jeff just didn't think he could pull the wool over his eyes. He would get caught for sure.

He took another swing at another weed when a voice startled him.

"Can I buy you breakfast?" The familiar voice came from behind him and he had been so busy thinking he hadn't heard the foot steps behind him. He spun around to face his benefactor.

Steven gave the boy a big grin. "Come on in with me. It's my treat."

Jeff looked at him, suddenly suspicious, "Why would you want to buy me breakfast?" he demanded.

"Well, now," Steven drawled, "you and I have been working together now for a while and it just seems proper for a man to buy his coworker breakfast. Of course, if you are too busy…"

"Oh no sir," Jeff hurried after the older man. "I ain't busy at all."

Steven held the door for the boy and then followed him in. They sat at the only table available, the one under the boarded up window. Jeff glanced up at his handy work ruefully.

Steven's eyes followed the boys look and he noticed the expression on his face.

"You're regretting that morning, aren't you?"

Jeff dropped his gaze and didn't answer.

"Son, there have been many things that I did in my life that I regret. There were times that I hated myself and what I had become." Steven paused as Elizabeth came over to the table with a cup of coffee for Steven.

"What can I get for you gentlemen?" she asked.

Steven looked at the young man seated across from him. "What will it be, Jeff?"

Jeff gazed at the display case lined with cakes, pies, doughnuts and other delectables. He spied a large roll with brown, sugary goodness dripping down the sides.

"Can I have one of those sticky buns?" he asked, pointing at the biggest one.

Steven let out a laugh. "Of course." He turned back to Elizabeth, "we'll have two of those, please, and I betting this young feller would enjoy a glass of milk, too."

"Yes ma'am, I would," Jeff chimed in.

Elizabeth smiled as she walked away and Steven continued, "there were many times I thought I couldn't get any worse and then I did something else that just added to the list of horrible things I'd done."

"What happened," the boy asked quizzically.

"Someone came along who actually cared about me." He stopped as the pastries were delivered and thanked Elizabeth before returning to the conversation.

"In spite of the fact that I was a terrible drunk, this man tried to help me out."

Jeff interrupted, talking more to himself than to the man across the table.

"My dad's a drunk."

"I know, son." Steven had a tender heart for the boy. "I knew your dad before you were born. I used to drink with him on Friday and Saturday nights. It's one of the reasons I am telling you this story."

Jeff dug into his roll while Steven continued, "I think you know the man that helped me out, his name is Eli."

Jeff looked up with sugar drizzle circling his lips. "The preacher?"

"The very same one." Steven replied. He took a bite of his roll and Jeff waited while he chewed. He swallowed the bite and took a sip of coffee before he spoke again.

"Eli fed me when I had nothing to eat. He gave me coffee when all I craved was liquor and he told me about a God who loved me so much that He paid the price for my sins and was willing to forgive me for everything that I have done or will do. He never gave up on me, even when I had given up on myself."

Steven went on to share how Eli had been bushwhacked and thrown on a train. He told of riding out to find the injured man and how he desperately needed a drink. He spoke of his cry to God and how God answered that prayer. He told his story and the young boy listened with rapt attention.

Meanwhile, Jeff had finished his roll and was draining the glass of milk. Steven's coffee on the other hand was starting to get cold and his roll had only a single bite out of it.

Steven paused to take a swallow of the coffee then turned his attention back to the boy.

"Jeff, I don't want to see you go the way of your dad. You have a choice to make and no one can make it for you. I hope that you are going to do the right thing."

Steven did not push the boy, he simply left him with a lot to mull over.

Elizabeth came over with more coffee and as she filled his cup she commented, "you haven't hardly touched your roll, is something wrong with it?"

"No ma'am, it is delicious. I was doing too much jaw jacking and not enough eating, but I'm going to take care of it right now."

She smiled at Jeff. "I see you didn't have that problem. Is there anything else I can get you, young man?"

"No ma'am. It was sure good. I'm plumb full up to here." He held his hand up to the level of his eyes.

Elizabeth laughed, "Well thank you Jeff. I'm glad you enjoyed it."

When Steven finished, he paid and the pair walked out the door. They stepped off the porch where they could enjoy the early morning sun on their faces.

Jeff finally broke the silence.

"I don't want to be like my dad."

Steven looked down at the upturned face.

"You don't have to be, but one thing is for certain, you can't do it on your own. We all need help from someone else at some time. If you ever need anything, you let me know. If I'm not around, you ask the Widow Franco or find Eli but don't try to go it alone. When you decide you want to make peace with God, you just ask and I will show you how."

* * *

When Eli finished setting up the saloon for the Sunday morning service, he hurried over to the church so that he could help Steven. Together they knelt in prayer even as the hands on the clock approached the hour.

As was the custom the service started out with hymns being sung and then Eli stepped to the pulpit.

"This week has been one of turmoil and redemption." He began, "I don't know if many of you heard, but one of the local saloon owners was shot and God healed him of his wound. He has now accepted Jesus as his savior as a result of this incident, but it has also laid a great burden upon my shoulders. As a result, Steven Bosco has agreed to fill in for me this week, to ease my work load. Please welcome Steven as he comes to give the sermon today."

There was a halfhearted clapping from the congregation as Eli and Steven traded places.

Steven cleared his throat, obviously uncomfortable with the stiff new collar that he was wearing. He had bought new clothes for the occasion but was now wishing he was in his old worn out trousers. It did not help his anxiety any, standing in front of the congregation which numbered nearly one hundred and twenty five people. Steven looked across the sea of faces and nervously thought the entire town must be seated out there. He swallowed but his mouth was so dry he nearly caused himself to choke. One finger reached up and tugged on the collar while an impatient parishioner coughed in the audience.

The silence was broken when Elizabeth stood up. "Mr. Bosco has asked me to read to you from God's Word today. Please open your Bibles to John chapter nine, verses one through seven."

There was a murmuring from some, as they were not used to a woman reading in church but she also heard the rustling of pages as the congregants began to search for the passage. Elizabeth waited, giving them time to find it, then began reading in a clear voice that was so sweet that it caused a chill to run down Eli's back.

"'And as Jesus passed by, he saw a man which was blind from his birth. And his disciples asked him, saying, Master, who did sin, this man, or his parents, that he was born blind? Jesus answered, 'Neither hath this man sinned, nor his parents: but that the works of God should be made manifest in him. I must work the works of Him that sent me, while it is day: the night cometh, when no man can work. As long as I am in the world, I am the light of the world.' When He had thus spoken, He spat on the ground and made clay of the spittle, and He anointed the eyes of the blind man with the clay. And said unto him, go, wash in the pool of Siloam, (which is by way of interpretation, Sent.) He went his way therefore, and washed, and came seeing.'"

When she was finished reading, Steven took a long drink from the glass of water that someone had placed at the pulpit, grateful to the unspoken hero. When Elizabeth sat down, Steven began to speak and even as he did, a calmness that was not his own covered his soul and he knew this was exactly where he was supposed to be at and what he was supposed to be doing.

"I suppose that when many of us read this passage, we focus on the fact that Jesus spit into the dirt, made mud out of it and with that, healed a blind man. That in fact is an extraordinary thing, but I want to point you to another part of this passage. Notice what Jesus said before he healed the man. 'As long as I am in the world, I am the light of the world.'"

Steven scanned the faces of the people in front of him, no longer nervous.

"I have heard people quote that last part of that verse, quite a bit," he launched into his sermon with vigor. "I hear, 'Jesus is the light of the world', but that is not what it says."

Now another murmur rose up across the room.

"What Jesus was saying is, *while I am still here on this earth*, I am the light of the world. But where is Jesus now? According to the scriptures, He is seated at the right hand of God the Father, in heaven. So if Jesus is in heaven and no longer here on earth, who is the light of the world?"

He let the question hang for a moment then continued on, "In Matthew chapter six, Jesus refers to His disciples as the light of the world. The disciples went out and changed the world with their message of hope. They truly were light in a dark, dark world. Men and women who were dying in their sin, found salvation in Jesus through the message of hope that the disciples took to them."

Steven was preaching without notes, but he did not need them for the subject was near and dear to his heart and he was speaking with passion.

"When we read the book of Acts, we see that the disciples went into most of the known world to preach God's message of redemption. They started churches and mentored men and women to carry on what they had started. And we see that the Holy Ghost filled those people that received Jesus as their savior.

But the disciples died a long time ago, over seventeen hundred years ago, so the question now is: 'Who is the light of the world today?'"

There was another rustling across the congregation as they whispered amongst themselves. Steven allowed the noise to die down to nothing before he spoke again.

"Friends, those of us who have accepted Jesus as our Savior, we are now His disciples. We are now the light of the world. In the book of Matthew chapter five, Jesus tells his disciples 'Ye are the light of the world. A city that is set on a hill cannot be hid. Neither do men light a candle, and put it under a bushel, but on a candlestick; and it giveth light unto all that are in the house.'

Are we a candle in a candle stick? Are we a city on a hill? Do the people around us even know what we believe, or do we just blend into the crowd?" Steven was not pulling any punches now.

"The task of winning souls to Jesus is too great of a task for just one man. Eli cannot do it all. It is up to us, you and me, to reach out to our neighbors, our friends, our family and share the good news of Jesus.

The message is very simple, 'That if thou shalt confess with thy mouth the Lord Jesus, and shalt believe in thine heart that God hath raised him from the dead, thou shalt be saved. For with the heart man believeth unto righteousness; and with the mouth confession is made unto salvation.' He was now quoting out of the book of Romans.

There it is my friends, the gospel message in a few words. The good news that the world needs to hear. I encourage you to take these words outside of the four walls of this church. Take them to the lost and the dying. Be a light unto the world. Shine brightly for Jesus, that no one around you when they stand before the judgement throne, has the ability to use the excuse of 'I never heard.'

Eli has shared this with me many times and I pass this truth onto you. It is not your job to convince people to accept Jesus. That is the job of the Holy Ghost. Your job is simply to share the gospel. Please, do not fail to do your part of the job, *because the Holy Ghost will not, cannot fail in doing His job!*"

Steven stepped down from the pulpit and took a seat in the front row as the song leader came up for the last hymn. Steven breathed a silent prayer of thanksgiving. He had been terrified and God had used him anyway. As the last verse of the Hymn was being sung, he walked to the door to greet people as they left, the way he'd seen Eli do it dozens of time before.

He overheard an elderly woman talking to her friend.

"I cannot believe that he is telling us that we are supposed to do the pastor's job for him."

"Edna," came the reply, "what in heavens name are you talking about? You are already doing the things he was talking about."

"Sadie, I don't understand."

Steven was having a difficult time paying attention to the man who was complementing him on his sermon, as he tried to eavesdrop on the women's conversation.

Sadie answered her, "Don't you knit a blanket for every newborn in this town? Don't you take meals to folks who are sick? You have never failed to tell them folks about the Lord when the opportunity presents itself."

Edna sniffed, "Well yes, but I don't preach at people."

"Maybe not with your words, but you do with your actions. When you do those things in Jesus' name, you are doing just what Mr. Bosco was preaching about."

A thoughtful expression replaced the look of disdain.

"I never thought of it in those terms before." Edna responded. "So I just need to continue to do what I have already have been doing."

"Until the day you meet the good Lord."

The two women reached Steven by then. Edna reached out her hand and as he shook it, she said, "That was a lovely sermon today Mr. Bosco, just lovely."

Steven just smiled, "Thank you ma'am. I truly appreciate that. I really do."

* * *

Eli finished preaching, excited to see Sam in the service for the first time ever. Ben had come to the Saloon to hear his dad preach and Naomi had taken the baby to the parsonage so he could take a nap. Elizabeth went with Naomi so the girls could get to know one another better.

After the service had finished Eli and his son were moving the tables and chairs around for the Saloons' opening time. Suddenly a commotion out in front of the establishment drew their attention. Eli set down the chair he was carrying and moved to the batwing doors, peering over them. Outside the door, two young boys were on the boardwalk, taunting a man who was riding in a buckboard, drawn by a matched pair of Clydesdale draft horses. The man was dressed all in black except for his white shirt. He wore a black flat brimmed hat with a domed crown but the cause of the boys' ridicule though was the strange long curls of hair that came down out of the hat in front of his ears.

Eli knew the boys as two of the young urchins who were constant pests around town. They never got into real trouble, but they were talented at making themselves a nuisance. They were so focused on the man in front of them, they failed to recognize the threat behind them and Eli took advantage of that. He swiftly stepped out the door and grabbed an earlobe in each hand, grasping them between his thumb and knuckle of his index finger and twisting. Two distinct howls of pain split the afternoon air.

"You boys get home and tell your parents what you have done, because tomorrow, I am going to visit them and let them know what I saw and what I heard. Do you understand?"

Both boys squealed out their acknowledgement of his order and with a push, Eli sent them off the boardwalk. They hit the ground running, each holding their sore ear in their hand.

Eli turned to the young man, who wasn't much more than a boy himself. "I am so sorry about that. Please don't judge our town based upon that reception."

"I am used to being ridiculed because of my looks, but I thank you for intervening for me. My name is Levi. Levi Kauffman."

Eli stepped off the board walk and offered his hand. "I am Elijah Exeter. It is a pleasure to make your acquaintance. Come on in. I can offer you coffee or a beer, if you'd like."

"Thank you," Levi responded, "but I was looking for the sheriff when I was accosted by those two boys. Could you please point me in the right direction?"

"You are not too far away." He told him how to find the Sheriff's Office and bid him farewell before returning into the saloon.

No more than a quarter of an hour had elapsed and Levi returned.

"I forgot that today is your Holy Day and found that the Sheriff is not in his office. This matter is of utmost importance and I believe your Sheriff needs to know." He took a moment to consider then continued, "I have found a body buried in a shallow grave south of town."

Eli drew a sharp breath, his mind immediately going to Matt's missing person report.

"Levi, I agree. Let me get my horse and I will take you to his house." He turned toward Sam and called out across the room. "Sam, I need to take this young man to see Matt. Are you okay with me calling it a day?"

Sam just waved for him to leave.

It only took a few minutes to get his horse saddled and ready to go. He and Ben rode alongside the wagon, but Eli purposefully kept the conversation away from the dead body. He figured it was Matt's job and he did not want to step on any toes.

"Levi, you spoke of my Holy Day, what do you consider a holy day in your religion?"

Levi turned his head, "I am a Jew and we celebrate the Sabbath. Here, you call it Saturday. It is why I could not come in yesterday to report my find."

Eli responded, "You are one of God's chosen people."

"Many Christians do not see us that way. For centuries, our race has been persecuted by people who call themselves Christians because they say we crucified their messiah." Levi had a dower look upon his face as he spoke.

"Seems to me that it was the Romans that crucified Christ. Sure the Jews asked for His death but it was the Roman governor Pilate who sentenced Him to death. Besides, the death and resurrection of Jesus was all in God's plan, so none of them really had a choice."

Levi grinned ruefully. "I wished everyone looked at it that way. If so we could live a peaceful existence alongside of others without persecution." He glanced over at Eli. "How is it that a Saloon keeper knows so much about my people and the one you call the messiah?"

Eli laughed. "I tend bar at the saloon, but I am also the town preacher. I am so glad I had the good fortune to meet you and would be honored to be called your friend."

"Sir, the honor is mine".

They rode in silence and Levi kept stealing glances at his two new friends. He was struck by the likeness that existed between the two men. There was no mistaking that they were father and son, although Ben was several inches taller than his dad and had a far stouter build, the resemblance was uncanny. Ben, he noted was much quieter than his father, a trait that was not altogether bad.

As the wagon and two riders came into the yard, Matt was already out on the porch, holding a carbine in one hand, casually but in a way that it could be brought in to play quickly. As soon as he realized who his visitors were, he let the hammer down and leaned it in a corner so it could not fall and accidentally discharge. He stepped off the porch as Eli dismounted his horse.

"What brings you all out here this afternoon?" Matt reached out and shook Eli's hand.

"Matt, this is Levi." He turned to Levi, "this is Sheriff Wheaton."

Levi leapt down from the wagon and put his hand out. "Sheriff, I am sorry to bother you on your Holy Day, but I have to report a body that I have found."

Matt exchanged glances with Eli then returned his attention to the young man. "Levi, where is this body at?"

"It is south of town, about an hour's ride with the wagon." Levi replied.

Becky came out on the porch to greet the visitors.

"Come in, please," she offered. "Have you had supper yet?"

Eli was the first to respond, "Thank you ma'am, but we don't want to impose upon you."

"Nonsense. We are just finishing up and there is plenty of food left," Becky responded.

Matt piped up, "I'm going to finish my meal before I head out so you might as well join us. That body is not going anywhere."

He turned to Joshua, "would you mind saddling my horse for me?" he asked.

Joshua had finished eating already and had been itching to get outside, but Matt suddenly changed his mind. "Forget the horse. Please hitch up the wagon if you don't mind."

"Yes sir." He started toward the barn then turned back to Matt. "May I come along too?"

Matt walked over to the boy and put his arm around his shoulder. They began walking toward the barn together.

"Don't you think you seen enough death to last you a lifetime?" Matt prodded gently.

Joshua dropped his head as he thought back over the last year and a shudder coursed through his body.

"Yes sir, I reckon I have."

"Someday soon, I'll let you come along, but this is not the right day for it. I'm sorry son."

Joshua nodded. "Okay."

He headed to the barn and Matt walked back to the house. When he got inside, Becky already had their guests served up. Matt sat down at his place and turned to the other men.

"We already said the blessing. Go ahead and dig in."

Becky sat down and Ben gave his fork a rest for a moment to address her, "ma'am, I did not realize how famished I was until I began eating this. Thank you. It is delicious."

Levi and Eli both chimed in their agreement.

Becky smiled at the praise. "Well thank you, gentlemen." She responded. "Can I get you more coffee?"

With mouths already full again they just shook their heads. The men wolfed their food down as quickly as a man can politely do in the company of a woman and then with repeated thanks, headed toward the door.

Joshua had the wagon ready to go when they got outside. Eli pulled him aside.

"I have an errand for you to run, if you are willing?"

"Of course," came the reply, "if I can."

Eli took a two bit piece out of his pocket and placed it in the boy's hand.

"I need you to ride out to the parsonage and let the Widow Franco and Naomi, Ben's wife, know that we will not be home for several hours."

Joshua pocketed the coin.

"Yes, sir!" He made a beeline for the barn.

Matt grabbed an extra canvas tarp and some rope which he tossed into the back of the wagon and together the four men began their morbid journey.

* * *

Steven walked to the door of the Saloon and peered over the top of it, looking for Eli. When he didn't see him, he pushed his way through and approached the bar. It was the second time he had entered a saloon during working hours, since he had been rescued from drinking nearly a year ago. The sounds and the smells began to waft into his memory and he was transported back in time. It seemed like yesterday, he could feel the burn of the liquor down his throat. He started to turn around, to walk away.

"Hey Steven, can I buy you a drink?" The cowboy at the bar was just being friendly, he meant no harm, but no one could have anticipated what happened next.

Sam's arm shot out across the bar and he grabbed the man's wrist and twisted it so his palm was face up. Grabbing a coin from the cash box he was standing by, he slapped it into his open hand. Then with a shove, he sent the startled and confused man stumbling toward the door.

"*Get out,*" he roared, "*and don't ever come back!*"

"My drink?" the cowboy stammered.

Sam pointed toward his now closed fist.

"I gave you your money back. Now git!"

The poor guy stumbled out of the bar, still not sure of why he'd been booted out. He stepped out into the sunshine, still shaking his head.

Sam turned to the rest of the crowd. "If any of you ever try to buy Steven a drink, the same thing is going to happen to you. Do you understand?"

He just got a bunch of blanks stares.

"*Well, do you?*" he bellowed out with a venom that none of the men had ever seen before.

This time all the heads in the room were bobbing up and down.

"Sam, you didn't have to do that for me." Steven was more than a little embarrassed, being unexpectedly the center of attention.

Sam turned his attention to the younger man, "son, if you were ever to start drinking again, it won't be at my Saloon. I happened to really like the man that you have become and I don't ever want to see the old Steven come back.

Steven murmured, "The old will pass away and all things will be made new."

"Huh?" Sam queried.

"Nothing." Steven responded. "Thank you, Sam."

Sam shrugged. "Can I get you some coffee?"

"No thanks. I was looking for Eli."

"He and Ben ran off with some stranger, a man I've never seen before. They were looking for the sheriff."

"Okay."

Back in the sunshine, Steven pondered his next move. He started walking and soon he found himself alongside the river. A light breeze was playing across the slow moving waters and the coolness it brought was refreshing.

A scream ripped through his thoughts and brought him back into the here and now as his attention was drawn a teenage girl who was watching something out in the river. He diverted his gaze and saw a young boy who was upstream from him, floundering in the slow moving current. Even as Steven located the source of concern, the boy's head dipped below the water and it seemed like a lifetime before it reappeared.

Steven was galvanized to action, kicking off his boots and stripping down to his undershirt. He dropped his gun belt onto the pile and sprinted for the riverbank, diving headlong into the cold water. With long, deep strokes in the water, he raced at an angle that would intercept the lad.

As he neared the exhausted swimmer, he too began to feel the tiredness creeping into his muscles. Though once a champion swimmer, the years of drinking had taken its toll on his ability and on his stamina. Steven grabbed the boy and the added weight lent more pain to his already aching muscles. He was determined not to let the young man drown, but suddenly realized that there might be two of them going to the bottom of the river. For a moment he considered letting the boy go and trying to limp himself back to the shore, but immediately dismissed the thought. He would rather die than to let the boy die. The decision made, he did the only thing that he could do, the only option that they had left. He began to pray.

"God, help me!" It was all he could get out.

His muscle screamed in protest of the unaccustomed work that he was calling upon them to do, but he would not quit. He was determined to stroke his way to the shore and would not stop until his muscle seized up or he made it. One more stroke. One more kick. The weight of his wet trousers were dragging him downward and he wished he had stripped naked to attempt the rescue, but it was too late to think about that. One more stroke. His head dipped below the water and he tried to push the boy up. Maybe the youngster had rested enough to make it to shore. Steven kicked one more time, got his head above water and was able to gulp another mouthful of air.

Without warning, his feet hit solid ground. With a startled exclamation of disbelief, he stopped trying to swim. He realized he was on solid ground, out in the middle of the river. Stunned, he stood neck deep in the lazy current, thankful that he had the water to buoy him up for his muscles were so exhausted that he could not have stood up on shore. His disbelief faded into the realization that God had answered his simple prayer. He held the boy in his arms, head above the water and with tears of exhaustion streaming down his face and he praised the Maker of heaven and earth for answering his prayer. Under his feet was a sandbar for him to stand upon. He rested chin deep in the water and held onto the whimpering child in his arms.

The girl who was on the shore, seeing they were safe, at least for the moment, called out to Steven asking him as to what she should do.

Steven was so tired, he could not make himself heard at first because he wasn't able to generate enough volume to give her an answer.

Nearly ten minutes passed before he mustered enough strength to make her understand that she needed to find someone with a rowboat to come out and rescue them. As she ran off toward the main part of town, Steven realized another issue was arising. Even though it was hot outside, the water, coming out of the mountains was relatively cold and now both he and the youngster were starting to shiver. He knew that if he got too cold, his muscles would cramp and sandbar or no sandbar, they would die.

He turned to the lad, "What's your name?" he asked through chattering teeth.

"Sammy." The young boy chattered back.

"Sammy, do you pray to God?" He could feel the tremors go through the boy's body as he held him in the flowing water.

Sammy nodded. "I go to Parson Exeter's church."

Steven replied, "Sammy, I think we need to pray right now that the cold water won't have any effect upon us. Can you do that?"

This time the boy just nodded. Steven noted that his little lips were beginning to turn a pale blue.

They took turns praying. Once they had prayed for their situation, Sammy began to pray for his mommy and daddy. He asked Jesus to watch over his sister Sarah.

Steven too began to pray for the special people around him, Eli, the Widow Franco, Sam. He even prayed for the Christian woman in St. Louis who he had sent a letter to. As the two stood in the water, chilled to the bone, they shared the communion of prayer. It kept their minds off their own predicament and allowed them to concentrate on the ones they loved.

So intent were the two on praying, they did not even realize that help had arrived until the splashing of the oars sent water spraying across them. Soon strong arms reached down and pulled Sammy into the boat.

As soon as the mission had been accomplished and Sammy was safe, Steven realized that the muscle cramps that he had feared could no longer be held at bay. As his calf muscle recoiled from overwork and cold, he could no longer keep his head above water. The pain from the charlie horse was so intense he went under without catching a breath of air. Steven began to thrash his arms in panic until he slipped into blackness as his entire head disappeared below the surface of the water.

"Oh no you don't." Adam, the hostler who employed Steven at the livery stable, shoved his hand into the river and grabbed at a bunch of hair, but missed. He plunged his entire upper body under the water and this time, got a hand hold on Steven. As soon as he brought the head up, the other rescuer grabbed him under the arm. They were grateful that Steven was a small man, but even so, it was quite a struggle as they yarded his limp body over the side of the boat. The violent maneuver caused a stream of water to flow out of his mouth as he hit the bottom of the boat but there was no other response from him.

It only took a few short minutes for their powerful strokes to bring the boat to shore. Sarah rushed to them, wrapping the still shivering Sammy in her arms. As soon as she grabbed him, the brave little boy burst into tears.

Harvey, Adam's rescue partner jumped from the boat.

"I'm going for the doctor." He bolted down the road.

Adam bodily lifted the limp body of Steven and carried him from the boat into the sunshine. He looked down at the unmoving form of his employee, not sure what to do. He knew that Steven would pray, but he was an atheist. He just couldn't believe in a god who would allow bad things to happen. He argued in his mind, right here was an example. Steven went to save that poor child and here he lay, lifeless on the ground. What kind of a god would allow such a thing to happen?

Even as he argued in his mind, Adam finally looked at the sky.

"Okay, God. If you are real, what are you going to do?"

Next to him, a young female voice piped in.

"God, thank you for saving Sammy. Please save Mr. Bosco. Please!" She began to sob along with her brother as they stood by the prostrate form on the ground.

"Please, God." The young boy cried, still shaking from the ordeal, barely able to stand even with his sister's help.

Doctor Mercer came running up, carrying his black bag.

"Out of the way!" He ordered.

He knelt down alongside the man whom he come to admire. He had seen Steven wandering around town as a hopeless drunk, despised by the towns folk. He was then miraculously transformed into an upstanding citizen of the community, saved from alcohol. He'd be hanged if he was going to let him die like this.

He placed the stethoscope to Steven's heart, but there was no sound. Balling up his fist, he brought it down like a hammer into the center of the chest. The patient responded with a violent fit of coughing, which caused water to spew out of his mouth and then there was a deep intake of air.

Amazed, Doc Mercer placed the stethoscope back on the heart, only to hear the thump, thump, thump, a healthy heart going at its rhythmic pace.

He shook his head. "I've never actually had that work before." he muttered.

Harvey came running up carrying the litter that the doctor kept behind the door. Together, he and Adam rolled Steven onto it and they carried his still form to Doc Mercer's office.

CHAPTER ELEVEN

Eli and Ben had tied their horses to the back of the wagons. Eli sat with Levi in his wagon while Ben took a place next to Matt. As Eli and Levi talked about the younger man's Jewish beliefs, Matt and Ben rode along silently.

Matt finally turned to Ben. "You don't talk much, do you?"

Ben grinned. "'Even a fool, when he holdeth his peace, is counted wise and he that shutteth his lips is esteemed a man of understanding'." He quoted from Proverbs 17.

Matt pressed on. "Your father does his fair share of talking, but I don't see him saying stupid things very much…In fact, I don't ever recall him ever putting his foot in his mouth."

Ben shrugged. "I guess wisdom comes with age."

Matt smiled. "I guess it does."

Just shy of an hour, the quartet pulled up. Levi pointed to a rock formation with a scrubby tree growing out of it.

"I recognize that," he declared. "We will pass that, turn east and there will be a wash with the sand caved in over the body."

They found the body, just as Levi had described it. Levi and Ben stayed with the wagon, while Matt and Eli approached on foot. They carefully check for clues as they advanced on the wash, but the wind had blown any evidence away.

The body had been pretty well covered, but the stiff winds of the last couple of days had blown the sand and the result was a portion of the forehead and the tip of a boot were uncovered.

Eli turned to Matt.

"That boy is pretty sharp, to recognize this for what it is with so little showing."

Matt nodded his agreement.

They both put on their leather gloves and Matt swept the sand away from the face. The skin was dried and had turned black in the desert heat so identification of the body was impossible. Together the men carefully removed sand from the rest of the decaying corpse. Once that job was completed, they began a thorough examination of the dead man. It wasn't until they went to roll the body over that they discovered that the lower back of the man's head was missing, blown out by the bullet which entered his eye and exited the bottom of his skull. The decomposition of the skin made it impossible to positively identify the entry wound.

Matt called out to Ben, who made his way over to the other two men.

"Can you tell how long this man has been dead?" He asked the young doctor.

Ben just shook his head.

"No, I honestly don't deal with people that have been dead this long so I really couldn't give you a clue." He answered. "But I can tell you that he didn't die here."

Matt looked up at him quizzically.

Ben continued, "a traumatic head wound would have bled profusely. There is no dried blood on the sand beneath him. I suspect he was brought here from elsewhere to be buried."

Matt nodded, "Good catch. That makes perfect sense."

Eli smiled, proud of his son's knowledge and wisdom. He nodded his agreement. He too had reached the same conclusion, but he was glad to see that Ben still knew how to use his head, even after all that book learning.

Matt began to go through the dead man's pockets, searching for any indication of who they were dealing with.

Levi wandered over, bored with sitting at the wagon. Eli looked over at him.

"How did you know this man had been murdered?" he asked.

Levi replied, "the way he was buried. If one of my family member's had died, I would have buried him properly. I assumed that whoever had buried this body here had done so with the intent of hiding it as opposed to having respect for their dead loved one. I didn't know for certain, I just suspected.

Matt paused his search. "Well you were spot on, son." He then casually asked, "when did you ride into the area?"

Levi smiled, "If you are wondering if I did this the answer is, 'No'. My family and I rode in here Friday afternoon. We were going to try to make it to town before the sun set, but I discovered this when I went to relieve myself away from the women. The elders discussed what we should do until it was too late to do anything."

"Where are they now?" Ben queried.

"Oh, we passed them about a mile back. We camped away from the main trail so there is less chance of being discovered by those who might try to make sport of us." Levi spoke with a tone of resignation, like it was just a fact of life to be dealt with.

Matt returned to his searching the pockets of the man's trousers, but found nothing that would help in identifying the dead man.

Above him on the top of the wash, he heard Levi call out, "gentlemen."

The three men left the body and scrambled their way up to Levi's position. He pointed to some sagebrush where he had discovered a slip of paper.

Matt stepped over and pulled it loosed from its entanglement. After reading it, he handed it over to Eli. Ben and Levi looked over his shoulder to read the message. In block printing it said, "MEET ME AT THE HOGS SNOUT. IF YOU DON'T WANT ME TO TELL YOUR WIFE ABOUT THE GIRL, YOU WILL COME."

Eli questioned, "The Hog's Snout?"

Matt replied, "it's a rock formation about a half mile from here. I suspect I will want to check that out, perhaps that was where he was killed."

They got the tarp out and laid it out alongside the body, pinning the corners down with rocks. Carefully, so as not to damage the corpse, they rolled the body onto it. Matt didn't want any of the extremities falling off during the trip to town so he wrapped the man up tightly then tied the package securely with the rope. Eli brought Matt's wagon over while he was preparing the body and the four men lifted the gruesome freight into the back of it.

When that was accomplished, Matt turned to Levi. "Thank you for all your help. Are you and your family going to stay in the area?"

"That I do not know." Levi responded. "The elders will decide where we are to settle."

Ben interjected. "You keep mentioning the elders. Who are they?"

"The eldest member of each family meets to make decisions about the group. We have seven families traveling together."

"What happens if you don't agree with the elder's course of action?" Ben asked.

"I could leave at any time." Levi answered as if he were surprised by the question, "But why would I? They are my people." He turned to Eli, "As you have already seen, we are not always accepted by outsiders."

Eli nodded. "Yes, but you are welcome here. Please don't let those two hooligans warp your opinion of our town."

Matt looked puzzled and Eli explained what had happened earlier in the day.

"I plan on having a talk with their parents tomorrow," Eli finished.

"Thank you." Matt replied. "They need to get those two under control."

The foursome began their trek back to town. Levi split off to reunite with his family and the other three continued on, unaware of the drama that had unfolded in their absence.

* * *

Once again, Jeff had escaped the house early, before his father woke from his drunken stupor. He engaged in his favorite past time, whacking the head off of weeds with a stick, although it was only a favorite by default. It was the one thing that he always seemed to be doing. He wandered down one of the alleys in town, looking for something to do, anything to alleviate his boredom. Oh how he wished he could do stuff with his folks like normal kids. Instead, he looked for ways to entertain himself. All of his friends, the few that he had, were in church and there was nothing for a kid to do. He picked up a rock and balanced it in his hand as he lazily contemplated breaking some windows on the closed businesses. He quickly decided against that and tossed the rock onto some empty crates. Last time he broke a window, he recalled, it did not work out so well.

All at once, he heard a whimper. Snooping around the crates which were stacked against a wall, he located a small brown and white puppy. The thing didn't look like it was big enough to be away from its mother, but here it was, whining for some food. Jeff put his finger down by the poor things mouth only to be rewarded with a lick and then the attempt at sucking. He laughed and scooped the little guy up in his arms.

Looking around, he didn't see any lactating bitches close by. He began walking around, looking for the puppy's mother but to no avail.

He was afraid to take the dog home, his pa would probably make him get rid of it, or worse yet, he might just kill the poor little thing out of spite.

Jeff pondered his situation. Just about everyone in town was at church. At least he figured they were though he had no idea what time it was now. He thought of Steven. Steven was the only adult friend that he had, but he too would be in church and then he thought of Joe over at the lumber store. Joe wouldn't be at church and even if his store wasn't open, he might be at his place behind it.

Jeff hurried to the lumber yard, the whimpering pup inside his shirt. Joe open the door on the third knock.

"Jeff!" He exclaimed in surprise. "What are you doing here?"

"Mr…" Jeff suddenly realized he did not know the last name of the man standing in front of him. "Mr. Joe, I found this puppy."

He held the dog out to the man. "I can't find his mom and he's hungry."

Joe started to ask the boy why he didn't take it home, but stopped himself when he realized he already knew the answer. He held open the door.

"Come on in," he said, "I think I might just have the thing."

Joe walked over to a rug on the floor, which he moved aside revealing a hatch with a recessed handle. He pulled it open, reached down into the cooling box and pulled out a jar of milk. He poured some of it into a dish and held it out to the young boy. Jeff dipped his finger into the milk and held it to the puppy's lips and as soon as his tongue touched the milk, he latched onto the finger like he was sucking on his mother's teat.

Joe watched with amusement as the young boy kept dipping his finger. Finally, he shook his head and grabbed a cloth off the sideboard of the sink.

"Here son, let's try this." He grinned at the eager pup.

Jeff pulled his finger out of the dog's mouth as Joe dipped the corner of the rag in the milk. When it was sopping wet, he put it into the puppy's mouth and watched as the animal went to town on this latest acquisition. When the rag was all but sucked dry, Joe handed the rag to the boy. Jeff followed the example of his elder, dipping and letting the young puppy suck it dry, over and over again.

Joe interrupted the silence with a question.

"So what are you going to name this poor little whelp?" He asked.

Jeff thought about his answer as he dipped the cloth one more time.

"I don't know, maybe Rock." He finally answered.

"Why Rock?"

Jeff hesitated for a long time.

"I don't know," he shrugged. "I just like the name."

There was no way he was going to admit to an adult that he was thinking of breaking windows with rocks when he found the pup.

Joe laughed his big laugh, causing the puppy to startle.

"Okay, I like it too." He grinned at Jeff which caused the boy to smile as well, lighting up his young face.

When Rock had his fill of milk, he waddled around the floor, snooping around Jeff's feet and ankles. Within moments he plopped down against Jeff's worn leather boot and promptly fell asleep.

Joe brought the young man back to reality with his next question.

"What are you going to do with him now?"

The face that had been beaming a moment before clouded over.

"I don't know." He was silent for a moment as he pondered his next move.

"Your pa won't let you keep him?" Joe asked.

"No sir, I don't think so." Gloom settled on the boy. "He ain't gonna let me have a dog."

Suddenly his face lit back up.

"I can see if Mr. Bosco will take care of him for me." Jeff remember how kind Steven always was with him.

Joe gave a sigh of relief. He had no desire to be saddled with a dog, his life was too busy to worry about any other living creature.

Jeff scooped the sleeping up critter and snuggled Rock in the crook of his arm. He started out the door but skidded to a halt with his hand on the door handle. He turned to the older man.

"Thanks Mr. Joe."

Before Joe could respond, the boy shot out the door and sprinted down the street toward the livery stable.

In a few short moments he arrived at the stable. He'd been here before, when he had snooped around a little one time when no one knew he was around. This was the first time he'd come here with a purpose.

He was surprised to find no one was around. When he received no answer to his knock, he stepped back out into the sunlight, squinting as he looked around. He figured with all the time he'd spent at Mr. Joe's place, it was well past time for church to be out and he was puzzled at the lack of a presence at the stable.

Rock woke from his nap and Jeff set him down so as not to get piddled on. The puppy did his thing in the dirt, while Jeff contemplated what to do next. He thought of exploring down by the river, but then he caught a movement out of the corner of his eye. It was Adam, the hostler who ran the livery.

"Sir," he called out as the man approached. "I'm looking for Mr. Bosco."

Adam stopped in front of the young man, taking the puppy in at a glance.

"He's not here." He responded, a worried look on his face.

"Where is he?" the youngster asked. He didn't like the feeling he was getting from the encounter.

"Jeff, why are you looking for Steven? What is he to you?" the burly man asked.

"Him and me, we work together at the Widow Franco's bakery." Trepidation filled the boy's mind and an eerie feeling began to settle into the pit of his stomach.

100

"Son, Steven nearly drowned today and he is over at Doc's Office. Doc says he's in a coma."

Fear flooded the boy's soul. "What's a coma?"

Adam hesitated, not sure how much to tell the boy.

"It's kind of like a deep sleep, but we don't know when they will wake up... or even if they will wake up." Until a couple hours ago, Adam had no idea what a coma was until Doc told him.

Jeff felt like the wind had been knocked out of him. He reached down and picked up the puppy so Adam would not see the tears welling up in his eyes. In a strangled voice, Jeff croaked his thanks before hurrying away.

Adam watched the back of the retreating figure, worried over the boy's reaction.

As soon as he turned away, the tears started flowing down the young man's cheeks and dripped onto the puppy as Jeff tried to decipher the emotions that he was feeling. He had never had someone who had spent time with him, talked with him the way that Steven had. He had connected with Steven in a way he had never connected with anyone before and now Steven was dying. For all he knew, Steven was already dead. Just the very thought brought renewed tears streaming down his face.

He found himself standing in front of Doc Mercer's Office, drying the tears on the back of his sleeve. He waited for his breathing to calm down and wondered if he should knock. Even as he considered his options, the door swung open.

"Son, do you need something." Doc Mercer stood in the doorway, peering over top of his glasses at the pair out in the street.

"Is Mr. Bosco okay?" Jeff sniffed to keep his nose from dripping.

"Son, I think you need to head home." Doc Mercer tried to head off the inevitable.

"Please, can I see him? Please?" the boy pleaded.

The Doctor sighed. "Come on in."

Nervously, Jeff walked up the steps to the doctor's office. He stopped at the door to peer inside.

"Come on. We don't have all day." Doc Mercer's worry came across as impatience.

Jeff stepped through the doorway, afraid of what he would find.

Steven was laying on the bed and appeared to be sleeping. Jeff approached the still form with trepidation. He sidled up to the bed.

"Mr. Bosco."

There was no response.

He turned to the doctor, "Will he be alright?"

"I don't know," the doctor replied. "Sometimes, people wake up and other times they don't. Nobody knows why."

Jeff silently stared at the unconscious figure on the bed. The puppy that was still in his arms began to wiggle and absentmindedly, the young man began stroking his head. Soon the puppy settled down and fell asleep once again.

Jeff sat down in the chair that was pushed against the wall. He turned to the doctor, "Is it okay if I just stay here and talk to him?" he asked.

Doc Mercer shrugged, "suit yourself."

He turned and walked back into the interior of the house, leaving the boy and his puppy in the front room with his patient.

* * *

Ben was riding slightly ahead of the wagon when the threesome entered town. He noticed a wagon coming toward them, loaded with freight. The approaching wagon hit a pothole, causing the rear end to bounce and one of the crates on the rear of the wagon to fall off, crashing to the roadway. Somehow, it remained intact, but the freighter appeared to be oblivious to the mishaps.

Ben galloped his horse forward and flagged down the white haired driver.

"Sir, you lost a box off your wagon."

The younger man dismounted by the wayward freight and tested the weight. It was not too heavy so he lifted it up, walked to the rear of the flatbed and set it back in its place by the time the old man was able to get off the wagon.

"Thank you my boy." the freighter cackled.

The old man grabbed the rope that had failed in properly securing his load and retied the crate into place.

"Yes sir." Ben replied. "You're welcome."

As Ben remounted his horse, he saw the smirk on the Sheriff's face. As the freighter drove away down the street, Ben glanced over at Matt.

"What's so funny?" he asked.

"That there is 'Molasses Mike'," the Sheriff replied.

"Molasses Mike?" Ben queried.

"Yeah," came the reply. "He got the nickname 'Molasses Mike' because he basically has two speeds, slow and slower. Never does anything faster than he has too. Even his team of horses just plod about.

"He's not that bad," protested Eli. "He can down a plate of food faster than anyone else in town."

Matt continued, "to hear him tell it, he is the fastest gun this side of the Mississippi and won the War Between the States all by himself."

Ben glanced at the two men to see just how serious they were and then just shook his head.

Matt pulled up in front of the undertaker's office and the other two men took their leave, heading toward the parsonage and the women that waited for them.

Together, the Sheriff and the Undertaker unloaded the body and took it inside. A number of big questions remained, whose body was it and who killed the man. It was a man's body that much Matt had determined. It could be Norris', but the decomposition was too great to determine that definitively. The note they found near the body was a good indicator it could be him. As much as he did not want to do it, but he was going to need Mrs. Swensen to try and identify the clothing. This was a part of the job that he really hated.

* * *

Eli and Ben found the women had been busy, preparing a meal, talking and taking care of the baby. They sat down and the delectable food was set before them. During the meal, both of the men took time to lean back and express their gratefulness for the ladies and how hard they worked.

After the meal, Eli and Elizabeth washed the dishes, allowing Ben and Naomi some time alone together while the baby slept. Eli found himself just reveling in the time spent with this lovely woman. Even as he thought about it, he realized that her beauty came from deep within and his previous ponderings were starting to crystalize in his mind.

When the dishes were dried and put away, the couple took a walk together in the cool evening air. Elizabeth had an early day tomorrow and Eli did not want to keep her out too late, but he did not want her to go home yet either. They were walking down the boardwalk and found themselves in front of the bakery.

Eli turned to the amazing woman by his side.

Elizabeth spoke before he had a chance. "I have been thinking about selling the farm and moving in above the bakery. With the money from the sale I should be able to turn the attic space into a functional home."

She smiled and Eli was amazed at how her face lit up.

"I think that is a wonderful idea," he replied.

Eli took both of her hands in his.

"Elizabeth," Eli hoped that she could not hear the pounding of his heart. "I have been thinking so much about you. About us. I want you to know that I love you and I want you to be my wife."

He wasn't sure who was more surprised that the words came out of his mouth, but no sooner were they uttered and he knew that this was absolutely right. He had prayed long and hard about this very thing and once he had spoken his intentions, peace flooded his soul.

If Elizabeth's face had brightened up before, now it completely glowed.

"Elijah Exeter. I have loved you for the longest time. I have waited for this day for nearly a year and I would be honored to be your wife."

Eli leaned forward to kiss her for the first time and the kiss was as magical as he had dreamed it would be.

But the spell was broken by footsteps approaching on the boardwalk. Eli turned toward the sound and found that it was Matt coming toward them. He looked as if he were on a mission.

"Eli, Elizabeth," Matt looked like he was having trouble saying what was on his mind. "Something terrible has happened." His voice cracked as he continued. "Steven nearly drowned this afternoon, saving a young boy. He is at Doc Mercer's office, unconscious."

Elizabeth gasped in horror, but Eli was already on his way to the Doctor's Office. The baker and sheriff hurried right behind him.

Matt and Elizabeth burst into the office right behind the preacher, but in their rush, none of them noticed the young boy seated against the wall. The doctor came into the room and directed his comments directly to Eli.

"After what I saw when Sam was shot, I hope you have something left over for Steven. I have done all I can do... It's in God's hands now."

Eli looked at his companions. "It is in God's hands. Let's pray for Steven."

The three bowed their heads and it was at that time Eli realized that Jeff was there. Jeff stood up and as he did so, the puppy that was still in the crook of his arm whimpered. He stepped up to the group and bowed his head as well.

Each in the group offered up their entreaties to the Lord.

Tears streamed down Elizabeth's face as she prayed for the man who had been her right hand at the bakery for the last year.

Eli felt the tears welling up in his own eyes. He had mentored this young man and the pair had become closer than brothers.

Matt had to really struggle to keep his emotions in check for he had known Steven the longest. He had been a young boy when he watched the man's slide into alcoholism and then his miraculous deliverance. He could not believe that God would bring the man this far only to take him home at this time. It was unthinkable to the human mind.

Jeff had cried himself out a long time ago. His was the simplest of prayers but none offered that night were more heartfelt.

"Please God, fix Steven." He blurted out.

In a world of rejection, the young man finally knew what it was like to be accepted just as he was and now he was in fear of losing it.

Doc Mercer did not participate in the prayer, but he stood by, watching as if he was expecting a miracle to happen. When there was no noticeable change in the man on the bed, he looked as if he was disappointed.

He caught Eli and Matt's attention and motioned with his head to have them step outside.

Outside on the boardwalk, the doctor turned to the two men.

"That boy in there has been sitting with Steven all afternoon. Do you know what the story is?"

Eli shook his head. "Not really. I kind of have an idea, but…"

Matt just shook his head.

Eli took the bull by the horns, abruptly changing the subject.

"What about Steven?" he asked.

Doc Mercer explained the circumstances of how Steven came to be in his care.

"He could come out of it at any time or he could die. I don't have the equipment they have in the big eastern hospitals. If he were in this coma long enough he will eventually die of dehydration. I really have no way of giving him food to eat or to drink water."

Elizabeth came out to join them. She was the one to enlighten them on Jeff's presence.

"He has been working with Steven ever since he broke that window in my shop and Steven has taken great interest in him. I believe he has been mentoring him."

"I am amazed that his folks haven't come looking for him." Doc Mercer commented.

Matt nodded, "Yeah, I probably need to take him home." He changed the subject. "Do you know the story on the puppy?" he asked.

Doc shook his head. "No, he was carrying it when he came in."

"Has that dog had anything to eat today?" Elizabeth asked.

Doc nodded. "Yes. I brought him some milk and that durned kid has been using the corner of a rag to feed that miserable critter. I can't believe he has kept it alive, that pup is so young."

Matt stepped back inside to get the young man. He heard Jeff talking to Steven and instead of interrupting, he just stopped and listened.

"...I can't. I don't want my dad to find out about him. He will probably kill him, or make him starve to death, but I don't think he will let me keep him. I ain't never had a dog before, but I know I can take care of him. Honest, I know I can."

Matt stepped into the room. "Jeff, I suspect you can," he interjected.

The boy turned toward him. "Sheriff, I can't take Rock home or my dad will make me get rid of him."

"Come on out, let's see what can be done."

Jeff stood up and followed the sheriff out of the building gently holding the animal to his chest.

Matt explained the dilemma that Jeff was engaged in and Elizabeth immediately wrapped her arm around the young boy's shoulder.

"Jeff, I have an idea! Why don't we keep him at the Bakery? You can care for him there and as he gets older, you and I will figure out a more permanent solution."

The boy's face lit up at the suggestion.

"That a great idea," he almost shouted in his enthusiasm. "Thank you ma'am." He was more animated than they had ever seen him before and it suddenly dawned on them how important this puppy was to the youngster.

Eli was impressed with Elizabeth. He marveled that she, in the midst of her own personal turmoil, could reach out with such compassion. She was indeed a rare jewel and that small act of kindness solidified in his mind the decision to marry her.

CHAPTER TWELVE

Monday morning dawned with ominous dark clouds obscuring the normally azure Nevada sky. Matt and Joshua saddled their horses for the ride into town, tying their slickers on behind, just in case. As much as they needed the rain, Matt was hoping it would hold off until the night time hours.

Quietly, they ate the breakfast that Becky had prepared for them and Matt decided to forego the multiple cups of coffee that he normally had in lieu of an earlier start. Together the two men mounted up.

Joshua broke the silence.

"What did you find out in the desert yesterday?" he asked.

Matt appreciated the fact that Joshua was interested in others around him and that he was not totally self-absorbed.

"We found the body of a man who had been murdered. He was shot through the head." He replied. "Someone tried to bury him by caving in the edge of an arroyo over him, but it appeared that the wind blew the sand off him."

"Do you know who it is?" Joshua prodded.

"I don't." Matt hesitated, wondering how much to reveal to the teenager. "I have my suspicions, but that is all they are. Today, I have to ride out to the place I think it may have happened."

Joshua took another look at the sky.

"You better pray it don't rain," he commented.

When they reached the fork in the road where they were to separate, Joshua gave a wave to his foster dad and rode off toward school. Matt turned his horse toward the desert and the rock formation known to the locals as the Pig's Snout.

Taking Joshua's suggestion, Matt began to talk to the Lord as he rode along, asking that the rain would hold off, that he would have wisdom in handling the case and that God would intervene on Steven's behalf. As he rode, he prayed for people who would come to mind. The time passed quickly and he found himself at his intended destination with no clue what he would find. The week that Norris had been missing, if it was his body they had found, was a long time for clues to survive out in the desert.

He started at the rock formation and almost immediately a glint of metal caught his eye. Peering down into a crack in the rock, he located a shell casing in the fissure. He had to hunt around for twig that was long enough and strong enough to hook it and get it out. The brass was shiny enough that he knew it had not been long in the crack. A weathered casing would have blended right into the greyish brown rock.

He put the find into his vest pocket and then surveilled his surroundings from the vantage point he found himself at. A person coming from town would come from the north and he viewed that direction. Someone would be visible for well over a half a mile. It would take someone with extraordinary skill to hit a rider at that distance, then he recalled that Norris, if it was Norris' body he'd found, was riding in a wagon.

If this was where it happened the shooter could remain hidden and take the shot at any time, even when their target was only a hundred feet away. The spot was well chosen by the sniper and Matt could appreciate the cunning of the person.

He left his horse and began walking. A head shot would probably have been taken when the target was closer, so he decided he could see more on foot. A slow methodical search revealed nothing of significance and he began zig-zagging back and forth when returning. By the time he reached his mount, sweat poured down his face from the humid conditions created by the overcast and heat. He was disappointed that the only thing he had discovered was a shell casing.

He wiped his forehead with his shirt sleeve then retrieved the brass from his vest pocket. It was necked down so the opening was smaller than the base. Whoever left the casing behind was shooting a .38-40 caliber which gave him pause. Who would use a .38-40 to ambush someone? The shooter would have to be one tremendous marksmen to depend upon on that small of a caliber. He was of course assuming that a rifle was used and not a pistol but regardless, it was not the round he would have chosen if he were to be lying in wait for a person.

He began to ponder what kind of a person would use such a weapon. A small, weaker man would be more inclined toward the smaller caliber with less kick. Maybe it was the only weapon available to the shooter. Other than that, he could not come up with any other reasons.

Matt jumped like he'd been kicked. He suddenly knew why he did not find any evidence. Again he was assuming his victim was Norris and if it was, he knew that Norris was in a wagon. A head shot would have knocked him back into the wagon and any blood or skull bits would have landed in the bed of the wagon. It would be no wonder that he had found nothing!

He began to feel encouraged, for finding the shell casing was the equivalent of finding a needle in a haystack.

Mounting his gelding, he began making his way back to town. He had just hit the edge of town when the first drops of rain hit the brim of his hat. He reached behind his saddle and by the time he got his slicker donned, the rain was coming down in sheets.

Once he got his horse put up in the stable and made his way to the office, the street was a sea of mud. It was then and only then that he realized that a number of his prayers had been answered. Hanging the wet oilskin and hat up, he breathed a prayer of thanks.

* * *

Joshua hustled to school and for the first time since coming to this town, he was excited to go. He had no idea what the day held for him but his hopes were high that he would have friends to talk to and to play with. He even admitted to himself that he was looking forward to seeing Michelle. Without realizing it, he reached up and touched his cheek where she had kissed him. He'd never had a girl kiss him before and he decided that he really liked it.

With the prospect of rain on the horizon, he removed the saddle and placed it in the shed, then walked into the school. The air was humid and he knew his horse would enjoy the shower along with all the other animals hitched out in the school yard.

As soon as he walked through the door of the one room school, several of the boys called him over to be included in their conversation. Joshua was amazed at how right Mrs. Wheaton had been. It was as if the stigma of his killing of the outlaw had been left behind at the picnic and he was a brand new man, at least in the eyes of his peers.

Miss Elliot smiled as she watched Joshua assimilate into the group as if he belonged. She was also happy to see that the boys he was with were some of the more virtuous at the school. At this point, he could have hung out with anyone in the room.

During the noontime break, Miss Elliott ate at her desk, perusing the afternoon's lesson plans while the children ran outside to play. The earlier rain had been replaced with sunshine and the soggy ground had dried into packed sand. There was very little evidence that the rain had even fallen a couple of hours ago.

Once she was satisfied that she was prepared, Miss Elliott stepped to the door. There were still a few more minutes before the class was to start and she wanted to get a moment out in the sun and the fresh air before they all dove headlong into work again. The teacher stood out on the front porch of the school house and shaded her eyes, scanning the playground and checking on all of her charges. Her eyes settled on Joshua and within the glare of the sun it took her a moment to realize who he was with. Jeff was talking with the much older boy and from the expression on his face the conversation was a serious one. She found herself extremely pleased that in spite of his new popularity, Joshua was taking time to reach out to the younger children, especially one like Jeff who needed good direction.

When the hands of the clock reached the half hour, she rang the bell, calling everyone into class.

* * *

Eli hurried through his morning and quickly made his way to the Doctor's office. To his extreme disappointment, there was no change in his friend's condition. He sighed but then reminded himself that God's timing was certainly not his and that faith meant trusting the Lord completely. Once again he offered another of many prayers on behalf of the still figure in the bed.

A noise behind him drew his attention and he turned to find Elizabeth coming in to check on Steven as well .She advanced across the room, taking Eli's hands in her own. He leaned down and gave her a kiss on the cheek. It was a bitter sweet moment for him, the first real touch of intimacy. What should have been a leap forward in their relationship was dampened by the circumstances that surrounded them. In spite of all of that, Eli reveled in the sweetness of it.

Elizabeth looked up into his eyes and for just a flickering moment forgot the world around them, the troubles and the sorrow. But that moment was not to last long.

"Eli, there is a crowd gathered outside and I think that you are needed out there. I believe for the first time, both of your congregations are all here in one place, drawn together by the same drastic event." She tried to smile but it was difficult considering what was going on.

"Would you come out with me?" he urged.

She shook her head. "No, I came to sit with Steven for a while to give Doctor Mercer a break."

Eli simply nodded. He held her hand for another lingering moment then took a deep breath and turned to meet with the waiting crowd outside.

* * *

The rain had stopped and Matt decided to ride out to Mrs. Swensen's Spread to talk to her some more. To his amazement in spite of the muddy streets, there was an immense crowd of people waiting outside the doctor's office. As he got closer, he could see that the covered boardwalk was blocked by a gaggle of women while the men created a semicircle around the face of the building, standing out in the soggy street. He nudged his horse closer and soon realized that Eli was addressing the assembly.

"… still in a coma and the doctor tells me that he hasn't a clue as to when, or even if, he will be out of the woods." Eli had his hat in his left hand and was using it to gesture as he spoke.

A woman on the walkway spoke up.

"Pastor Exeter, can we pray?" She asked.

"Mrs. Horton," Eli responded, "That is about the only thing we can do."

Even as he spoke the men in the crowd began removing their hats. Everyone bowed their heads as Eli began lifting his friend up to the Lord. It was a simple prayer, like a man who was having a conversation with a friend. He finished and one of the ladies started praying. She spoke with a few more flowery words, but her heartfelt entreaty was truly sincere. When she finished another person began their supplication. Each time one person finished another would chime in to continue the request, each one lifting Steven up to God, each one praying for his healing.

Matt sat astride his horse, hat in hand where he too joined in the prayer for his friend.

The impromptu prayer meeting lasted close to an hour. A large number of the crowd prayed aloud, but there was also a group who silently supported what was being said aloud.

When it was apparent that everyone was finished, Eli closed with a simple, "Amen".

* * *

Elizabeth walked over to the bed and gazed down at the man who was her employee and a friend. She reached over and retrieved the chair that was against the wall moving it over so she could sit down near him. Once seated, she removed an envelope from her handbag. She looked at the handwriting on the outside before tearing it open.

"I don't know how much you can hear or understand," she said to the motionless figure on the bed, "but this came for you on the train today. I figured I would read it to you."

She scanned the contents to make sure it was not bad news before she began.

"Dear Mr. Bosco,

I received many responses to my advertisement, mostly from farmers or ranchers searching for a wife to care for their children. Out of the multitude of letters I received, yours was the only one that spoke of your love for Jesus and how you were looking for a woman to complete you, to make you whole. You told me that you are looking for love and companionship, just as I am.

I know that I need to be absolutely honest with you so I need to tell you that I am not what men would call pretty. I have a birthmark upon my face that has marked my appearance significantly and has been a detriment to my relationships. I believe it has kept me from getting married.

After praying over the letter that I received from you, I decided to respond. My prayer is that you are looking for a woman of faith and that you love the Lord as much as I do.

What I can tell you is that I have been a Christian all of my life and my only comfort in my loneliness is to spend time in fellowship with my Lord. He has been the rock upon which I can stand and I trust Him completely."

Elizabeth continued to read the lengthy letter which outlined the many struggles of the woman from St. Louis and how each one had increased her faith in Jesus, for He was the only one in her life that had stood by her, who never had failed her. As she read, Elizabeth began to develop a deep appreciation for the woman who had reached out for companionship through the local newspaper. She hoped that Steven could appreciate the maturity of the young woman from the east, who was baring her soul in a letter of open frankness. The letter was signed, "Evelyn Pritchard."

She set the letter aside and used a clean sponge that she dipped in water to wipe out the inside of Steven's mouth, the way that the Doctor had showed her. He had shared with her that his concern was not about starving to death, a person could go weeks without eating, but in dying of thirst, which could happen in a matter of days. As a result, whoever was tending to the man was constantly providing water in the manner that Elizabeth was now. She was amazed how he reflexively swallowed, despite being unconscious. The idea of dying from lack of water was unthinkable to the tenderhearted woman.

Even as that thought crossed her mind, Elizabeth realized that Steven might not even come out of his coma that he might just die in his peaceful state of sleep. The thought made her shudder and a wave of grief swept over her. So she did the only thing she could. She set the sponge aside and bowed her head to pray.

* * *

As the men and women began dispersing, the Sheriff nudged his heels into the flanks of his gelding, guiding the horse over to the Preacher.

"Eli, what just happened here?" he asked.

Eli shook his head, "I don't know, but look at how many lives Steven has touched. Men left their jobs to come here in the middle of the day. Women came out in the rain and the mud. It's the first time since Steven got baptized that both churches have come together in unity. Matt, it was an incredible thing!"

Matt nodded, "yes, it was pretty amazing." He changed the subject.

"I'm headed out to talk to Mrs. Swensen, I need to show her the clothes from that body we recovered yesterday. Are you up for coming out with me?"

Eli shook his head. "I better not. I have things to do around here and with Steven sick, Elizabeth will need some help over at her bakery. I do appreciate you thinking of me. Maybe next time."

* * *

Matt rode up the lane toward the house, the items that had been taken from the body were rolled up in a blanket and tied on behind the saddle. Mrs. Swensen was walking back to the house from the far edge of her huge garden. In her hand she was holding a jackrabbit by the hind feet.

Matt rode up to her and when she saw him looking at the animal, she commented. "As long as I ave to shoot dem to keep dem out of my garden," she explained, "I might as vell eat the meat." She changed the subject. "Ave you found my husband yet."

He redirected the conversation.

"Ma'am, I have some things that I would like to have you look at." He spoke as he swung down from the saddle. He reached up and removed the bundle from behind the saddle.

"Is there a place I can lay this out?"

"Ov course," she motioned toward the house. "Ve can lay dem out on the table."

Matt followed her in and as she pulled back the curtains to allow more light in, he unrolled the package.

Mrs. Swensen turned and as she did so, her hand flew to her mouth and she gasped.

"Those are Norris,'" she stated. "Vere did you find them."

Right now, Matt was wishing Eli had come along for he really did not do well dealing with grieving people.

"Mrs. Swensen, please have a seat." He pulled out a chair for her and after she sat down, he took a seat himself. "We found him in the desert late yesterday. He passed away some time ago and…" He didn't know how to continue or even if he should continue at this point.

A single tear slid down her cheek.

"He is dead?"

"Yes ma'am. I'm so sorry."

She was trying to remain stoic, still several more tears escaped from the corners of her eyes.

The sheriff was in a quandary. He did not want to be cruel, but there were questions that needed to be asked. He allowed her some time to process the news and then proceeded with as much tact as he could.

"Mrs. Swensen, ma'am, did your husband have any issues with anyone that you know of?" Matt kept his tone of voice soft in an attempt to ease her discomfort.

"No, No. He vas a hard verker and got along vith everyone."

Matt guessed that she was unaware of the fight her husband had at the River Saloon. He wondered how many of his other activities that she was unaware of? Even more importantly, how many secrets had he hidden that Matt was unaware of?

* * *

Matt hitched his horse in front of the River Saloon. He caught a few glances from the patrons as he walked to the bar, but he had gotten used to that in the years since he pinned on the badge. It came with the territory.

The daytime bartender nodded, "Afternoon, Sheriff. What can I get you?"

"Coffee, please." Matt replied.

When the cup was placed in front of him, he retrieved a coin from the pocket of his vest and handed it to the man but before he could turn, the sheriff stopped him.

"The fight that Norris Swensen was in, what was it about?"

"I don't know. I don't stick my nose into other people's business." The man replied, piously.

Matt raised an eyebrow at the pronouncement. "Well, if that is true, that makes you the only person in this town that does."

The man gave the Sheriff a look of disdain. "Look, like I told you before, there are so many fights in here, I don't have time to figure out why the men are fighting."

"Maybe if you stopped letting them get so drunk, you wouldn't have so many fights." Matt suggested.

The bartender snorted, "I'm not their mother. Besides, how am I to make any money?"

He turned his back on the sheriff and started cleaning glasses.

Matt looked around the room and then asked the back of the man, "Where can I find Peggy."

"Last time I let you talk to her, you hauled her out of here and pointed a gun in my face."

"Maybe you should have learned to stay out of other people's business earlier." Matt was determined not to let the fool in front of him push him into something he would later regret, but he couldn't resist the jab.

"I don't know where she is, it's her day off."

"Okay," Matt persisted, "Who was Norris fighting with?"

The bartender turned with an annoyed look of on his face. He sighed, then pointed to a man seated at a table across the room.

Matt had this sudden urge to put a fist into the bartender's nose but instead, he quelled his own feeling of anger and moved across the room to the person indicated.

The neatly dressed man was seated by himself, a glass and a bottle in front of him, shuffling a deck of cards. Matt took note of the fact that even though the glass was full, the only amount missing from the bottle was in the glass and the man was not drinking any of it. This was a man who was baiting his victims for a fleecing.

Matt sat down across from the gambler who simply bobbed his head toward the lawman.

"Would you like to play cards, Sheriff?"

Matt smiled, "not a chance, my wife would kill me."

The man gave a knowing grin and nodded.

"What can I help you with?" he asked.

"My name is Matt Wheaton," he offered

The man replied, "My friends call me Dusty."

Matt looked at the man's black hair and queried, "Dusty?"

"When I was a youngster, I rode trail herd. I was the newest and youngest hand on the drive and ended up riding drag most the time. Every evening I came up to the chuck wagon with a layer of dirt from head to toe, so one of the older fellers nicknamed me that."

The Sheriff chuckled. "I understand you are acquainted with Norris Swensen." He ventured.

The man spat out a foul name. "He's a clumsy oaf," he add emphatically.

"I hear tell the two of you got into a fight. What was it about?"

"That dirt farmer got himself all tanked up one afternoon and spilled his drink down the front of one of my finest suits." Dusty spoke with disgust.

"When was the last time you saw him?" Matt asked.

"He was in here a week ago, on Monday and I haven't seen him since. Why all the questions? Is he in trouble or something?"

"Something." Matt was there to get information, not to give it.

"Well, if he never comes back here again that would suit me just fine."

"Thanks for your time." Matt pushed his chair back and walked to the bar.

Dusty's contempt for the man was all too evident and the Sheriff noticed that he spoke of him as if he were still alive. If he'd have killed the man, it stood to reason he would have tried to hide his dislike. Besides, if he'd been here when Swensen left, there was no way that he could have made it to the ambush.

The bartender showed his impatience. "What now?"

"Was Dusty here last Monday?"

"All day and late into the evening. He was seated at that table almost the whole time playing cards." Came the reply.

Matt sighed and walked out of the saloon. His prime suspect had an airtight alibi.

* * *

Joshua finally came riding into the yard and a very concerned Becky hurried out to meet him.

"Where have you been young man? You're nearly an hour late and I was getting worried." Frown lines furrowed her brow.

"I'm sorry ma'am, I stayed a little late at school." Joshua as looking at the ground as he spoke.

"Did you get into trouble?" Her worry turned to consternation.

"No ma'am, everything is fine. I was just playing stickball with some of the guys after class."

Becky's face broke into a huge smile. "Joshua, honey, that's wonderful."

He looked into her eyes with a twinkle in his own. "Yes ma'am, you were right. The picnic was a grand idea. I have a bunch of new friends at school now."

"I am so glad. Come on in and get a snack and then you will have to hustle to get your chores done before Mr. Wheaton gets here."

Supper was an animated affair as Joshua filled them in on his day at school, actually wanting to tell them all that happened. Matt on the other hand and overly silent, his mind seemingly elsewhere.

Becky finally confronted him. "Matt, you have hardly said a word and you're just fiddling with your food. Have you even heard a word of the conversation tonight?"

"I'm sorry Joshua. I was listening…sort of. I'm so happy you're now enjoying the other kids at school. I guess I'm just preoccupied."

"Is it the thing with the dead body?" Joshua asked.

Matt gave him a lopsided grin, impressed with the boy's perceptiveness. "That is exactly it."

He explained to them that he had determined that the body was that of Norris Swensen and how his only suspect has a solid alibi.

"Maybe you should look at the wife?" Becky suggested.

"I've thought of that, but it doesn't really make sense." Matt replied. "She could have killed him and buried him on their place and no one would be the wiser. Why go to all this elaborate scheme to get him out into the desert and shoot him, then drag the body to the arroyo and bury it? Besides, she's the one who reported it to me."

Becky countered, "Yes, but if she had not reported it, someone would have gotten suspicious when he failed to show up in town and then people would ask why she had said nothing."

Matt pondered that a moment and then asked, "Why would you suspect the wife anyway?"

Becky stood to take the dishes in and as she did so, she answered, "There are lots of women who want to kill their husbands."

Matt leaned back in his chair, "Oh really." He said with a smile. "So do you want to kill me?"

Becky leaned over and kissed him on the top of the head.

"Not lately." She responded as she carried the dishes to the sink.

Matt glanced over at Joshua.

"Wipe that smirk off your face."

* * *

Matt was on the road early the next morning. As he rode out toward the Swensen place he contemplated what Becky had said last night. He knew that she had been teasing him but then again, was there a note of seriousness in her comment? They had been married for a number of years now and he asked himself how good of a husband he really was. He worked hard and provided for his wife and now for Joshua, but other than that, was he the husband that God had called him to be?

His ponderings went back to one of the Wednesday morning Bible studies he had attended. He remembered something that Eli had said. The preacher had been referring to a conversation that Jesus had with a Pharisee in which He had been asked to name the most important commandment. Jesus said it was to "Love the Lord your God with all your heart and to love your neighbor as yourself."

In talking about marriage, Eli quipped, "love the Lord your God with all your heart and love your wife more than you love yourself."

Matt thought about that. Did he love his wife more than he loved himself?

He wanted to. The truth was, if he was honest with himself that his own selfish desire won out more often than not. He began to question himself about how he treated his wife. He admitted that often he took her for granted. He did not recognize all that she did, simply because he was so focused on the things that he was doing. He wasn't trying to be self-absorbed but in the hustle of daily life, he definitely got distracted.

He was so caught up in his thoughts that he did not realize that there was a person riding up behind him until it was way too late, had there been any ill intent. Fortunately, when he finally looked around, he saw that it was Ben. He stopped his horse and waited for the other man to catch up.

"Ben, what brings you out so early this morning?"

"The baby kept Naomi up most of the night. She finally got him to sleep early this morning, so I decided to take a ride and let the two of them rest. Are you out here on business?" he asked.

"Yep. I'm going to talk to some of Mrs. Swensen's neighbors. Yesterday, she positively identified the clothing as Norris'." Matt filled him in on his dead end at the Saloon the previous day and Becky's assertion that it must be the wife.

Ben laughed, "so do you think it is the wife?"

"No. I kind of think that Becky was trying to make a point and I have to admit, it really has me thinking. That was why I was so preoccupied with when you rode up." Matt replied.

"What kind of a point was she trying to make?" Ben asked.

"She commented that a lot of wives want to kill their spouses and it got me to thinking how I do not want to fail her as a husband."

"Do you have any words of wisdom to share?" Ben glanced sideways at his riding partner, assessing his response.

Matt measured his words before he responded, "your wife is a treasure. You need to treat her as such and never, never forget."

They rode in silence for a while, so long that Matt was beginning to wonder if Ben had forgotten what they were talking about.

Out of the blue, Ben spoke, "I couldn't agree more."

The silence resumed and they just enjoyed the sound of hooves on the road, the wind in the bushes and numerous birds chirping in the cool of the morning.

Suddenly, Ben reined his horse in and Matt followed suit. He looked over at Ben, expectantly.

"I think I will ride back before the baby awakes, so I can be there to take care of him. I would like to let Naomi get some rest." With that, Ben touched a two fingers to the brim of his hat in a quasi-salute, turned his horse and began the ride back to town.

Matt grinned and continued on in his journey.

* * *

"What can you tell me about Norris Swensen?" Matt was talking to the Swensen's closest neighbor.

"He would give you the shirt off his back if you asked for it."

Ira Torkelson was a homesteader who raised a few pigs, goats and cows. He had a couple of acres of oats in the back and was simply trying to make a go of it.

"Last year, I broke my wrist and for five weeks, Norris came over every morning to help me. He would pitch hay, milk the cow and do any other chore I was unable to. If it hadn't been for him, we would have gone belly up. He is the only reason we are still here," he reiterated.

His wife chimed in. "Yes, God bless him."

Hattie was a slender wisp of a woman, with weathered hands and face from too much time in the wind and the sun. Matt had no doubt that she worked hard, based on the callused hands but she was not built for the heavy work. He could see how Norris' help would have been invaluable.

She continued, "I think Mrs. Swensen resented him coming over here so much. She will hardly talk to us anymore."

"Did their spread suffer because of it?" Matt was curious.

"I don't know if their farm suffered, but I am sure that their relationship did. He would never say anything against her, but I feel like as the time went on, he became more sullen."

"Hattie, quit gossiping." Ira looked uncomfortable.

He turned his attention back toward Matt.

"She is a nice enough woman." He continued, "But I think that coming here was a difficult change for her. She came from money over in the old country and it was hard for her to barely scrape by here in this land."

"Money?" Matt prompted.

"They came from Sweden where her father raised championship horses. I understand he was very successful and they were quite wealthy. Mrs. Swensen was quite an accomplished rider from what I have gathered. I once saw a number of ribbons that she had won as a young girl."

"What about Norris, was he also from a wealthy background?" Matt queried.

"No, not from what I gathered. His father was a farmer and he followed in his dad's footsteps. Norris once told me that he met his wife when she was a teenager. They fell in love and got married against her parent's wishes. Her father disowned her so they moved over here to the States." Ira apparently did not want his wife to gossip, but he was more than willing to disseminate information.

Matt appreciated the background information, but he really wanted to get back to Norris in the present.

"Do you know of anyone that Mr. Swensen had issues with?"

The two exchange glances and finally Ira spoke.

"Sheriff, he didn't seem to have issues with anyone. His wife on the other hand had issues with most everyone. If anyone had a problem with Norris it was because his wife had caused hard feelings. In spite of what she was like, he stood by her."

"Is there anyone in particular?"

"Sheriff," Mrs. Torkelson interjected. "It would be shorter to list the people that she got along with. Every neighbor around here had troubles with Mrs Swensen. No one would have harmed Norris, though, he was such a sweet man."

When Matt finally took his leave, he again felt as if he had raised more questions than answers. Something in the conversation left him with the nagging suspicion that he was missing something, but he could not put his finger on it. He rode back to town with a shadow idea that refused to come to the surface.

* * *

Joshua left for school early. He had a purpose in mind and the very thought of it scared him half to death. His mouth was dry, his pulse pounded and his breathing came shallow and fast as he contemplated his plan. He was relieved that he was the first to arrive and quickly cared for his horse as he rehearsed just what he would say.

The other students began filtering in and he studied each one closely as they were afar off. Finally, a figure approached that he was certain was the right person, only to be disappointed once again.

"Good morning, Josh." Michelle plopped down on the front steps next to him.

Surprised by her sudden appearance, Joshua forgot everything he had planned to say.

"Aren't you even going to say Hi?" she asked.

"I, I, I, uh, hi," he stammered.

"You're cute when you're embarrassed." She jumped up, looking at the other girls across the school yard.

"Wait!" Joshua finally found his voice.

"Yes?" She smiled sweetly and her big doe eyes made him want to melt right there.

"Can I walk you home after school?" He was blushing furiously.

"Of course." She flashed him a big smile then raced across the yard to her friends.

* * *

Matt was nearly to the edge of town when his mind connected with what was bothering him. He made a beeline to the mercantile.

The store keeper was helping another customer when Matt walked in. Impatiently, he looked at the hardware hanging on the wall as he waited for the woman to quit yammering about what type of yarn that she needed for her current project and get out of the store.

Finally, after making her choice and paying the merchant, the little old lady turned to leave.

"Hello there Sheriff Wheaton," Edna smiled, "did you hear that the Anson's just had a little baby boy? I get to knit him a blanket today."

She hurried out the door before Matt had a chance to answer.

The clerk gave a hearty laugh when he saw the look on Matt's face. "That woman will probably have it done today if I know her. What can I help you with?"

"The other day when Norris was in here, did you help him load his wagon?"

"Of course, he had a couple of weeks' worth of supplies he bought." The man replied.

"Did you notice his team of horses?" Matt asked.

"Sure did, they were a matching set of Bays that he just traded for. They were a couple of beauties." He spoke with great enthusiasm.

"Did you happen to see what the brand was on them?" Matt pushed.

"That I did. It was the "Rocking G"."

"Great. What about his wagon? Was there anything you noticed about it? Any distinguishing features?"

The question gave the grocer pause as he contemplated, glancing up as if he were trying to look into his mind.

"I really can't recall anyth…wait, he had a broken slat in the tailgate, 'cause he mentioned that he was going to have to fix it that night when he got home." The man hooked his thumbs under his suspenders and grinned as if he was so proud of himself

Matt nodded, "You have been a tremendous help. Thank you."

He headed back to the office and sat down at his desk and began writing out a list of what he knew about the case. At the bottom of the list, he wrote a name in block letters, then drew a circle around it.

CHAPTER THIRTEEN

Matt walked through the doors of The Saloon, taking note everyone present before quietly slipping to the bar. Eli met him at the end.

"What can I get you?" he asked.

"When you have time, I would like to run this case by you again." Matt was excited to share his revelation.

"Why don't you grab that corner table and I will join you in a minute." Eli offered.

Matt had not even seated himself when the door burst open. A heavy man, in a suit and bowler hat, stood there breathless, looking around until he spotted the sheriff.

"Sheriff, you better get out here, quick." Without waiting he lumbered back out the door he had just come in.

Matt sighed. It never failed. Instead of following the man though, he headed for the rear door. He didn't know what was going on, but he did not wish to be ambushed coming out that front door.

Cautiously, he slipped out the door and headed along the alley, gun in hand. He stopped short of the corner and crept forward, looking right then left as more of the street became visible. He reached the boardwalk and saw the messenger looking expectantly back toward the front door. Satisfied that he was not in danger, Matt holstered the pistol and stepped onto the walk.

"What do you need? I don't see anything out here needing my attention?" Matt was brusque. The man was only known to him by sight and it irked the Sheriff that he had run back out and not taken time to tell him what was so pressing.

The man pointed down the street to another saloon. "Right there Sheriff, I saw him." The man still gave off an air of urgency.

"Who? Who's down there?" the Sheriff demanded. Now he was starting to get annoyed.

"Irv Carter. I'd know him anywhere. I saw him once down in Abilene. If he's wanted, I get the reward." Greed showed in his eyes.

Now Matt was angry, "if he's wanted and you bring him in, you get the reward. There's no reward for just seeing."

The man's jowls sagged. "You mean I gotta bring him in?"

"If he's wanted. I haven't seen any posters on him since I've been in office." Matt got distinct pleasure in watching the man deflate.

"Oh, I thought I was going to get rich." Disappointment was written all over his face.

Matt walked away, toward the saloon the man pointed out. He did not care for bounty hunters all that much, but this man was lower than a bounty hunter. He was simply a coward, wanting to make money off another man's life without risking his. He was the kind of man that Matt despised.

Irv Carter. He had not heard that name for…well, since he was a little boy. Every young boy dreamed of being Irv Carter, the Texas gunman. There was even a dime store novel written about the man. Legend had it that he had killed seventeen men, all in fair, stand up gun fights. Matt imagined that the number was highly inflated in the retelling of the stories, but regardless, Carter was indeed a legend of the old west, even if it was decades ago.

He entered through the back door and stood in the room for nearly a minute before the bartender noticed him. In fact, only one man saw him when he slipped into the room. The old man was seated at the corner table, a glass of whiskey in his left hand, and his right hand under the table, resting on his thigh mere inches away from his gun. Matt crossed the room and could feel all eyes in the room following him.

"May I?" he asked, gesturing toward a chair.

"Be my guest." The man's voice had the sound of boots on gravel.

"Mr. Carter, I am Sheriff Wheaton."

"You know who I am, I'm flattered," came the response.

Matt chuckled, "I reckon, truth be told, everyone around here knows about you. You made a name for yourself back in the day."

"I never intended for that." Carter replied. "I was just trying to keep my bones out of boot hill."

"Yes, that I can certainly understand. I'm just trying to do the same. " Matt abruptly changed the subject. "Sir, may I ask why you are in town?"

"Sheriff, normally I would tell you that is none of your business and in fact it ain't, but I figure you can help me out. I'm looking for a sky pilot."

"Sky pilot?" Matt queried. This was a term he'd never heard before.

"The parson."

"Well now, that I can help you with. Where are you staying? I will let him know you're looking for him." Matt did not intend to send any surprises the way of his friend.

"How 'bout you point me in the direction of the church?" The look Irv's face relayed his annoyance.

"Because I know for a fact that he is not there. We do not have a full time preacher and right now he is working at his other job. I would be glad to send him your way though, when he gets off work." Annoyed or not, Matt was not going to be pushed.

The old gunman studied the steely eyed gaze of the young lawman seated by him and decided that there would be no backing down.

"I'm staying in the boarding house at the end of the street, only the lady of the house don't know who I am and I would like to keep it that way."

"That is not a problem. Who should I tell the parson to look for?"

"John Smith."

Matt chuckled, "That there is mighty original." He continued, "the preacher's name is Elijah." Matt rarely used the full name but he felt a slight misdirection was appropriate for the time being.

"Elijah what?" The gunman was persistent.

Matt could not bring himself to lie. "Exeter."

The change in the man's demeanor was immediate. His eyes narrowed as he held up his glass and peered through the amber liquid.

"Eli Exeter. This should be interesting."

"Do you know Pastor Exeter?" Matt was suddenly nervous over the change wrought in the man.

"You just tell him I will see him after he gets off work."

Irv tossed down the whiskey, stood up and headed out the door, leaving the Sheriff wondering what position he had just left his friend in.

* * *

"Irvine Carter." Eli shook his head. "After all these years."

"Do you know him?" Matt was still concerned.

"Only by reputation." Eli looked pensive.

Matt was not convinced. "You're holding something back. What's going on?"

"Irvine Carter was a fast hand with a gun. It was thought that he rode the wrong side of the law a time or two but nothing was ever proven. For all I know he has been an upstanding citizen all of his life." Eli paused, "His brother on the other hand, he rode the outlaw trail from the time he was able to throw a leg over a horse."

Matt interjected, "and what does that have to do with you? Did you put him in jail?" he asked.

Eli gave him a crooked smile. "I wish that was all that it was."

"What do you mean?"

"Matt, I put him in the ground. I killed the boy. I had no choice but still, I killed him."

Matt simply waited for Eli to continue.

"I was a young sheriff and a pretty good hand with a gun. Back in those days, I didn't carry my father's heavy old Dragoon, I carried a couple of Peace Maker's that were much easier to use. Over the years, several would be gunslingers tried to coax me into a gun battle. They were looking to make a name for themselves. Durned fool kids who thought they wanted that kind of a reputation. But I learned to use my words and the vast majority of them I was able to reason with. I was able to talk them out of a fight. In fact, I convinced all but this one…" Eli's voice trailed off.

Matt waited for more but nothing came.

Eli stood up. "Would you do me a favor?"

"Of course." Matt did not even hesitate.

Eli unbuckled the gun belt and handed it to his friend.

"Would you hold onto this while I visit Carter?" he asked.

"You're going to go see him?" Matt was startled.

Eli was nothing if not practical. "He did not come into town looking for Eli Exeter. He came in looking for a preacher. The man has something weighing on his mind and I intend to do what I can for him. Based upon what I know of his reputation, I don't believe he would shoot an unarmed man."

* * *

Matt took the gun and holster to his office and secured it where it would be safe. Eli had stopped carrying his father's ancient relic of a sidearm when he moved from the shed next to The Saloon to the parsonage where he could keep it under lock and key. Now he carried the Colt .45 that he inherited last year. Matt immediately left the office and he went straight to the telegrapher's office and had Bert send a telegram off to the Territorial Marshall, requesting information on Carter. Once that was accomplished he sent another one, a personal telegram to Judge Middleton.

* * *

Joshua waited for the school day to end, nervous and excited all at the same time. As it got closer to the time to go home, suddenly he began to feel panicked. What would he say to her? What if he just ended up making a fool of himself? The more he thought about it the more he thought he should run away when school ended. His palms felt clammy as he contemplated what he was going to do.

"JOSHUA!"

Startled out of his rambling thoughts, the young man realized that Miss Elliot was speaking to him.

"Do you know the answer to number thirteen?" She repeated.

He glanced down at his math primer, relieved that he did know the answer.

"Seventy two." he said.

She smiled, "very good." Her face took on a stern look. "Please pay attention during class. You will be dismissed soon enough."

Joshua colored slightly as a twitter of laughter rippled through the room.

Miss Elliott glance around the room. "That will be enough," she reprimanded.

Unfortunately that was all it took for her to lose control of the class. The girls began whispering and the boys started throwing spit wads at each other. Glancing at the clock, she realized that it would be hopeless to try to accomplish anything more today.

"Class!" She called out loudly, getting the attention of the group. "Your reading assignment is chapter seven. Do your math homework and I will see you back here in the morning." She recognized that they were really a good group of kids, but once they got distracted, it was a difficult task to rein them back in and today she just did not have the energy for it. It was best to let them out to burn up all of that youthful exuberance outside and not in her classroom.

Joshua gathered up his books and homework, but he was walking slow, dragging his feet because he did not know what to expect. What was he going to say to Michelle? He felt like he was tongue tied when he was in a group of people so how was he going to be with a pretty girl?

Michelle skipped over to him with her books under her arm.

"Would you like to carry my books for me?" she asked.

Joshua wasn't even sure what he mumbled, but he reached out and took the offered bundle, tucking it under his other arm.

Michelle chatted cheerfully as they walked a meandering route toward her home. As she continued her steady course of conversation, he began to relax, interjecting a question or a comment every once in a while. They stopped in the shade of one of the few trees that were available and the young girl turned to face her escort.

"I have been doing all the talking," she said sweetly, "now it is your turn to tell me about you."

She had made him feel so comfortable that he found it was easy to open up to her and tell her about the death of his father, shot out of the saddle by the gunman, Rob Handy. He shared how he and his mother struggled to get by and when his mother got sick and died, how he began his quest to hunt down the killer of his father. Most everyone in town, unless they were new, were aware how he had shot and killed the gunman outside of The Saloon that fateful morning last year, so he did not talk to her about it. Michelle had other plans though.

"What's it like to kill a man?" She was young and still too immature to realize that it might not be a thing that he wanted to dwell upon or even discuss.

To his credit, Joshua did not take offense.

"It's hard," he replied. "It weighs heavy on a man, to know that you done took another man's life." He looked down at the ground and scuffed the sand with his boot.

Josh continued, "I thought I would feel better, getting revenge for my pa. Instead, I felt nearly as bad as I did when I lost him, only in a different way."

He had never really talked to anyone about it before. When the Wheaton's tried to get him to talk about it, he would clam up even though he didn't really want to. For all of the nightmares that Mrs. Wheaton had helped him through, he still could not even tell her about it. Yet here, for some reason he felt like he could talk to the girl that was standing in front of him and for the first time he began to open up.

Michelle reached out and took his hand. "I am so sorry for you."

Before he realized what was happening, a tear trickled down his cheek and suddenly he wished that the ground would just open up and swallow him. What must she think of him right now?

To his surprise she did not laugh at him, instead she reached up and tenderly wiped the tear from his cheek.

"When you first came to school, I was so scared of you." She spoke softly and her voice had a sweet, gentle quality to it. "I am so happy to know that you are not scary and I'm even more glad that you're my friend."

With that she stood up on her tippy toes and gave Joshua a big hug.

CHAPTER FOURTEEN

Eli knocked on the door of the hotel room and a voice on the other side bade him enter. He made sure his hands were visible when he stepped into the room. He did not want any mistaken intentions to be relayed to the occupant of the room. As soon as he opened the door he realized what a disadvantage he had. The curtain was pulled back from the window and the sunlight caught him in the eyes, momentarily blinding him. By the time his eye adjusted to the room and he located Irv, the man could have shot him had that been his intention. He was seated to the side of the window that was farthest from the door, giving him all of the advantage. Eli was beginning to realize why the old gunman was still alive.

"Mr. Carter, I'm Pastor Exeter." There was no sense in delaying the inevitable.

"I know who you are. You killed my brother." Apparently Carter felt the same way.

"Yes I did," Eli responded. "But I didn't want to. In fact, I did everything in my power to prevent that gun fight from happening. Quince was determined that he could beat me in a gun fight and the truth of the matter is that he got his gun out of the holster first. His shot hit the dirt right in front of me. My shots all hit their mark."

To his surprise, Irv just nodded. "That sounds like Quince. He was always in too much of a hurry and once he set his mind to something, there never was no talking him out of it."

"Well, I want you to know that I am sorry. I did not want to shoot him. I never wanted to kill anyone." Eli was truly sincere.

The older man simply replied. "I appreciate that."

"It stands to reason that you did not wish to see me about that. You wanted a pastor. Is there something that I can help you with?"

The gunman pointed to a chair and Eli sat down opposite of the man as he offered to pour some whiskey from the bottle next to him. Eli simply held up his hand to stop him from filling a glass.

"I do have some questions," Irv began. "I'd like to know what is going to happen to me."

Puzzled, Eli queried, "what do you mean?"

"When I die, what is hell going to be like?" Irv was totally serious.

Eli pondered his response before replying.

"Hell is a place of eternal torment," he answered. "Souls will be eternally condemned to burn in the flames. There will be no relief. Ever."

Irv sat there stone faced, mulling over what he'd just heard.

Eli continued, "But there is no reason why you have to spend eternity in hell. Jesus came to save us from hell, to give us eternity in heaven with God our Father, our creator, our brother and friend. He will save you if you only ask him."

Irv snorted in derision, the first emotion he had shown.

"God is not going to save someone like me. If you knew all the things I've done, you wouldn't even have suggested it."

Eli smiled, for this was not the first time someone had expressed this mistaken belief to him.

"There is nothing so bad, nothing so heinous that you have done that God will not forgive you. Jesus, as he hung on the cross, bloody and broken, skin torn to shreds by the lashing he had received, forgave the very men who beat him and drove nails into his hands. Let me ask you this, if Jesus, who is God, forgave the people who killed him then don't you think He will forgive you of all that you have done?" Eli let it sink in a moment. "I'm telling you He will and it is as simple as asking Him for forgiveness and committing your life to Him."

Irv smirked and commented, "What's left of it."

Eli gave him a questioning look and waited.

"The Doc in Virginia City tells me I have the cancer. He only gave me a couple months to live." Irv continued. "I wanted to find out what I have to look forward to."

The preacher leaned forward in his chair, "You need to understand that you have a choice and that choice is yours alone to make. If you want to be saved from your sins, I would happily lead you in prayer."

"I sure don't want to rot in hell for eternity."

"And you don't have to. In a way, you have an advantage over so many others." Eli pointed out.

"How do you figure?" Irv asked.

"A lot of people put off getting things right with God, figuring they will take care of it when they are old and grey, but there is no guarantee that anyone is going to live until they are old. You know that the end is near and you know what you need to do. The question is, are you ready to make things right between you and God?"

The grizzled gunman put his whiskey down on the side table next to him and leaned toward the preacher.

"I am." He said simply.

Together they prayed a prayer of repentance and for Irv to receive Jesus into his life.

When they were done, Irv commented, "it seems too simple."

Eli responded, "that was just the salvation portion of it. You are now forgiven and going to heaven, but each day you are going to have to choose what or who you are going to love and live for. It's either the world or Jesus. Sometimes it is so easy to get caught up in the living of life that we place our relationship with Jesus on the back burner so to speak. To keep our walk with Him out front, first and foremost can become very difficult."

"How do you do it?" the dying man asked.

"I begin my day by reading the Bible. I had a friend once tell me that the Bible is God's love letter to us. It explains what it is to be a Christian and how we are supposed to live, what we can do to honor the God who gave everything for us. "Eli continued, "and then I spend a lot of time throughout the day in prayer, just talking things over with my closest friend, Jesus."

"It sounds like a lot of work," Irv replied.

Eli thought for a moment before answering. "The Christian life is not an easy one. Many people have died for their faith, because it's not the accepted religion for where they live. But it is a fulfilling life, one in which you experience peace in the midst of turmoil, joy when you should be sad and even satisfaction when you have nothing. When you choose to live your life in a way that places God first, all the other things that we tend to worry about fall into place. God protects us and blesses us when we are fully devoted to him."

"It sounds like magic."

"It is actually miraculous."

CHAPTER FIFTEEN

It was early Saturday morning and Eli quickly finished his chores around the Saloon. With Sam's miraculous recovery, he had returned to his previous routine of working off his Sunday morning rent by assisting around the place. This morning, Eli recalled his earlier conversation with Joe at the lumber yard. If Joe was willing to come to church only if Kelly Guiness came, then Kelly was probably going to be a hard nut to crack. Eli contemplated the task ahead of him. He knew it would not be easy, but if he could get Joe to church, to introduce him to the gospel, then it was well worth trying.

Eli had never personally met Kelly but he had heard about him through the grapevine. This was still a very small town and very little of what happened here went unnoticed. Guiness had moved in a couple months ago, a single man who had taken over a homestead west of town. He did not frequent The Saloon, so Eli had only seen him from a distance. He was a large man which made him stand out where ever he was.

But before he went to Kelly, he had one more errand to do. He had brought a new Bible with him and he headed to the boarding house.

It took several knocks on the door before it swung open. Irv stood on the other side, looking pretty well used up.

"Are you okay?" Eli was suddenly concerned.

"I have good days and I have bad days. This morning is one of the bad ones." His gravely tone matched his appearance.

"Is there anything I can do for you?" the preacher asked.

"No, today I just need to rest. Mrs. Harkness is keeping me fed," he replied.

Eli held out the Bible. "I brought this for you. Each new convert gets one," he said.

"Convert," Irv chuckled. "I guess that's better than convict. Thanks Eli. I 'ppreciate it."

* * *

The ride out to Kelly's house was pleasant in the comfortable morning air. Eli loved the desert and even though many felt it had nothing to offer, in his experience the desert was teeming with life and he enjoyed the rich beauty it provided.

As he rode up into the yard, a giant of a man came out of the barn to see who was visiting.

"What can I do for you, stranger?" The Irish brogue was unmistakable.

"Kelly, I'm Eli Exeter, the pastor in this town," he responded. "I have come to invite you to church tomorrow."

"I am Catholic." He announced as if that proclamation settled the matter.

Now that he was next to him Eli realized the immense size of the man, in spite of the fact that the preacher was still seated on his horse.

Eli grinned at the man. "I promise I won't hold that against you."

Apparently Kelly did not appreciate the attempt at humor, for his face looked as if it were carved from stone.

"As long as you are not a priest, I will not be coming to your church," he spoke with finality.

Eli asked, "Don't you think that it would be better to fellowship with those of similar beliefs than to have no fellowship at all? Someday we might have a Catholic church in Scorpion Wells, but until then I would be proud to have you come to our church. You could see how the other side lives."

Kelly's face was expressionless.

"I have too many things to do. Tomorrow, I have to split all that wood over there." He gestured toward a wagon with a huge pile of wood on it.

Eli swung down from his horse and it was only then that he truly recognized the Goliath he was facing. Kelly stood over six foot eight and tipped the scale well over three hundred seventy five pounds. He had his shirt sleeves rolled up revealing arms that were bigger around at the bicep than Eli's thighs. Up until now, Eli had always thought of the Irish as men of small stature. After today, he would not make that mistake any more.

He looked up into the chiseled face of the Irishman.

"I'll make you a deal. I will work with you on the pile of wood for a couple of hours and that will give you the time that you would need to come to church. How about it?"

Kelly made his counter offer. "If you want me to come to your church, you split the entire pile, by yourself."

Eli was encouraged that the big man had at least budged slightly, so he came back with his reply.

"How about I split wood for four hours. That should make a large enough dent in this pile to give you the time to come to church tomorrow."

Kelly was relentless. "The whole pile, or nothing. Take it or leave it."

Eli eyed the pile then turned back to his horse. He took off the gun belt and hung it from the saddle horn then removed the spare pistol from the back of his waistband and put it in the saddlebag. He removed a pair of gloves from the other saddlebag and slipped them on. Finally he shrugged out of his vest and placed it atop the guns. He figured with a good, sharp double bitted axe and a splitting maul and sledge, he had a chance of getting the job done before he had to be back at The Saloon to help Sam.

"You have the tools?" he requested of the behemoth.

For the first time, a huge smile split the face of the giant and he turned as he headed toward the barn. Eli understood the smile when he came back out. In the man's hand was the largest double jack that Eli had ever seen. The hammer head alone must weigh eighteen or twenty pounds! In his other hand he had a splitting wedge but no axe.

Eli realized that he had been played the fool. To swing that sledge hammer for an hour, the average man would be exhausted. Obviously the tool had been custom built for the man who now held them and the preacher almost turned around in defeat.

Instead he reached out and took the tools from Kelly. If this was the only way to get the man to hear the gospel, then he would do his best and if he failed, it would not be for a lack of trying.

Without a word, he walked to the wagon and rolled one of the larger rounds at the back of the wagon off the edge onto the ground. It landed on its side, so he tipped it over and wiggled it back to a position under the lip of the tailgate to use as a platform. He carefully maneuvered the next piece so that it dropped down on top of the first. He did not want the wedge to be driven down into the dirt and dull the edge. At least the man had given him a sharp tool to work with.

As he was setting up, Kelly walked back into the barn with a large smirk on his face. He had to give the preacher credit. It took courage to even start this project, but there was no way on God's green earth that man was going to handle that hammer for an entire day.

Eli dropped a huge round off the wagon to give him something to stand on so he was not lifting the hammer as high each time he used it. If he was going to make this work, he had to be smart about it. This job was not for the faint of heart. The three foot in diameter log gave him a significant platform to work from.

Grabbing a fist sized rock from a pile nearby, he used that to drive the splitting wedge into the log inside a natural fissure. He raised the sledgehammer and brought it down with all his might. The wedge drove down into wood, sending a crack across the face of the log. A second blow increased the size of the crack and the third hit succeeded in breaking the round in half. He then started on the halves, splitting them into quarters and then into eighths. Once the log was cut into eight pieces, he tossed them aside into a pile and started on the next one.

By the time an hour had passed, he had spilt a fair number of the rounds. He had removed his outer shirt and sweat was pouring down his face and upper body. Pine logs are typically easy to split but because of the girth of these rounds, they were gnarly and he was having great difficulty with a majority of them.

He walked over to his horse and grabbed the canteen off the saddle. He had not brought lunch with him as he had no idea he would be out here for the day. The water would have to suffice. Fortunately, there was a well in the yard, so he would not have any lack of water and he was going to need plenty of it.

By the end of the second hour, the muscles in his arms and shoulders were protesting the unaccustomed work that they were being called upon to do.

The third hour found him over half way done and in spite of his aching body, the preacher was not going to give up until either the job was done or he dropped from exhaustion. Even though he had been drinking water with abandon, he had not used the outhouse once, for the sweat poured off of him like rain, drenching his clothes and dripping to the ground around him. He was now well into the heat of the day and felt the brutal sun beat against his undershirt.

Well after the fifth hour, his muscles were starting to cramp up and he had to stretch them to ward off the charlie horses that wanted to knot up and render his arms useless. His hands could barely hold the handle any longer, but there were only two rounds left. He used the method he had developed to finish off his base and then his stand. Even cutting the logs into eight pieces, they were still rather large chunks of firewood.

Eli dropped the tools where he stood and with great difficulty, grabbed the canteen to wash his out his dry mouth then poured some in his hand and splashed it over his face. Finally, he knocked his hat off his head with a clumsy swing of his arm and dumped the remainder of the water over his head and shoulders. It had taken him over six hours, but he had succeeded in the impossible. Using the tools of a giant he had split the entire load of logs. And not a moment too soon for he had just enough time to make it back to his job at The Saloon.

Kelly must have been keeping an eye on him for he came from around the barn and approached the exhausted man. Eli had no idea what the man had been up to for the better part of the day because he was focused on the task in front of him but now he met him next to the pile.

"I will see you at church tomorrow." Eli didn't even recognize his own voice, he was so weary.

"You're not done. These are too big to fit into my stove." The smirk was back on the man's face.

Eli stared at him in disbelief. He had been set up! Kelly never had any intention of coming to church. The pieces were large, but they should fit in any wood burning stove. He simply wanted to get free work out of him and it took all of Eli's willpower to bite back the angry retort that he desired to make. Instead, he turned back to his horse and proceeded to put his gear back on. It took several tries of his weary arms to even sling the gun belt around his waist. With difficulty, he got his shirt and vest on. He placed his hat back on his head and then calmly turned toward the Goliath that he faced.

"You never struck me as a man who would go back on his word."

"WHAT!" Kelly's face turned red with anger and he stepped toward the preacher, towering over him.

Eli was too tired to even respond to the implied threat. If the man chose to strike him, there was nothing that he could do to defend himself. Even the use of a gun was out of the question, for he did not believe he had the strength or dexterity to get a gun out of the holster. Kelly could beat him to a bloody pulp and there was not a thing Eli could do to protect himself. That did not stop him from talking though.

"You are a giant of a man, in physical stature. But the true measure of a man is his character. We had an agreement and I kept my side of it. If you choose to welsh on yours, that's up to you but you remember you're the one that will have to live with yourself. Just keep in mind that I know the truth."

"If you spread that story around town, I will hunt you down and kill you with my bare hands." The Irishman was livid.

"I'll do no such thing. I am not a man to spread rumors, but you know what happened out here today. If you are any kind of a man, you will be in church tomorrow. The service starts at eleven at The Saloon."

Eli turned his back on the man, too exhausted to care what happened next. He had to grab behind his knee and lifted his leg with his hand to get it into the stirrup. Even then it took several attempts to get onto the animal. He reined the horse around and without another word, began his ride back to town.

* * *

"What happened to you?!" Sam was stunned by the wreckage of the man who sagged before him.

Eli mumbled, "You might say I bit off more than I could chew."

Sam just shook his head. "I'd say you better just head to bed. I'll take care of things around here tonight."

Eli tried to argue, but it was of no use. He had no energy left to even begin to fight so he just turned and stumbled to the shed behind the saloon where he used to stay. He would never have made it back to the parsonage. The exhausted man slouched down in a chair that had been left behind when he moved across town and promptly fell into a deep, muscle twitching sleep.

Eli awoke to a hand shaking him. Normally he would never sleep this sound as to let someone walk up to him, but exhaustion had taken its toll. His muscles were screaming their protest every move he made and it took all of his will to open his eyes to see who was waking him. To his surprise, there was a dark eyed beauty standing over him.

"Honey," she said, "Wake up. I'm here to take you home."

Eli tried to sit up, but he was in too much pain to get there on the first try. To make things worse, sleeping in the chair left a crick in his neck that made him want to cry out in pain just moving it. Finally he eased himself into a sitting position and looked over at his intended bride.

"What are you doing here?" he croaked.

"Sam sent a messenger to let us know you were here." She replied. "Ben was out doing an errand and it was just myself, Naomi and the baby at the house. I decided to bring the wagon and get you home."

"Thank you!" He forced himself out of the chair and stood, swaying on his feet.

Elizabeth hurried over to him, wrapping her arm around his waist to support him. To her credit, she made no issue of the odor that emanated from him. Together, they made it out to the waiting buckboard. Once she got him up, she tied his still saddled horse to the tailgate and together they made the trek to the parsonage.

Inside the house, she helped him with his boots and the weary preacher laid down, fully clothed. As soon as his head hit the pillow, he fell into a deep, fitful sleep with dreams of logs, wedges and gigantic hammers.

Elizabeth stepped out of the room to find Ben had returned. Once the wagon and the horses were cared for the three of them assembled around a pot of coffee that Naomi prepared.

"He has not been is such bad shape since last year, when he was attacked and left for dead." Elizabeth confided. "Even then, I did not see him until he was mostly healed." She filled her listeners in on the attack of the previous year.

Ben shook his head, "I would have thought that leaving the Sheriff's office would have been a precursor of easier times. Instead, he has had more trouble than you can shake a stick at. Did he tell you what happened today?"

"He just said something about splitting wood," she replied. "He splits wood all the time. I don't understand what was so difficult about today."

When they finished their coffee, Ben offered to escort the older woman home. Naomi put her foot down. "You'll do nothing of the kind. It is late and there is an extra bed here. She can stay the night here."

Elizabeth was tired as it had been a long day. She was grateful for the offer and thankfully accepted. The trio exchanged their goodnights and took to their beds.

* * *

The roosters crowing roused the sleeping parson, who struggled to get out of bed. A good night's sleep did wonders for the aching muscles, but they were not going to relinquish their pain that easily. With an audible groan, he swung his feet to the floor. It was Sunday and he needed to get ready to preach, yet here he was nearly an invalid from all the work of the previous day.

It took some doing to shake all the kinks out and to get moving. But Eli was not going to leave a job undone just because he was uncomfortable.

He was moving slowly but also trying not to make too much noise. He did not want to wake the rest of the family as he got ready. He washed the dirt, grime and smell of the previous day off then put on his best suit for the early service. He would lose the jacket and string tie for the service at the saloon, where he was expected to be less formal, which suited him just fine. The bath had taken extra time and he was running late, so he slipped out the door without any breakfast. He hobbled across the yard from the parsonage to the church and as he turned the key in the door, a voice behind him startled him. He was upset with himself for being so unobservant. Fortunately, it was the voice of his betrothed.

"When was the last time you have eaten?" she asked.

Eli tried to give her a smile, "sometime yesterday morning."

"You come with me. I am going to make you breakfast." Even though she spoke softly, there was something in her voice that made it very clear that there was no room for argument.

That did not stop him from negotiating.

"Let me make sure that everything is ready for church and I will be there as soon as I am done."

She gave him a disapproving look, but did not argue.

"You need to take better care of yourself," she ordered, hands on her hips. "I want you around for a long, long time."

Eli leaned down and kissed her on the forehead. "I don't plan on going anywhere."

Impulsively, she wrapped her arms around his waist and hugged him tight.

"I was so worried about you. Please don't scare me like that ever again."

He grimaced as his sore muscles screamed for mercy, but he held her tight and whispered, "I am so sorry."

When she let go, he was surprised to see her eyes were glistening.

"I love you, Elijah Exeter."

With that she turned and hurried away, reaching up to wipe a tear from her cheek.

* * *

Matt walked with Eli to The Saloon after the first church service was finished. They arrived to find that Sam had coffee on and the tables already arranged. Eli looked at him in surprise.

"I figured after yesterday, you'd be in no shape to do this all yourself."

"Thank you. I can't even begin to tell you how much I appreciate this."

They had time for coffee and Eli was going to take advantage. He sat down with the other two men and relaxed. The Sheriff watched with an amused look as Eli made faces each time he brought the mug to his lips.

"It's pretty sad when a man can't even drink a cup of coffee without wincing in pain. What in heavens name happened yesterday?"

Eli set the cup down. "I cut a deal with someone that I would split their pile of wood if they would come to church."

"Who?" Matt asked.

"I don't want to say." Eli responded. He was going to remain true to his word, even if Kelly refused to keep his.

Matt shook his head. "I don't get it."

"Let's just say that I had the opportunity to save the souls of two men. I took the chance and now we'll have to see if it pans out."

The Sheriff shrugged, "okay. I guess I'll have to take your word for that."

As the men began to filter in for the church service, Sam took care of serving the drinks and allowed Eli time to relax his battered body. The clock approached the top of the hour, when the batwing doors of the saloon swung open and the bulk of the man in the doorway totally blocked the sunlight. Eli looked up and a smile lit up his still weary face.

"Welcome." He offered as Kelly entered the room.

Kelly nodded to Eli, "Preacher." He said in greeting. He walked to the bar and ordered a whiskey from Sam, then went and sat down at one of the tables.

The last man to enter was Irv Carter. He sat down in the back where he could keep an eye on everything around him.

It took Eli a couple of tries to get out of his chair, but at this point, he had no regrets about the previous day.

When he first began his church, he had kept the sermons to fifteen minutes, but over the last year, he had discovered that his congregation was more than willing to listen longer. This morning, he finished in a little under twenty five minutes and after the closing prayer, most all of the people stayed as it was lunch time and the smell from Sam's cooking had wafted through the room for most of the message. It was rare for anyone to leave after church these days. They all stayed around to eat, talk and drink, although no one seemed to get out of hand on these lazy Sunday afternoons.

Eli had worked the kinks out and was moving well, albeit, slower than normal. He was carrying several plates of food to one of to a table where three cowhands were waiting. Seated at the next table was Kelly, deep in conversation with his neighbor. The big man had his back to the preacher, but that did not stop Eli from overhearing what he was saying.

"I didn't figure he would be able to last an hour with that hammer, but he stayed on it for more than six hours. Six hours, I tell you. Dang, I don't think I could last that long swinging that hammer anymore. I'll say this for your preacher, the man has guts. Shoot, if he was willing to do all that to get me to this church, I had no choice but to come."

Eli moved quietly back toward the kitchen, not wanting Kelly to know that he'd overheard the conversation. Suddenly, a grin split his face as he realized that now it was time to go make sure that Joe kept his side of the bargain. Eli had been trying to get him to come to church for most of a year and now he had the leverage to make it happen.

By one o'clock in the afternoon he was able to say his goodbyes and then slip out the door. He decided to walk to the lumberman's house as movement seemed good for the overworked muscles.

Besides, he did not want to make the effort to find his horse and saddle the animal. It would be easier and faster to walk.

On the second round of knocks, Joe opened the door. When he saw who his visitor was, a slightly puzzled look shown on his face but true to the code of the west, he swung the door wide open.

"Come on in preacher." His normal tone of voice always sounded like shouting, probably due to hearing loss from all the work he did at the sawmill as a young man.

Eli limped into the house and took the offered seat, immediately wondering if he was going to be able to get himself out of it.

"Can I get you anything? A cup of coffee or some whiskey?"

"Coffee, if you already have it made," Eli responded.

Joe walked to the stove and poured a cup for his guest.

"Hope you don't mind me being blunt," he said as he handed over the coffee. "But what brings you here? You ain't been to my house since I told you I would not come to your church."

Eli took a sip of coffee and replied, "Well, because that is going to change."

Joe snorted with derision. "That's never going to happen."

Eli took the same tact as he did with Kelly.

"Joe, you have the reputation around town of being a man of your word."

The puzzled look returned to the merchant's face.

"I am a man of my word," he said forcefully. "I never go back on it."

"That's good," Eli responded, "because I am here to make sure you follow through on your promise."

"What in tarnation are you talking about?" The color was starting to rise in Joe's face, evidence of his rising consternation.

Eli smiled, "Kelly came to church this morning."

As the comment registered in the man's brain, he exploded, "WHAT? That ain't possible!"

The preacher leaned forward in his chair.

"Not only is it possible, it happened. I just wanted to give you some time to get used to the idea so you can be ready to come to church next Sunday."

"Well I'll be dad gummed." The flummoxed host was regaining his composure. "I never thought it could be. How did you do it? How did you get Kelly to come to church?"

"He runs a hard bargain. That's all I can tell you."

He finished his coffee and groaned as he pushed himself out of the chair.

"If you want to know more, you'll need to ask Kelly yourself. Meanwhile, I will see you at eleven o'clock on Sunday morning at the Saloon. I'll even buy you the first beer."

He hobbled out the door, leaving the lumberman shaking his head in wonder.

* * *

Jeff snuck out of the house that morning and made a beeline for the Café. He had brought milk with him in a Mason jar, so he cared for Rock and cleaned up after him, as he had been by himself all night. Holding the puppy in the crook of his arm, he made his way to the doctor's office. Without knocking, he slipped in through the door as the ancient lock was no match for the town scamp.

Soon he was seated next to Steven. He placed the puppy on the bed next to the comatose man and Rock immediately began to lick the still face, evoking a twitch of movement from the man. The dog quickly tired of his unrequited attention, so he snuggled up against Steven's neck and promptly fell asleep.

Jeff told the still form about all the things going on in his life. He spoke of Joshua's willingness to take time to speak to him at school and how he had encouraged Jeff to pray for Steven's recovery. He shared how Mrs. Franco was taking care of the puppy for him and how he was continuing to work for her to pay off the animal's keep.

He had brought the rest of the milk from home with him and the only time he left his friend's side was to take the puppy outside for a break and to feed him some of the milk in the jar.

Throughout the day, different people came in to see the stricken man, to pray over him and ask the doctor how he was. Without fail, each of them would pull the doc out of earshot of the boy and ask him about the child. He filled them in on what he knew and most everyone seemed to understand as pretty much all of the folks knew about Jeff and his life at home. In a small town, nothing was really secret and it came as no surprise to anyone that he had attached himself to a man like Steven.

* * *

Elizabeth hurried over to her shop that Sunday morning, right after she had prepared breakfast for Eli and made sure he ate. She had forgotten about the puppy and was worried about what she would find. She walked in to discover that all the messes were cleaned up and the blankets inside the wooden crate were neatly folded up.

She smiled as she realized that Jeff let himself in as if he owned the place, but she was grateful that he was taking such an interest in this poor little orphaned pup.

Making sure everything was in order for the following morning, she locked up the shop and headed to church.

Elizabeth was thrilled to be in the congregation seated with Eli while the song leader led them in the hymns. The church had a very talented pianist and years ago the congregation had bought a spinet piano from a pioneer who was traveling through to California. The man had finally convinced his wife that the extra weight in his wagon would kill the mules if they tried to take it over the Sierra Nevada's. She in turn was accepting of the loss since it was going to a church. She could not bear the thought of leaving it alongside the trail, somewhere in the desert.

After the sermon, Elizabeth stood with her beau as he greeted the parishioners who exited the church. She marveled at his patience, even though he had another service to attend to.

At the last minute, when he absolutely had to leave, Eli leaned over and kissed her lightly on the cheek, being as discreet as possible. He whispered his love into her ear and then hurried toward the Saloon. Well, he hurried as much as his tortured body would let him. She had a worried smile on her face as she watched his back in the distance. She still did not know all of what happened yesterday. He had remained tight lipped about the incident, only saying that he had given his word. She was proud of him for being an upright man, but she was still concerned over his safety.

Ben and Naomi were the last to leave the church and they waited for Elizabeth as she locked up the building. Little Elijah had fallen asleep during the singing and had slept through the service. Coming out into the sunlight, he was starting to stir and fuss.

Elizabeth met the trio at the bottom of the stairs.

"Elizabeth, what are your plans for the rest of the day?" Naomi asked.

"I was going to visit Steven, then I am open for the rest of the day. How about you?"

"I was hoping you would join us for the afternoon. Father should be coming home at a reasonable time and I have a roast I'm preparing for supper." Naomi wanted to spend as much time as she could with her future mother-in-law.

"Naomi, I would love that. Thank you." In turn, Elizabeth looked to Ben.

"Ben, could I impose upon you to come and take a look at Steven? I have the utmost confidence in Doctor Mercer, but I feel that a second set of eyes could not hurt."

Ben nodded. "I would be happy to as long as I am not stepping on toes. Steven is Doctor Mercer's patient and the good doctor has the final say. I will grab my bag and escort you over there."

He leaned down and kissed his wife and then the top of the baby's head. "We'll be back in a short while."

Within moments, Ben and Elizabeth were on their way and the short walk was pleasant, even though the morning was heating up quickly.

Doctor Mercer was very receptive to the idea of having another qualified physician check on his patient. Jeff was ushered out of the room while Ben made a thorough exam. When he had completed his prodding, listening, checking of the pulse and all the other things that needed to be done, he slung his stethoscope around his neck with a practiced movement and turned to his fellow doctor.

"Doctor Mercer. I find him to be in excellent health, aside from the coma. He seems to be well hydrated."

"I have been giving him shots of water, sodium chloride and bicarbonate several times a day," the elder man answered, "and all of his attendants have been wetting his mouth almost constantly."

"Well you are doing an incredible job, I would not change a thing you are doing." Ben spoke with confidence.

"Thank you. It's a relief to know that I have not missed anything. This is not something that I deal with on a regular basis… In fact, it is something I have never dealt with." Doc Mercer replied.

They walked out of the room and Jeff slipped past them to resume his vigil.

* * *

Eli left Joe's place and headed straight to the Doctor's Office. He tapped on the door and then entered only to find Jeff still in the same place he'd last seen him. Earlier in the week, he found the boy doing his homework alongside of Steven's bed working on memorizing a poem that Miss Elliott had assigned. Now he was just sitting there having stopped his one sided conversation with Steven when Eli knocked on the door.

"How is he doing?" The preacher asked Jeff.

Surprised, the boy answered, "There is really no change. I'm not sure if he can hear what I am saying or not, but I still keep talking to him." The boy paused, a thoughtful look on his face and then continued. "I keep praying, but I don't think God is listening to me."

"He hears you."

Puzzled, the boy asked, "What?" He was looking straight at the parson, but his lips never moved.

"Yes Jeff, He hears you."

Jeff turned his attention to the bed and whooped, "Steven! You're awake!"

Eli stepped to the bed as well. "It is good to hear your voice my friend. How are you?"

"Good… I think." He looked over at the young lad. "I have heard most of what you said to me. I kept trying to answer but just could not get my mouth to work."

He pulled the sheet part way down off him and grimaced, "Oh, I really need a bath."

Eli laughed with joy. "I think that can be arranged. Welcome back to the land of the living."

Steven looked over at Jeff. "Jeff, don't cry."

The boy was snuggled up with his puppy, tears streaming down his face. He sniffed before he responded.

"I'm sorry, I don't mean to be a baby."

Eli dropped a hand to the young man's shoulder, but it was Steven who replied.

"You're not a baby. You are a true friend. I know how you came every day to spend time with me. That is the sign of a man who is closer than a brother. Thank you."

Jeff sniffed again. "You think of me as your brother?" he asked.

"No. You are more than a brother...better than a brother. You are a true friend."

Jeff's face lit up at such high praise from a man that he respected.

Steven turned to look at Eli, "Can I ask a favor?"

"Of course."

"Would you go to my place and grab a clean set of clothes for me?"

Eli motioned toward a chair in the corner, "It is already done."

"Oh thank you. Can you see if the doctor has a bucket and a wash cloth so I can sponge off before I dress?'

"Perhaps," Eli suggested, "We should let the good doctor know that you are awake."

"Perhaps." Steven responded.

Eli walked to the door that separated the office from the doctor's residence and knocked. When it opened, he addressed Doc Mercer.

"You might want to check on your patient. He is getting a little antsy."

The Doctor hurried over to the bed to see Steven with eyes wide open and then turned to the other two.

"Okay, out. Out, both of you."

When the room was cleared, he turn back toward is patient.

"How do you feel?"

"Good...A little weak, but good. I really want to get washed up and into my clean clothes."

"That will have to wait a moment until I check you out," the Doctor replied.

He grabbed his bag from a cabinet and did an exam of his patient. When he finished, he put his instruments away and turned toward Steven.

"All that praying must have some sort of effect because you seem as good as new. No bedsores and no noticeable side effects." He shook his head. "Every time that parson gets hisself involved, things happen that ain't supposed to happen." The normally articulate doctor slipped into the regional vernacular in his exasperation. "It ain't natural."

Steven looked up at the doctor and spoke with simple frankness.

"If you became a follower of Jesus, you would have the same power available to you. Jesus' disciples went around healing the sick, making the lame to walk and raising the dead. You could do the same thing."

"I don't know." Doc looked skeptical.

"What don't you know? Look at some of the things that have happened around here in the last year. I was saved from the grips of alcohol. On the same day I 'just happen' to find Eli, in the dark in a desert that is thousands of square miles. That was an absolute miracle. Then there is Sam. His healing is another act of God and there is nothing else to explain it. Now there is me. How long have I been laying here? Four or five days?"

"One week. One week ago today you nearly drowned and should not be alive. The extreme cold and your lungs full of water, the length of time it took to rescue you."

"And yet here I am," Steven interjected. "Another miracle. Doc, what is it going to take to open your eyes to the hand of God? He is doing a work in this town, but you are trying your best not to see what is right in front of your face. What, are you waiting for? Him to hit you in the back of the head with a board, because that may very well come next?"

No longer feeling weak, Steven was animated as he tried to get through to the man in front of him.

"No, that won't be necessary. The evidence is all right here in front of me. What do I need do to be saved?" he asked.

Steven smiled. "The gospel is simple. We are all sinners and someone has to pay the price for our sins. God's sentence upon the whole world for turning their backs on him was death. Jesus, the perfect Son of God, came down and took our sentence upon himself. He was crucified on a cross, dying in our place. He was buried, along with all of our sins that he took upon Himself. He was resurrected from the dead three days later and now sits at the right hand of God the Father. The debt has been paid, but we still have to accept the gift that Jesus offers. The Bible tells us that if you confess with your mouth, Jesus as Lord and believe in your hearts that God raised him from the dead, you will be saved."

He continued, "Doc, the word Lord means Master. We are asking for the salvation of God through Jesus, but then we let Him be master of our lives. That means we live our lives in a way that glorifies God and points people toward Him daily. But it is not enough just to live good lives, it also means that we are confessing Jesus before men so that they understand the reasons we live our lives the way we do."

He paused a moment then asked, "Are you ready to ask Jesus to forgive your sins and to follow Him for the rest of your life?"

Doctor Mercer nodded, "How do I do that?" he asked.

"We pray. I will say the words and you repeat them after me."

Together the men bowed their heads and just like Eli did with Steven a year prior, Steven led Doctor Mercer in a pray of confession and repentance. In the stuffy little office with the rank smell of body odor, medicines and tonics, the older man finally let go and turned his life over to Jesus.

* * *

Eli burst through the door of the Parsonage, startling the three inside. "Steven is awake!"

The announcement brought about a flurry of activity as supper was forgotten for the moment. It was decided that Ben and Naomi would stay at the house and take care of the food so that it would not go to waste. Eli and Elizabeth would go get Steven and bring him back for supper.

All his muscle pain was forgotten as Eli hitched up the buggy then saddled his horse because Elizabeth's buggy could only carry two people. When they reached the Doctor's Office, they found Steven standing near the Doctor deep in conversation. Elizabeth was too excited to follow societal protocol, instead, she raced across the room and gave Steven a big hug.

When she let go, he was surprised to see tears sparkling in her eyes.

"You men," Elizabeth glanced over to Eli, "both of you have got to stop this. If you keep giving me frights like this I am going to grow old before my time."

"Miss Elizabeth," Steven responded, "I can honestly say, I don't ever want to go through anything like this again."

She sniffed and dabbed at her eyes with a kerchief.

Doc Mercer interrupted. "Before you all haul my patient away, I would like to tell you something."

All eyes turned toward the doctor and he continued. "Steven and I have been talking and I have decided to accept Jesus as my Savior."

Eli was the first to respond. "Doc, that is the best news yet."

Elizabeth took the older man's hands in her own and looked up at him. "Today, two lives were saved and we all have a lot to celebrate."

The old man's eyes twinkled as he looked down at the beautiful woman in front of him. "I would have done it a long time ago if I'd known I would get this kind of response."

Elizabeth felt the heat rise in her face as she began to blush.

Doc turned toward Eli. "In all seriousness, Steven and I were talking about me having someone show me the ropes on this Christian thing. I was wondering if you could help out in that."

Eli smiled and shrugged. "You know, Steven and I have been meeting a group of men for the last year. I think it is time for him to disciple you on his own. I will be available for anything that arises, but he is more than capable."

Doc nodded. "That is fine by me."

Elizabeth turned toward the group. "Naomi has supper waiting, gentlemen would the three of you care to join us?"

Jeff didn't need to answer, he was all in. His folks wouldn't even notice if he was gone a little while longer.

Steven nodded, "yes ma'am."

It was the Doctor's turn to grin, "young lady, nothing would make me happier right now than to dine with you. Let me get my hat and my coat."

"Doctor Mercer," Steven interrupted, "how much do I owe you?"

"Oh, I figure the bill will come to about eighteen dollars."

Steven sighed. "Okay, I will have to get that to you later, if that is okay?"

Before the Doctor could reply, Elizabeth fished in her drawstring hand bag and pulled out a twenty dollar gold piece.

"This should take care of it." She said as she handed it to the Doctor.

Steven turned to his employer. "But…"

Elizabeth looked him in the eye and said earnestly, "over the past week I have come to realize how much I depend upon you and how much you do around the bakery. Consider that part of the raise in pay that you will be receiving."

Before he could respond, she turned toward the door. "We better hurry or dinner will be ruined."

CHAPTER SIXTEEN

Matt looked down at the paper on his desk and sighed. Everything pointed to Mrs. Swensen, but for some reason, he was reluctant to talk to her. As he contemplated it, he realized that he had never accused a lady of something so terrible before. He also was seeing the whole thing through the perspective of his own life and Becky would never do something so despicable so it was difficult for him to imagine another wife doing such a thing. It was for this reason alone that he had delayed questioning her for so many days. He also realized that he had a lot of circumstantial evidence, but no hard proof.

He wanted to continue to put it off, but he had already wasted nearly a week. He needed to do something and he needed to do it now.

He scanned the list again of what he knew. Mrs. Swensen was not well liked by any of the neighbors because she had an abrasive personality. She was a crack shot with a rifle as evidenced by the rabbit she'd shot when he was last there. He estimated the distance at about fifty yards and she had hit the critter in the head. Finally, she was an expert horsewoman, yet she had played dumb about the horses that her husband had bought. What he did not have for her was a motive. He knew about Norris' dalliance's with the prostitute, but was his wife aware of it? Did Inga Swensen know about her and suspected far more than what had been really going on?

What about the horses and the wagon? What had become of them?

Even as the question came to mind, a plan began to take shape.

With a sudden burst of resolve, Matt pushed back from his desk and unlocked the gun cabinet. He took out his spare pistol and checked the loads before tucking it in behind his back, under his black vest. He grabbed his hat off the rack and jammed it down onto his head then headed out the door. In spite of his hurry, he had lost none of his caution.

The ride out the Swensen spread was uneventful and the Sheriff used the time to finish putting together his plan of action. He rode off the road prior to the turn off for the Swensen place and painstakingly worked his way to the back of their property. He stayed in the low areas, the gullies and washes, staying out of sight of the house as he made his approach. He kept the barn between him and the main structure.

He was able to ride within a couple hundred yards of the buildings before he had to dismount and tie his horse. Staying in a low crouch, he darted from trees to bushes and shrubs, staying out of sight the best he could.

Matt reached the corner of the barn and paused to reconnoiter the area. He located Mrs. Swensen in the garden hoeing weeds. There was no way to make it to the door without being seen so he hunkered down to wait. From his vantage point he was able to take stock of his surroundings. The house had a front door and two windows facing the barn. From his earlier visit, he was able to recall that the barn had the large doors for the animals and on the end furthest from him, there was a smaller man door. There was a smaller out building behind the house. He had no idea how he was going to search that. He decided to cross that bridge when he got to it.

Nearly forty five minutes elapsed before the widow finally began walking toward the house. The sheriff waited until the door closed behind her and then swiftly sprinted to the man door of the barn. He did not want to chance opening the larger door as it would take too long and he really did not want to be seen.

Inside, he waited for his eyes to adjust to the dim light. He did not want to trip over anything in his haste. The last thing he needed was for one of the animal to startle and give out a warning. Once he could see well enough, he slowly advanced forward picking his way carefully toward the back of the barn.

He figured that if Mrs. Swensen killed her husband, she might have taken the wagon and the horse back home after burying the body. If so, he would have all the evidence that he needed. He decided to risk a match and reached into his vest pocket to retrieve one. He raised his right leg to tighten up the course cloth of his pants to strike the match on when the door of the barn swung open and framed in the sunlight was the widow Swensen, her rifle aimed at the center of his chest.

CHAPTER SEVENTEEN

Joshua was happy. In fact, he was happier than he had been in the longest time. Michelle was… well he wasn't exactly sure what she was in relation to himself, but he knew that when he was with her she made him feel all strange inside, not that he would ever admit that to anyone. Still, he knew how he felt about her and he thought she felt the same way about him. He didn't know what love really was but he knew he was smitten.

On top of that he was being accepted as part of the crowd at school and was no longer an outsider, standing on the edge looking in. Finally, he had the Wheaton's, who were as kind to him as if he was their own son. All in all, life was really good.

When the school bell rang, he gathered up his books and followed the group outside. It took him a moment to isolate Michelle, but when he did, he made a beeline to her.

Without asking, he took her books and tucked them under his free arm and together they began their familiar walk toward her house. For once Joshua was doing all of the chatting and Michelle was strangely quiet. But like most boys his age and many men much older, he didn't notice the change. He finally ran out of things to say and now the silence was starting to get awkward. Not sure how to respond to the nothingness, he finally stopped walking and turned to Michelle.

"Is everything alright? You ain't hardly said a thing." Now he was feeling a little worried.

Michelle's frown spoke volumes as the ball of fear in the pit of his stomach began to grow.

"My father says I can't be friends with you any longer." Her eyes began to fill up with tears.

"Why?" Joshua didn't know what else to say, so he blurted out the only thing he could. "Why?"

"My father says you…" Michelle hesitated, not wanting to say it out loud. "He says you are a killer." Her voice cracked with emotion, even as she spoke the words.

The need to defend her father along with her desire to be with Joshua spurred her on.

"He doesn't know you like I do. He doesn't know how kind and sweet you are. All he knows is what he has heard from others." The tears had escaped and were spilling down her cheeks. A sob welled up from deep inside as she fought conflicting emotions. She loved her father but Joshua was her new best friend.

Joshua struggled with his own desire and personal shame. If he could change the past, knowing what he now knew, he would have done it in a heartbeat. Rob Handy was a thief and a murderer, but Joshua had to live with the consequences of his own actions and killing the outlaw weighed heavy on his conscience. Unfortunately, the young man did not know how to intimately share those emotions with the girl that stood before him.

As the tears streamed down her face and the sobs came from deep in the depth of her soul, Joshua wanted to reach out and hold her, to comfort her in her sorrow, but his own pain kept him from doing so. Without warning, Michelle spun on her heel and ran as quickly as she could toward her home.

Dejected, Joshua headed back toward the school and his horse. He was half way there before he realized that he still had his sweetheart's books under his arm.

* * *

Becky was taken aback when Joshua came in, dumped an extraordinary amount of books on the table and took off out the door without a word and without touching the sandwich she had waiting for him. She always teased him about having a hollow leg, so when he ignored food, she knew something was really wrong.

She was new to the job of being a mother, so she bided her time, contemplating how to approach this new development. Often times, when unsure of a situation, she would ask herself how her mother would have handled such a conundrum with one of her brothers. Drawing upon her mother's wisdom had more than once taken her through these uncharted waters.

She had an overwhelming desire to fix all of Joshua's problems for him, but life had taught her it simply was not possible. There were just some things that he was going to have to figure out on his own. She hated the fact but resigned herself to the reality of the situation.

Becky did not rush out immediately. She had decided to let the boy stew in his own troubles for a while. He knew he could talk to her when he was ready and she was determined to let him try to figure this one out on his own. If he could not, she would be there for him when he was ready to open up. It nearly killed her not to act, but she knew that if he was going to grow up and mature, this was part of the process.

As she nervously waited for Joshua to open up to her, Becky had no idea what kind of situation her husband faced. Something prodded her to go into her bedroom and close the door. She knelt down alongside the bed and earnestly prayed for the two men in her life.

CHAPTER EIGHTEEN

Matt stared at the bore of the rifle that was pointed right at his heart. His mouth had gone instantly dry and it took a moment for him to realize that he was holding his breath. He exhaled even as he considered his next move.

"Vat are you doing in my barn?" the widow demanded.

The Sheriff thought about throwing himself to the side and going for his gun. He dismissed the idea as soon as it entered his mind for even if he was fast enough, how would he explain to the town council why he had killed the woman in her own out building? He was in a precarious predicament, caused by his own foolish behavior and now he needed to face up to it.

"Ma'am," Matt spoke carefully. "I'm here looking for clues into the killing of your husband. I have run out of leads and am simply hoping to find anything to help." His hands were up at shoulder height. He did not want her to have any reason to squeeze that trigger.

"Vy did you not just ask me?" she responded. Suddenly, a look of realization flashed across her face.

"You tink I killed him, don't you?" she demanded.

Matt had the feeling of a boy caught with his hand in the cookie jar but before he could say a thing, she continued on.

"Get out! Get out ov my barn right now." Tears streamed down her face as she screamed at him.

Matt's gut sank as he realize that he had made so many mistakes, especially to assume the wife killed her husband based upon such flimsy, circumstantial evidence.

Feeling foolish and stupid, the Sheriff slunk out of the barn and lost no time making his way back to his horse. He felt like an idiot and his first inclination was to lay the blame on his wife for suggesting that the widow was the culprit, but he soon acknowledged to himself that the blame laid squarely on his shoulders. Any attempt to lay it elsewhere was cowardly and he felt a wave of shame wash over him.

The ride back to town seemed much longer than it really was and Matt had plenty of time to think. After he got past mentally kicking himself, he began to think of the case and it occurred to him that he had become so focused on the wife that he overlooked another option.

Matt rode directly to the telegraph office and sent out messages to each of the local sheriffs in the area, asking for information on the two missing horses. He gave the description and brand information. As he paid Bert his fee, he added an extra coin. "Please, let me know if you receive any answers that will lead me to those horses, okay?"

Bert nodded. "Of course Sheriff. Do you want me to send a messenger to your house if you're not in town?"

"Absolutely!" Matt replied. "I don't care what time it is." He turned to walk away, then paused. "Bert... Thank you."

Bert grinned. "No problem, Sheriff." He did not get much excitement in his life, so anything out of the ordinary was welcome.

Matt found Eli over at The Saloon. He tossed his nickel on the bar. "Can I have a beer please?"

The preacher filled a clean mug and slid it over to his friend.

"Do you have a minute?" Matt asked.

"Sure." Eli grabbed his cup of coffee and together they headed to an empty table.

When they were both seated so each had a view of the door, Matt opened up to his mentor and shared with him the events of the last couple of hours. Eli for his part did not pass judgement on his friend, instead, he listened with a sympathetic ear.

"Eli, I felt like a full blown jackass when she started crying and screaming at me to get out. I'll never be able to face her again. It was terrible." Matt was looking pretty forlorn.

"Unfortunately, it probably won't be the last time you feel that way. Matt, we all make mistakes, but it is important that you don't keep beating yourself up about it. Learn from it and move on my friend."

Matt gave him a lopsided grin. "I'll try, but I ain't making any promises."

Eli changed the subject. "I wanted to let you know that Elizabeth and I are getting married."

This time Matt's grin went from ear to ear. "That's fantastic." He burst out enthusiastically.

"Thank you." Eli smiled.

"Wait one minute, didn't you just start courting her a couple weeks ago?" Matt's face wore a puzzled look. "You move mighty fast, don't ya?"

Eli chuckled. "I'm not getting any younger and I certainly can't afford to waste any time. I know in my heart this is God's will for us and Elizabeth feels the same."

"Have y'all set a date?"

"No, we simply want it to be sometime before the kids head out on the wild frontier. "

Matt laughed. "Remember when they used to call Nevada that?"

Eli nodded. "I'm not so sure we still aren't," he replied.

Matt stood up and slapped Eli on the shoulder. "Well congratulations buddy. I'm happy for you. For both of you. It's about time, if you ask me."

Matt headed for the door and Eli stood up and made his way back behind the bar.

The dinner rush had not yet begun and Sam was relaxing at a table with a couple of his customers while the smell of dinner simmering on the stove permeated the room. Eli began heating water to wash dishes from the lunch hour. He set the dirty plates into the tub as the steam began to rise from the surface of the water.

The door burst open and a preteen boy rushed in. Eli called out to him, "Percy, what are you up to?"

"I'm lookin fer the Sheriff." The boy was panting.

"He left short while ago. Did you check his office?"

"Yep, he ain't there." Percy was starting to get his wind back, the advantage of being young.

"He probably headed home for supper." Eli postulated.

The boy looked crestfallen. "That's a long way," he groaned.

Eli laughed, "You can do it son. I have faith in you."

Percy's face lit up. "Yes sir." He turned and by the time he hit the door he was once again at a dead run.

* * *

"Joshua, you haven't said a word all evening. What in the name of heaven is going on?" The teenager had a morose look on his face and Matt couldn't take this moping any longer.

"I don't want to talk about it." Joshua figured it was his problem and he had to find his own answers. He couldn't keep running to the Wheaton's like a little baby.

Matt and Becky exchanged glances, but nothing more was said.

When the meal was finished, Joshua looked up from his plate. "May I be excused?" he asked.

Matt pushed back from the table. "Come with me," he ordered.

Joshua followed him outside, not sure what was coming.

The two men sat down on the front stoop at Matt's direction. Matt had his cup of coffee in his hand and he took a sip before addressing the younger man.

"Joshua," he began, "We are a family here and as such, we bear one another's burden. When you are hurting, as you obviously are, it creates," Matt paused, searching for the right word, "…a break down in our small family. Whatever is going on, you don't have to go through it alone. "

The silence that follow hung heavy in the air. Finally, Joshua opened up.

"I like someone at school, a friend, but their pa won't let me be around them anymore."

Matt pondered this for a moment, suspecting he already knew the answer to the next question.

"Why is that?" He asked.

Joshua was studying a knot in the wooden stair tread during the conversation. Now he looked up. "Cause he says I'm a killer."

Matt sighed with trepidation. He was afraid that this would happen and in fact, he was surprised it had not come up earlier. He paused for a while as he thought of his response.

"Son, we can't change the people around us," he began. "There are those who will make assumptions, based upon the things that they have heard and sometimes there is just no changing their minds."

Joshua burst out, "Yeah, but I like her."

Everything came into perspective for Matt. He studied the anguished face of the boy next to him before he continued on.

"Josh, who is the girl?" he asked.

Joshua felt his face turning red, but he couldn't take back what had already been said. "Michelle." He uttered quietly.

Matt grimaced. Her father, Wilfred Youngblood was a self-righteous son of a...he stopped himself from blurting out how he really felt about the man.

"Son, if this is that important to you, I can see if I can talk to him. There are no guarantees that he will listen, but I'm willing to do what I can."

For the first time that evening, Joshua felt a surge of hope. He turned to his surrogate father and nodded. "Yes sir, it is important to me. Ever since the party, Michelle and me have..." he searched for the right word but couldn't find it, so he left the words hanging.

Matt nodded his understanding. "Alright, I will try to figure out where we go from here." He stood up. "But remember, you need to talk to us when you hit hard times. Mrs. Wheaton and I, we will be here for you...always."

* * *

Matt was getting ready to head back into town when Percy came trotting up to the house.

"How can I help you young fella?" he asked.

Percy held out the telegraph that he was carrying. "Mr. Bert told me to get this to you as quick as I could," he panted.

Matt retrieved a coin from his pocket and handed it to the lad. "Thank you, son." He said. "This is really important so I appreciate you bringing it."

As Percy turned back toward town, Matt called out. "Can I give you a ride back?" he asked.

The youngster came back. "Yes sir," he replied enthusiastically.

Matt swung up into the saddle, then reached down and grabbed the outstretched arm reaching up toward him. With a heave, he swung the boy up behind him. Together the pair rode back into town.

Once the boy had been delivered to his front porch, the sheriff rode to his office where he took a look at the telegraph. He was surprised that he received a response so quickly and as he scanned the message, he realized that the investigation which had gone stone cold had just heated back up. He stuffed the telegram into his pocket and walked out to begin his rounds.

He rattled the doors on the shops that were closed for the night and looked through the windows, making sure no one had broken in. Matt was thorough in his duties, but he made sure that he would make it to The Saloon before Eli finished his shift.

The preacher looked up from his work when the Sheriff made his entrance. "Fancy seeing you in here twice in the same day. To what do we owe the pleasure?" He called out.

Matt walked over to the bar, pulling the paper out of his pocket as he approached. He tossed it onto the planks with a little flick of the wrist so it spun as it landed letting Eli read it without putting down the glass he was drying.

He set down the towel and glass, picked up the note and re-read it. Looking up, he queried, "What gives here?"

Matt was excited. "After the debacle today, I telegraphed all the local lawmen, asking for information on those two horses. They were sold to a rancher who only lives about a three hour ride from here." He looked his friend in the eye. "I was wondering if you were up for an early morning ride."

Eli squinted as he thought about his plans for the following day. "I'll talk to Steven about leading the prayer meeting in the morning. If he's up for it, I think I can do it."

"Good." Matt replied. "Meet me at the southern fork at daybreak if you can make it. If you're not there, I'll head out alone."

Eli nodded. "Hopefully I will see you there."

CHAPTER NINETEEN

The morning sky was lit up with yellow, red and orange hues on the bottom of the clouds as the two men began their journey. Eli had to admit that there were times that he missed his old profession and he was grateful that Matt would include him in these forays.

Matt on the other hand was happy to have the years of experience by his side. He had learned much of his craft through trial and error and to have someone to help guide him through the process was in some ways a relief.

Neither men spoke much. Eli had a late night and the early morning was not conducive to edifying conversation. The silence was welcomed by both.

By the time they reached the town of Briarbush, the sun had warmed the day and their coats were off, tied behind their respective saddles. The ride home promised to be a scorcher.

The two men walked their horses down the middle of the street, scanning both the buildings and people as they looked for the Sheriff's Office. It was a small town, consisting of one street and it was not difficult to find what they were looking for.

Dismounting in front of the Jail they noticed a man seated on the boardwalk. He had his hat pulled low, shading his eyes, but it was apparent that he was watching them.

Both Eli and Matt were wearing tied down guns. Eli had his second gun tucked in behind his back, while Matt had his in a double holster set up. If it weren't for the badge pinned to Matt's chest, they could have been mistaken as trouble makers. The pair wondered if they were looking at one of the towns riff raff and whether they would have to deal with him before they got out of town.

Keeping a close watch on the man out of the corner of their eyes, the two men made their way inside, only to find the office empty. Matt was a little perturbed until he realized that he had not replied to the telegraph and the Sheriff had no way of knowing they were coming. He turned to his friend, "So, we have a choice. We can wait or start trying to hunt him down."

At that moment, the door swung open and the man whom they had been watching moments ago, stepped over the threshold. Matt's hand hovered over the handle of his right pistol while Eli let his hand hang casually near his gun which had the handle facing forward. The illusion of the left handed cross draw was intentional, as he was proficient with drawing the gun with his right hand with deadly accuracy.

The intruder raised his hands shoulder high. "Whoa, boys. I'm Sheriff Jackson. It probably would not bode well for you gentlemen if you were to shoot the Sheriff. We haven't had a necktie party around here for a long time and I don't think y'all would want to be the guest of honor."

Matt visibly relaxed while Eli kept the same easy readiness as before. Jackson carefully reached up and pulled back his vest to reveal a badge pinned to his shirt. "Welcome boys. I assume you are here about two horses?"

He was a wizened man of an undetermined age with a fringe of hair showing beneath his cowboy hat. When he removed the hat, his bald pate glistened with the sweat of the day. His bushy grey mustache hid a mouthful of yellowing teeth. He was slight of build with a bit of a potbelly going.

Matt reached out a hand. "Sheriff Matt Wheaton and this is my friend, Eli Exeter."

At the mention of the name, Sheriff Jackson took a second look. He studied the face for a moment.

"Elijah Exeter? Used to be a sheriff in Utah?"

A faint smile was his only give away. "Maybe," he replied.

"Andrew Jackson. It is a pleasure sir."

It was Eli's turn to look at the other man over. "Do people around here call you Old Hickory?" he asked.

"Ha. Good with a gun and funny too." The older Sheriff chortled.

Matt shook his head, "Okay you two, before you sit down to a game of checkers and a beer, how about we get some information on those horses. Can you tell me where to find the man who bought them?"

Jackson grinned. "You know, everyone in town were so upset when Clancy got them there horses. Some people seem to have the golden touch and that's Clancy for sure. He seems to fall into the most lucrative deals and this certainly was one. Them horses would sell for forty dollars apiece. He got them and a wagon for fifty bucks. Fifty bucks I tell you."

Matt was impatiently waiting for the information he wanted. "Where can I find this Clancy?"

"Well, he lives about twelve miles south of town here."

"Great. Just tell me how to get there and we will be on our way." Matt's frustration was beginning to show.

"Let's see. You head south until you see the broken tree. Top blew down about a year ago in one our Washoe Zephyrs. About two dozen paces past that you take the road to the east and eventually you will run into his ranch. You can't miss it."

"Thank you." Matt turned to head out the door and just as Eli was getting ready to follow him, Andrew spoke up.

"But you won't find him there," he announced.

Matt turned around with an exaggerated sigh. Meanwhile, Eli just grinned. He really kind of enjoyed watching the old man torture the young bull.

"And why won't we find him there?" Matt's annoyance was evident and Eli suspected this was Sheriff Jackson's intent all along.

"Because he is across the street at the bar. This is the day he makes his trip into town for supplies. Once he's loaded all his stuff, then he heads to the bar for a beer or two before heading back. I would hate for y'all to make that long ride for nothing."

Matt's angry glare said what he *wanted* to say, but the words that came from his gritted teeth were simply, "Thank you very much."

He turned on his heel and flung the door open so furiously it bounced off the interior wall.

Eli extended his hand to the local sheriff. "It was a pleasure to meet you." He made it to the door and turned to Jackson. "You know, I will have to put up with him the entire ride home... but I wouldn't have missed that for the world."

Andrew flashed him a great big smile. "Aw, he's a young buck, but he'll learn. It was my pleasure, sir." He drawled.

Eli tipped his hat and followed Matt out the door.

Together they pushed through the batwing doors of the local cantina. While their eyes became accustomed to the dim interior, Eli put his hand on his partner's forearm. "Maybe you better let me do that talking here," he suggested.

Matt gave him a puzzled look and Eli continued.

"You're a little upset right now and we don't need to ruffle any feathers here. I understand the information you need and I promise you that I will ask the right questions."

Matt had to swallow his pride, but he conceded that Eli was correct. "Okay. Ask away. I just want to find this killer."

Eli continued. "Keep your badge hidden for now."

With a stealthy movement, the Sheriff reached up and removed the piece of metal pinned to his chest and slipped it into his vest pocket while Eli stood in a manner that blocked his movement from the rest of the room.

They approached the bar and when the bartender came over to them, Eli placed his money on the bar. "Two beers please," he requested.

When the mugs were placed before them, Eli spoke again. "Sir, we are looking for the luckiest man alive. Is there a man by the name of Clancy around here by chance?"

The bartender's gaze flitted across the room to a corner table and then he asked, "What do you need him for?"

Eli turned and looked at the man whom the bartender had unwittingly given up. He returned his attention to the man in front of him. "Well sir, I'm feeling really lucky today."

He turned to the table and walked over to the man who was nursing a beer.

"Sir, my name is Eli. I was wondering if I could sit down and talk to you for a moment."

The man motioned toward a chair across the table, but Eli pulled out the one to the man's right instead. The man's pistol was in a holster on that side and if there were any issues, he wanted to control the arm before it came down to gunplay.

Matt in the meanwhile was still at the bar nursing his beer but also keeping an eye on the room.

"I understand that your name is Clancy and that you are the luckiest man around."

A broad smile lit up the man's face. "There are people around here that say that of me."

"Can I buy you another beer?" Eli asked.

"I'll never turn down a free drink." The man declared as Eli flagged over the bartender. When the beer arrived, Eli turned back to the man.

"I heard a rumor that you got one heck of a deal on a couple of horses and a wagon. Is there any chance that you would want to sell them?"

"Two hundred fifty dollars and they are yours." Clancy didn't even blink at the exorbitant price.

"Can I take a look at them?"

"Sure. They're at the stable right now." He quickly drained the beer. "Come on, I'll take you there."

Eli motioned Matt to follow and as they stepped out the door, he introduced him. "Clancy, this is my partner, Matt Wheaton."

"It's a pleasure, sir." Clancy responded.

"So who did you buy this outfit from?" Matt interjected.

"Some lady said she was coming from Missouri headed to California. She told me her husband died on the trail and she just wanted to get rid of the horse and wagons. She just needed enough money to ride the train the rest of the way."

Matt and Eli looked at each other, then Eli continued with the questions.

"I heard you only paid fifty dollars for the entire outfit. Isn't that kind of taking advantage of a widow?"

"I would have paid more for 'em. A lot more. Thing was that she was in an all fired hurry and that was all the cash that I had on me."

By now they had arrived at the stable and together they inspected the animals. Matt checked the brands and nodded to Eli who continued with the negotiations.

"Can we move them out into the sunlight so I can get a better look at everything?" He suggested.

Clancy was more than accommodating, seeing as this pair wanted to buy them for five times what he paid for them. The pair hadn't even tried to bargain him down in price.

Out in the daylight, they inspected the wagon. The tailgate still had a broken board and in the bottom of the wagon, Matt found a large brown stain. Now he began to comb over the interior of the vehicle with a fine tooth comb,

"Hey, what are you doing?" Clancy demanded.

Matt reached into his vest pocket and pulled out his star. He held it up for the man and replied, "The woman's husband did not die on the trail. See this brown stain? That is his blood. He was shot in the head while driving this wagon. So right now, I need to see your bill of sale for this team and wagon."

Suddenly, Clancy did not look like he felt so lucky. In fact the expression on his face reminded Eli of a man who had just lost everything in a poker game.

"The bill of sale is at my ranch," he whined. "We'll have to ride there to get it."

Eli looked at Matt. "I'll get the horses," he volunteered.

He returned in a few moments and Matt turned to Clancy. He reached over and pulled the man's gun from its holster. "I'll hold on to this until we are finished. I wouldn't want you to get any ideas."

Clancy's face showed his displeasure at the turn of events. Matt decided to play his hand out. He pointed over to the preacher and said, "This here is Elijah Exeter, in the flesh. You try anything, and I'll let him take care of you."

Clancy began to look a little green around the gills while Eli threw Matt a look that could have withered a desert rose.

The ride to the ranch was uneventful and they went into the house with the rancher. He retrieved the bill of sale from his desk drawer and handed it to the Sheriff. Matt looked at the signature then handed the document to Eli. Eli glanced at the bottom of the paper, then turned his gaze to his friend.

"It looks like you've been hornswoggled," he said.

The anger on Matt's face was unmistakable. "I bought her act, hook, line and sinker."

The signature on the bottom of the document was that of the Widow Swensen.

CHAPTER TWENTY

Steven addressed the men that surrounded him at the bible study. They were assembled at the unopened bakery, using the chairs and tables where the customers were served. Meanwhile, Elizabeth was busy baking pies, cakes and her locally famous gooey rolls in the back.

"You all know who Jeff Simpson is?" he asked. It seemed every week the number of men increased in the group.

Almost every one of the men present nodded their heads in the affirmative. Steven continued, "I've been working with Jeff here at the bakery and the boy really needs our prayers. His father is an alcoholic, every bit as bad of one as I once was. The result is that he makes Jeff's life a living hell. I'm afraid that if something does not change, Jeff will be headed down the wrong path."

Once or twice a week, in the early morning hour Steven would share a few thoughts from the Bible, then as a group they would spend some time lifting up one another in prayer. Today, they bowed their heads and as they prayed for the town and those around them, they also prayed specifically for young Jeff.

The men started leaving for their respective jobs as soon as the "amen's" were said. Steven poked his head in the back and thanked his boss once again for the use of the facility. He headed out and locked the front door behind him so she would not have any surprise visitors then headed to the livery.

Steven finished his chores at the stable then washed and changed for his job at the bakery. He found himself standing in front of the bakery for the second time this morning, with time to spare. On an impulse, he walked on by and within a couple of minutes he was at the front door of Jeff's house. He walked past the broken down gate and up to the front door. Here he paused, for he had no idea what he was going do or even what he was going to say, but he felt like he had been led here for a reason.

He offered up a silent prayer then knocked on the door. What seemed like an eternity, but was really only a few short moments, the door opened a crack. Mrs. Simpson looked out the partially open door and even the little part that Steven could see of her looked pale and gaunt.

"Can I help you?" Her voice quavered as if she were scared she would get caught talking to him.

"Yes ma'am," Steven replied. He introduced himself then continued. "I was a friend of your husband back in the day and I was wondering if I could talk to him?"

The mousy woman seemed taken aback. "Just a minute." She quickly shut the door behind her, leaving Steven to wonder if he should have come at all.

It was several minutes later that the door opened, this time Hiram Simpson stood there. Even though it was only mid-morning, he had a bottle in his hand and swayed slightly as he stood in his trousers and dirty, stained red union suit. His hair was uncut and uncombed and stood out wildly in every direction. Hiram had not shaved in days and the image that stood before Steven took him back to his own life of not that long ago.

"Hello, Hiram." Steven greeted the man before him.

"Steven!" Hiram seemed genuinely pleased to see him. "Come on in and have a drink with me."

"I'm not drinking liquor anymore," Steven announced.

Hiram's eyes narrowed to slits as he contemplated this revelation.

"No kidding?" he asked.

"No kidding. I came to tell you how God saved me from my destructive drinking."

As the realization of what Steven said sunk in, the look on the other man's face turn surly. "Get out of here," he snarled. "If I wanted your religion, I would have asked you for it. Get out of here," he repeated. The venom in his voice caught Steven off guard.

"Okay, I'm leaving, but if you ever need to talk, I'm willing to listen."

He was cut off before he could say anymore as the larger man stepped toward him, menacingly.

Steven stepped off the porch, not out of fear, but simply because he wanted to be a witness to the man. There was no room for pride in the equation.

He walked away from the house, extremely saddened by the man whom he once called a friend. He realized that their friendship was based upon their mutual need for liquor and not because of any brotherly love. Hiram's slide down that slippery slope may have taken a little longer, but the outcome was certainly no better. Steven's heart was heavy as he walked back the way he'd come.

Much to his surprise, Elizabeth met him at the door. She held out an envelope with suppressed excitement that caused her eyes to sparkle.

"Look what came on the morning stage for you." She declared.

Steven looked at the writing on the outside and immediately recognized the flowing handwriting as that of Evelyn. He had reread her previous letter so many times that he had her beautiful cursive script memorized. He was stunned that she had already sent another letter as he had only sent his reply a few days earlier.

He tore the envelope open and laboriously struggled with the cursive, but Elizabeth's tutelage made it possible for him to get through it. She waited as patiently as she could, but at this point she had a vested interest in this relationship and found it was difficult to contain herself.

Steven looked up from the paper with a stunned look on his face. He held it out to his boss and as she took it, he blurted out, "She's on her way here."

Elizabeth scanned the document and looked up at her right hand man. "Are you ready for this?" she asked.

He let the thought soak in for a few moments then nodded his head. "Yeah, I'm ready." He considered it another moment. With a big smile he added, "Really ready."

CHAPTER TWENTY ONE

Evelyn stood on the train platform, her outward demeanor was calm. Meanwhile, on the inside the anxiety welled up and to quash it she silently prayed. Her father had passed away eight months earlier and had left a number of debts. In order to pay his creditors, she had to sell the house, which barely covered what he owed. Now with very little money in her purse and no place to live, she was leaving St. Louis and headed to the town of Scorpion Wells in Nevada.

Evelyn had a very voluptuous figure, with the kind of curves that made men take a second look. Her hair was a honey brown color, which she wore extremely long. In an era where many women wore their hair piled up high on top of the head, or partially pulled back, Evelyn wore her's down in an attempt to hide the purple birthmark that she had been born with. The port-wine stain covered her lower jaw on the left side of her face and spread back to her neck and under her ear. She could hide a good portion of it with her long hair but a section of it was always exposed. Men might take a second look but interest waned when they saw the disfigurement.

It had been the same story all of her life.

Her father had been her rock. He loved her no matter what she looked like and it was his steadfast love and their faith in Jesus that had carried her through. Like him, she developed a great love for God and she followed her father's example of trusting the Lord for all her needs.

This trip to Nevada was truly an exercise in faith. As she watched the train approaching in the far off distance, she bolstered her resolve.

"Lord, not my will, but Your will be done," she prayed. "Show me the way."

She picked up her valise and left her trunk for the conductor to stow aboard. She showed her ticket to the man and in turn he grabbed the box that contained most of her worldly goods.

Evelyn drew in a long breath then exhaled in a deep sigh. With that she climbed aboard the train and stepped into her new life.

* * *

Matt looked at the door of the house in front of him. Wilfred Youngblood was a successful man, with some sort of connection to the silver mining industry. His large home spoke to his wealth as well as his self-importance in the town. There were no other houses in town that were bigger or nicer than the one Youngblood lived in. He was a man who wanted people to fear him which Matt did not. In spite of that fact, he was not looking forward to this encounter.

He knocked on the door only to have it be opened by the manservant moments later.

"Can I help you sir?" the butler queried.

"I would like to talk to Mr. Youngblood."

"Have you an appointment sir?"

Matt gritted his teeth. The man in front of him knew full well Youngblood's schedule and therefore, he knew that there was no appointment. He quelled his irritation though and answered.

"No, I don't. I was hoping I could have a few moments with him is all."

"Let me see if he is available." The door shut in his face, leaving him standing on the front porch. The sheriff eyed the settee for a brief second but thought better of sitting down on it. Idly he wondered where it had been imported from.

When a significant amount of time had elapsed, so much so that Matt was beginning to wonder if he'd been forgotten, the door opened again.

"This way sir." The man servant began walking through the house, leaving the guest to shut the door and hurry after him. Matt's boots clacked hard on the wooden floor as he took long strides to catch up to the man.

He was ushered into a sitting room where Wilfred was seated behind a large maple desk. He did not bother to look up from a stack of papers he was studying when the Sheriff entered. The butler offered Matt a chair and as he sat down, he realized that the man at the desk had purposefully set up the room so he sat a couple inches higher than anyone else, framed by the large window behind him. Evidently he thought of himself as some sort of a king.

Once the servant left and shut the door behind him, Youngblood looked up impatiently. "I'm a very busy man, so I only have a few minutes," his tone raised the hackle on the back of Matt's neck and forced him to suppress the urge to dive over the desk and wrap his fingers around the man's fat neck. "What do you want?"

Matt breathed a silent prayer before he spoke. "I would like to talk to you about Michelle and Joshua. They are good friends and…"

Youngblood cut him off. "I don't want that killer whelp anywhere near my daughter. Do you understand?" Wilfred spoke with the expectation of immediate compliance.

"That's not up to me." Matt was suddenly calm. "And you really have no say in the matter either."

Wilfred glared at him but before he could interrupt, the Sheriff continued.

"These are two fine young people who have the ability to make their own choices about who their friends are. You can try to keep a tight rein on your daughter, but eventually she will rebel and you'll lose her forever. Meanwhile, you will stunt her ability to mature into the woman she was meant to be."

"I would disinherit her if she ever does anything like that." The venomous look on his face matched his tone.

"Well maybe what is important to you is not important to her. Maybe, just maybe, she would rather pursue friendship and love, instead of money." Amazingly, Matt was able to keep it at an even keel, not allowing his emotion to dictate the conversation.

Wilfred on the other hand had no such compunction.

"She will obey me," he shouted. "You keep that boy away from her, or else."

"Or else what?" Matt's voice suddenly took on a deadly calm and too late, the man across the desk suddenly realized that he had crossed a line.

"Just keep him away from her." Some of the wind was gone from his sails, but he was not going to relent.

Matt stood up and rested his hands on the desk, leaning in toward the man. Involuntarily, Wilfred leaned back in his chair. When the Sheriff finally spoke, the tone was low and menacing.

"I view Joshua as my own son. If anything were to happen to him, anything at all, I'm going to have to assume that you were behind it. I will come back and I will not be wearing this badge." He tapped the tin star. "You better pray that boy of mine doesn't get hurt in any way. If I believe that any wrong was done to him, I will come back and exact my vengeance. I will not wait for the Lord."

He spun on his heel and strode out of the room, leaving the white faced silver baron trembling.

CHAPTER TWENTY TWO

Eli looked up from the book he was studying to see Levi entering the bakery. A large smile crossed his face as he motioned to the young man to join him.

"You're still here," he declared. "I hadn't seen you and thought you and your family had left the area for good. I'm glad to see you."

Levi responded with a grin of his own "It is good to see you as well. We have been checking out this area and the decision has been made to stay here. I've been looking for you and was told you might be here."

"How can I be of service to you?" Eli spoke sincerely.

"We would like to buy a place, somewhere not too far outside of town that is big enough for all of us." The younger man responded.

"My betrothed has a ranch outside of town. She has talked to me about selling it and moving into town. Would you like to talk to her about it?"

Levi nodded. "I would," he replied, "are there any other places for sale?"

"Not that I know of," the Preacher answered, "but I will ask around for you if you'd like."

Elizabeth was headed toward the table holding the coffee pot and another cup. She set the cup on the table in front of the young man and asked, "Would you like some coffee?"

"Yes ma'am," he replied.

As she poured, Eli interjected. "Elizabeth, I would like you to meet Levi Kauffman. Levi, this is my wife to be, Elizabeth Franco."

Elizabeth dipped her head slightly. "It's a pleasure to meet you," she said sweetly.

"Likewise, ma'am."

"Dear," Eli continued, "Levi and his family are looking for a place to buy and I was telling him about your ranch. Are you still considering selling it?"

"Oh my, I am thinking about it, but I honestly don't know what its value is." She responded.

The trio discussed the possibilities with the conclusion that in the morning, Eli would meet Levi and the elders out at the ranch and if the location was to their satisfaction, they would meet and discuss money."

* * *

Matt thoroughly intended to head out to the Swensen spread, but the incident with Wilfred Youngblood left him trembling in anger. He decided to go to the office and calm down before heading out there. Unfortunately, it was not to work out that way. He had people coming in to report this or complain about that and by the time he made his rounds, the sun was sinking in the western sky.

'Tomorrow will be another day.' He told himself as he mounted his horse and headed home for supper.

The ride home seemed extraordinarily long and the headache he was fighting wasn't helping in the least. By the time he rode up to the house, his head was throbbing and he could feel the harsh raspiness in his throat when he attempted to swallow. He dismounted and did something he never had done before. He walked into the house and addressed Joshua.

"I'm sorry, I don't feel well. Would you care for my horse please?"

Becky glanced up from her cooking and took one look at her husband. With sudden urgency, she pushed the pan to the back of the stove and rushed over to him. Reaching up to put her hand on his forehead, she gasped. "You're burning up."

Joshua had not immediately responded when Matt came in but now he stood up and hurried toward the door. "Don't worry about the horse. I'll take care of him." He assured his foster dad as he made his way outside.

Matt began to shake as the chills overtook his body. Becky hustled him into the bedroom and soon had blankets piled on him and a bucket next to the bed. She figured that he would need it sooner than later.

Once she had him settled in, she went back out to the kitchen and resumed cooking. When Joshua came back in from outside, she set a plate in front of him and dished another one for herself.

After they were both seated, she turned to the young man. "Since you're the man of the house tonight, would you pray over the meal, please?"

Joshua stumbled his way through the blessing, not being accustomed to praying aloud. To his credit, he did what was asked of him.

By the time they finished their meal, Becky could hear her poor husband in the other room getting sick. She turned to the young man sharing the table.

"Joshua, I have another favor to ask of you." She was reluctant to make the request, but it needed to be done.

"Yes ma'am?" he responded.

"Would you be willing to ride back into town and notify the mayor that Mr. Wheaton is very ill and won't be making his rounds tonight?"

He nodded seriously, "Yes ma'am, of course." He pushed his chair back from the table and headed straight for the door.

Becky called out, "Let him know that he might not be in for a day or two."

* * *

Eli had finished his work up at the Saloon. Now that Sam was focusing more on the meals that he served and less on selling beer and whiskey, clean up took longer, but Eli found there were fewer issues with the customers. He ended up getting out of there much earlier than he normally would because earlier in the evening he had been approached by the mayor to fill in for the Sheriff while he was sick. Sam released him from his duties, so he would have time to make a quick round of the sleeping town.

He walked along in the warm evening, when the sound of a scuffle reached his ears. He slipped his Colt out of its holster and cautiously moved up to the alley ahead. He paused before rounding the corner, so he could listen carefully. He had no desire to step into another ambush, once was enough.

"…Stay away from her, ya hear." The voice was menacing.

A second voice chimed in. "Yeah, you go near her again and we'll be back and…" He paused mid-sentence when he heard the sound of a pistol hammer being cock next to his ear.

"Up against the wall both of you." Eli reached out and grabbed the shoulder of Joshua's shirt and pulled him back and behind him, out of harm's way. He removed a match from his vest pocket and as it flared up he looked into the face of two young men who were unfamiliar to him.

"What's going on here?" he demanded.

"None of your business." One of the men decided to be brave. It bought him a gun barrel alongside the head and as he crumpled to the ground, Eli turned to the other man with the gun aimed between the eyes.

"I'm not going to ask again." His voice was fraught with danger and it brought a whining response from the man.

"Nothing. " He cowered from the man in front of him. "We was just having some fun."

The pistol dropped swiftly and the bullet struck the dirt between his legs, eliciting a shrill scream from the man.

"Alright, alright," he cried. "We were hired to keep this kid away from the boss's daughter." The scream was reduced to a snivel.

"I have a message for you to take back to the boss." The left handed punch flattened the man's nose and bounce his head off the wall behind him. The second body landed in a heap along the foundation.

Eli turned to the young victim. "Joshua, are you okay?" he asked.

"I think so." Joshua's voice quavered, but somehow he held it together. The boy was not going to cry in front of this man.

"Let's go." Eli stepped out of the alley, but he had not lost any of his caution. As expected, the gunshot brought a mess of town folks running to see what was happening. It never ceased to amaze him that people were drawn to gunshots instead of running away. It lent credence to the old saying, 'curiosity killed the cat.'

He spotted one of the men who sometimes worked as temporary deputies. "Tom, you might want to check those two men in the alley. They may be in need of a bit of doctoring."

Tom just scurried past him into the alley way.

Eli guided Joshua into the light of a nearby window and did a quick check of his injuries. The boy had a contusion on his cheek and there was no doubt he was going to have a shiner on the left eye in the morning. His lip was split and bleeding and there was a good chance he was going to be feeling more pain later on. A lot more pain! Yet Eli was impressed with the young man. He had taken quite a beating by two grown men and still had not given his attackers the satisfaction of seeing him cry.

"Now it's your turn, kid. What happened back there?" he asked.

Joshua spit out some blood into the sandy dirt. "They told me not to see Michelle anymore." He looked up at his rescuer. "Mr. Exeter, we were just friends. I didn't do nothing."

Eli felt emotions well up inside him as he looked at the young man in front of him. A year ago he wanted the boy to leave town, now he only felt compassion for him. He had an idea of what the teenager was going through and was suddenly connected to him in a way he never imagined.

"Joshua, son, I want you to go home and take care of," He hesitated because Joshua was technically not adopted, but he knew how Matt felt about the boy. "Take care of your mom while your dad is sick. I'll take care of this in the morning. I promise."

"Yes, sir. Thank you." Joshua wiped the blood from his lip with the tail of shirt.

"Come on with me. You need to get cleaned up a bit before you go home."

Eli walked him to the parsonage, where Ben doctored the wounds and Naomi took over cleaning up and fussing over the youngster.

Once Joshua was on his way home, Eli located Tom again.

"Do you know who those two were?" he asked. He wanted to verify what Joshua told him.

"I do. They are a couple of handy men that work for Mr. Youngblood." He replied.

Eli nodded. "Thank you. How are they?"

"They'll live." Tom answered. "Parson, I don't think I ever wana cross you. You certainly did a number on them two." He said it with a bit of admiration.

Eli grimace. "I have to admit that seeing them two beating up on that young kid really took me back to my sheriff'in days. I didn't feel much like a preacher in that alley."

Tom quickly responded. "I didn't mean nuttin by it. You done did what needed to be done."

Eli gave him a lopsided grin. "I appreciated that Tom, but it was not my proudest moment. Me and Jesus, we will be having a talk later tonight... Thank God for forgiveness."

Tom nodded his agreement. "Yes sir. Thank God... Goodnight Parson."

"Goodnight."

* * *

Day break found Eli riding out to Elizabeth's spread to meet the elders. Elizabeth had left to go into town hours prior to begin her baking. The Preacher arrived moments before Levi and his clan. He showed them the property and the house. They were impressed with the layout and all of them were in agreement with purchasing the property, if the price was right. Eli promised the group that he would mediate the sale and as they headed back to their camp, he headed back to town. He still had a promise to fulfill to Joshua and he was not going to let him down.

The Preacher rode straight to the Youngblood mansion and dismounted. The incongruity of his appearance did not escape notice. Most preachers did not carry a gun on their hip, but his former life made it a part of his everyday outfit without seeming out of place. At least not to him.

He knocked on the door and was received by the same manservant that had ushered Matt in the previous day. Eventually he was shown to the same study.

"Mr. Youngblood, I'm going to get right to the point." Eli started the ball rolling. Wilfred was a regular on Sunday morning.

"Pastor, what can I help you with?" Mr. Youngblood wanted to keep up his appearances in town and what better way than to receive the pastor of his church?

"Wilfred, I'm embarrassed for you," Eli was not going to pull any punches or try to smooth things over. It was not his style. "In fact, I'm ashamed for you."

"Whatever are you talking about?" Wilfred maintained his outer composure, while his mind tried to determine what the preacher was referring to.

"Last night, I pulled two of your hired guns off a young boy. I think he's a friend of your daughter."

"My daughter doesn't keep company with killers." He spat the words out with vehemence.

"Then why do you go to my church?" Eli demanded.

"What?" Wilfred was startled by the change of direction.

Eli stood up and leaned on the desk, similar to way the Sheriff had done the day before. "I'm a killer. Not a murderer but a killer." Eli proclaimed. "I've killed more men than I care to remember. Not one of them am I proud of, but I was given no choice in the matter, it was kill or be killed. Regardless, I killed them. So I ask you once again, why are you going to my church?"

Youngblood stammered, "But, but you were a Sheriff."

"So what!" Eli slammed his fist on the desk. "What difference does that make? I'm a killer. There's no way around it! Joshua may not have had a badge pinned to his chest, but he killed a man who was a murderer and that man had a poster out on him – Wanted, dead or alive. Did you wish to have Rob Handy stay around this town?"

"No, no. He was a not the kind we need around here."

"Yet you would send your henchmen after a young boy who did the work of a bounty hunter. That young man avenged his father's death by killing a man that you didn't even want around this town. You need to make up your mind. Would you rather have a boy who killed for a justifiable reason, or a man who murdered without rhyme or reason? Well, which one?"

Youngblood looked down at the desk. "Neither," he answered.

Eli glared at him. "That ain't one of the choices." He stated emphatically. "Move back east if you want to live that kind of life. You chose to live out on the frontier and you either learn to accept what is dealt or get out. You can't have both. I don't care how rich you are. There's no way to buy yourself out of this." He tapped the star pinned to his chest. "You're lucky I'm not taking you in for hiring men to beat up a teenage boy." His tone softened. "This morning, I wanted to come to you as your minister. Joshua is not the same young boy that rode into town last year. He has changed. He has been redeemed by the good Lord, just like you and me. My desire is to see you repent, Wilfred, I want to see you do the right thing. That is why you are talking to me and not to Sheriff Wheaton. In fact, you really don't want to see him right now."

He did not bother to mention that Matt was out of commission. Eli was suddenly struck by how much grace and mercy God extends. He could not even imagine how much wrath that his friend would have brought into the equation.

Youngblood had lost all of his bravado. Somehow, the words of the preacher had cut him. They had sliced him all the way to the bone.

"I just want to protect my daughter," he replied weakly.

"Sir, I don't think you need to protect her from Joshua. Let me tell you about that boy. Last night, I pulled your two thugs off of him. He was battered and bleeding, but the young man never cried. His only concern was for your daughter. That boy is a man in every sense of the word. Honestly, I can't think of a nicer young man for her to be with. He is always a gentleman. Please, give him a chance. Get to know him. Don't judge him for one act of passion. He lost his father and avenged that, but inside, he is a stalwart young man." Eli spoke with feeling as he tried to convey his desire to the man in front of him.

With a choked voice, Wilfred replied. "I'll try. I promise, I'll try."

"You're going to have to do more than try. Call off your dogs or my next visit will be as the acting Sheriff and money or no money, you'll be in jail and find yourself in front of a judge."

* * *

Eli rode out to the Wheaton spread to check on Matt and Joshua. It was Becky who met him out on the porch.

"Pastor Exeter, what is going on? What happened to Joshua?" Eli had never seen her this rattled before.

He explained what had transpired the night before and that morning. "I know Matt is feeling poorly and I hope you don't mind that I intervened on your behalf without asking."

Becky looked up into his face, "Feeling poorly is putting it mildly. He was up all night retching. He has nothing left in his stomach to bring up. I keep forcing him to drink water, but it just keeps coming back out. I'm very concerned for him. As for Joshua, he wouldn't tell me what happened to him. It hurts that he feels he has to bear these burdens by himself.

Eli smiled down at her. "He knows he doesn't. I told him I would take care of the situation. He's quite a man, I want you to know."

Becky nodded, "That he is."

Eli changed the subject. "Let's pray for Matt."

Together, they bowed their heads and lifted her husband up to the Lord.

Joshua came from the barn while they were praying. Respectfully, he stood with head bowed until they finished. Eli looked up and saw the bruising and swelling on Joshua's face. "How are you doing?" he asked, the concern evident in his voice.

Joshua tried to smile, but it was too painful and came out as a grimace.

"I'm sore," he admitted. "I skipped school today because I couldn't get my chores all done in time. Mrs. Wheaton had to help me." His look spoke of the shame he felt for needing help.

"Son, we all need help, sometime or other. Someday, it will be your turn to help someone else out." Eli spoke from experience and the boy was well aware of it.

Eli continued, "I don't think you'll have any more trouble from Mr. Youngblood. I actually believe he was remorseful over what he did, but if you have any more problems, you let me know."

CHAPTER TWENTY THREE

It was three days before Matt could even get out of bed and another two before he was able to return to his job. Monday morning, he rode into town and found Eli at the bakery, drinking coffee with Elizabeth.

"Join us." Eli offered.

Elizabeth got up and came back with another cup of coffee for the Sheriff. She refilled Eli's and her own cup before sitting down again.

"I'm sorry to interrupt you two," Matt started. Now he directed his comments to Eli. "But since the town council put you on temporary status, I was wondering if you would be willing to ride out with me to arrest Inga Swensen for the murder of her husband?"

Elizabeth's face registered a look of surprise, but the preacher simply nodded his concurrence.

As Matt had done once before, the men made their approach from the back side of the barn. Knowing everything that they now knew, they were not going to take a chance on getting shot out of the saddle. Together, they approached the house with rifles out, at an angle that made it difficult for any occupant to see them. When they got alongside the door, both of them lay their rifles down against the wall and drew their pistols which were much better suited for close work. On a prearranged signal, Matt pushed the door open and rushed in to the right. Eli, right on his tail, dodged in to the left. It did not take long to discover the house was empty. A thorough search of the property revealed the same of both the out buildings. All the animals were missing. The place had been cleaned out.

They went to retrieve their rifles from the porch so Eli holstered his sidearm. He looked over at his partner, "She must have cleared out as soon as she realized she was a suspect."

Matt had reached the same conclusion. "She's had a week head start on us now. Even if she is trying to drive all them critters, there's no way we can catch up to her."

During the ride back to town they discussed Matt's options for the case.

"I would suggest you get the judge to swear out a warrant and put out some posters. She is a woman by herself and may try to settle not too far away."

"I sent a telegram to the judge a while back." Matt replied. "I'm expecting him any day now. I just need to get my report updated." He hesitated as he contemplated the posters. "I have no idea how to draw and I'm not sure who in town could even do that."

Eli drew on his knowledge of his growing congregation.

"I believe you should talk to Miss Elliot. I've seen her work and I think she could render a more than satisfactory drawing."

They lapsed into silence for the rest of the ride, separating ways so Eli could return to the Saloon and helping out Sam.

Matt began his quest to obtain a warrant and get posters made. The town council was not going to authorize a reward for a murder that happened outside of town, so he needed to wire the territorial Marshall as well.

For his first day back, he had his work cut out for him.

CHAPTER TWENTY FOUR

Evelyn clutched her valise on her lap, holding it close to her chest. What little money she had left was inside a wallet stashed down at the bottom of the bag. For emergencies, she had sewn a twenty dollar gold piece into the lining of her dress. Her life savings totaled just over two hundred dollars and was pretty much all she had left of her old life.

She had never traveled by train before and she had trouble viewing it as an adventure. Instead it caused her much anxiety and it was a whole day before she allowed herself to even begin to relax. Still she was nervous about this mode of travel and spent much of the time reading her Bible and praying. It was all that kept the tremendous stress at bay.

Early morning of the second day, a well-dressed man approached. He swept his hat from his head revealing a cascading mane of brown hair highlighted with silver streaks.

"Ma'am, would you care to join me in the dining car for lunch?"

"Oh thank you," she smiled cautiously. "I brought food with me."

She didn't reveal that she was trying to save the little money she had for living expenses. She didn't have any idea how long it would take to get established and find a job. She didn't know if Steven would take one look at her blemished face and never want to see her again. There was so much that was up in the air. She dare not share any of this with the stranger.

"Ma'am, please, you can save your food for later. I insist," he continued, "it is my treat." He flashed her a broad smile that helped put her at ease. "I'm sorry. Where are my manners? My name is Robert Bouche' and to be honest with you I simply hate to eat alone. I would love the company and conversation, if you are so inclined." He bowed slightly which had the effect of endearing him to the frightened girl.

He held his hand out to her expectantly.

Evelyn had never had anyone so charming pay attention to her, yet here was a handsome older man who was looking right at her birthmark and still wanted to keep company with her. She reached out her hand and let him help her to her feet.

Still holding the valise, she followed him to the car where they were to dine. During the meal, he told her fascinating stories of his travels and asked her about herself. She shared with him the basics of her story without going into great detail. She shared with him her love for Jesus and how He had been her rock throughout all the trials of her life. For the first time since she boarded the train, Evelyn began to relax.

She turned to her companion. "Thank you."

"It is I who should be thanking you. I do not know how I could be so fortunate to find such delightful company on a trip such as this. I just assumed that I would be rubbing elbows with cowboys and the like. Instead, I had the good fortune of meeting you. I hope that you will join me once again for a meal. I assure you that my intentions are honorable. The cost of a meal is certainly a small price to pay for such charming company." Evelyn felt self-conscious over such attention, but she finally had to admit to herself that she was enjoying it.

When the meal was finished, she returned to her seat. The anxiety she felt before melted away as she reveled in the realization that she had found a new friend. She estimated that he was at least twenty years her senior yet he did not seem to be pursuing her as a sexual conquest. Indeed, he was every bit the gentleman and she was grateful for the company.

Dinner was an elegant affair and the conversation was stimulating. Evelyn found herself having fun for the first time in months, maybe years. She felt she was able to open up to this incredible man and did not feel like she was being disrespectful of Steven. As she shared more and more about her situation, he also confided in her and it was during one of those conversations that he revealed that his father had a similar birthmark and Robert did not find it unattractive in any way.

The rest of the trip flew by in an exceedingly short period of time. Robert was there to bid her farewell as she stepped off the train in Scorpion Wells. She said her good byes then collected her case from the baggage car. She had not communicated to Steven when she was to arrive, so there was no one to meet her at the station. She approached the man behind the ticket window.

"Sir, is there a place in town that is safe for a lady to stay?" she asked.

"Yes ma'am. The Silver Strike Hotel is only a short way from here," he replied.

"Is it expensive?" Her thoughts returned to the limited amount of funds in her wallet. Even at a dollar a night, with other living expenses, her money would not last long.

"No ma'am. I believe it is very reasonable. "

"Thank you." She smiled her gratitude.

"You're welcome. Would you like me to have your trunk delivered there?"

"Oh yes, please." Everything was falling into place in an incredibly easy manner.

With that issue resolved she began her trek to the hotel with a new wave of confidence. The man behind the desk at the hotel was pleasant and helpful. She signed the registration book and reached into her valise to retrieve her wallet when he asked for the four dollar which would cover her first week stay.

In an instant, her confidence vanished. Her face turned white with panic and she set her valise on the floor, knelt down and began rummaging through it. It was not there. Her wallet was missing and suddenly she recognized Robert for who he really was. He was not a friend at all. He had gained her confidence only to take from her all that she had.

A sob rose up deep from inside, creating a even greater sense of embarrassment.

"Miss, is there something wrong?" The clerks question brought her to her feet.

"I've been robbed." She sobbed.

The clerk turned to one of the young men loafing around in the lobby. "Sammy, go get the sheriff."

Without a word, the kid ran off lickety split.

Within a few minutes, Matt strode into the lobby.

"I'm Sheriff Wheaton," he began, "Please, tell me what happened."

"There's nothing you can do." Evelyn was doing her best to keep her emotions under control. "He befriended me on the train and took my wallet. There was two hundred dollars in there. It was almost all the money I had."

Matt was practical. "Who is 'he'?" he asked.

"Robert Bouche'," she responded. "He acted like he was my friend. He was nice and charming, but it had to be him. He is the only one who could have taken my wallet.

"Please, tell me what he looked like." Matt pushed.

She described him in great detail and the Sheriff jotted it all down in the tally book he carried for such a purpose.

"I cannot promise you anything," Matt told her, "but I will do what I can."

She dried her tears. "Thank you, sir." She changed the subject. "Do you know Steven Bosco?" she asked.

"Is he a friend of yours?" The Sheriff was suddenly very curious.

"He and I have been writing back and forth and I came here to meet him," she replied.

"So he knows you are here?" Matt asked.

"I wrote to him," she shared. "I don't know if he got my last letter. My circumstances changed and I had come now before I ran out of money." She explained.

"He's a good friend of mine. I am more than happy to let him know that you are here." Matt replied.

"Thank you so much." After all the things she had experienced, it was so good to meet someone who took time to show compassion to her.

* * *

Steven was ecstatic to hear that Evelyn had arrived but was immediately concerned over her present circumstances.

"Matt, what can you do?" he asked.

"I've already wired ahead to the next stop." Matt replied. "Unless he jumps off between here and there, there is a good chance we can grab him. The Sheriff there has his name and description. God willing, we can get this guy."

Steven reached out and put his hand on the shoulder of the sheriff. "Matt, thank you. This is important to me."

Matt grinned. "I've got it. I promise you, I will do everything within my power. Meanwhile, don't you think you ought to get over to the hotel? That poor girl needs a friendly face right about now."

It wasn't until after Steven left that Matt realized he never asked what the woman looked like. Matt was able to gather that this was a relationship consisting of exchanged letters, yet Steven's only concern was for the young lady. It was a revelation to him that the man was truly in love and that he only cared about the welfare of the lady, nothing else. Matt began to wonder if Steven knew of mark on her face and how he was going to react to it.

He thought for a moment of what to do and then made his way to the bakery.

As was often the case, when he wasn't working, Eli was at the bakery studying his bible. It allowed him to be close to his betrothed while he completed the things that he needed to get done. Matt slid into the seat to the side of him. The problem with being the second one to the table left him in a seat that had the lesser vantage point.

"Were you aware that Steven had been writing to a woman from St. Louis?" he asked when Eli looked up from his book. He knew the preacher saw him come in but apparently he wanted to finish reading the portion he was at before disengaging from the tome in front of him.

"I had no clue," came the surprised response. "How do you know this?"

Matt couldn't help but feel a bit satisfied that he knew something his friend did not.

"She arrived in town today on the train. A swindler stole her wallet with all of her money in it," he replied.

Eli glanced down at the table. "You know, I don't feel comfortable gossiping about this," he responded.

Matt shot back with, "I came to you with this not to gossip. I figured this young woman is in trouble and was wondering if there was a way the church could help her out."

Elizabeth had come over with a cup of coffee for the Sheriff and overheard the last part of the conversation. She turned to the man she loved.

"Honey, is there anything we can do for her."

The fact is that Eli excelled in the role of a problem solver and the wheels of his mind immediately began to turn. He pushed his chair back so suddenly that it startled the other two at the table.

"I have an idea," he announced. "I'll be back."

He hurried out the door, leaving Matt and Elizabeth puzzled, shaking their heads.

* * *

The hotel clerk showed Evelyn to a settee in the lobby where she discreetly cut open the hem on her skirt and retrieved her precious remaining coin. With it she paid her weekly rent and after receiving her change, she was shown to her room. Now she wished she had stashed more of her money in her clothing.

While she waited for her trunk to be delivered, she sat down in the single chair and began to pray. As she lifted her sorrow and pain up to the Lord, she felt a sense of peace wash over her.

When the knock came at the door she opened it to collect her box and found a man there but no trunk. Puzzled, she asked, "May I help you?" After all of her adventures she was feeling a bit pensive.

"I hope so," came the sheepish reply. "Are you Miss Evelyn?"

"I am." She suddenly became hopeful. "You're Mr. Bosco, aren't you?"

Steven smiled with a sense of relief. She hadn't slammed the door in his face and in fact, she seemed excited to see him.

She actually towered over the slightly built man by several inches but that didn't matter to her. He had a pleasant face with a mop of light brown hair that was recently slicked down. What struck her most was his shy smile that made her want to give him a hug. Instead, she followed proper etiquette and stepped out of the room closing the door behind her. A lady would never receive a gentleman into her room and as excited as she was to meet him she did not forget her manners.

Her fear of meeting Steven and having him turn and run had not come true. Indeed, he seemed like he was scared that she might not like him.

Awkwardly, they stood in the hall, neither of them knowing what to say. It was Evelyn who broke the silence.

"Is there a proper place we can go to talk?" she asked. "There is so much I want to know about you."

Steven's shyness began to evaporate, "I have the perfect place," he replied.

He offered her his arm and she placed her gloved hand in the crook of his elbow and allowed him to guide her down the stairs. As a couple, they walked the boardwalk to Elizabeth's café and throughout the journey heads turned to look at the couple. Some looked to see who this new woman in town was but mostly they were looking at Steven. The once town drunk now had a woman on his arm and a smile on his face that was amazing to see. It had been years since anyone saw Steven with a woman and it was causing quite a stir with the town folks.

Evelyn was suddenly struck by the realization the Steven was in no way trying to hide the fact that she was with him. It seemed to her that he was proud that she was on his arm and wanted to show the whole town. The revelation that her birthmark did not phase the man one bit, but that he wanted to be with her made her heart glow. The letters they had exchanged may have been few, but they were full of intimate details and the payoff was this man who accepted her as she was.

When they walked through the door of the bakery, it took only a moment for the proprietor to rush over and take her by the hands.

"You must be Evelyn." Her eyes sparkled with excitement. "I'm Elizabeth. Welcome to my place."

Evelyn was taken aback by the unabashed friendliness of the people here.

"Miss Elizabeth, thank you." Evelyn felt a tear starting to well up.

"My dear, you just call me Elizabeth. You two follow me." She led them to the same corner table that she and Eli shared when Jeff shot out the window above them. Even as Elizabeth seat them, she realized that whole incident seemed like it happened ages ago.

Evelyn opted for a cup of coffee, still thinking of her shrinking wealth. She was not willing to burden Steven with her plight, unbeknownst to her that Matt had already filled him in.

"Are you sure you don't want anything to eat?" Elizabeth queried. "I have some ham and cheese in the back. I would be glad to make you both sandwiches." The shop owner was bound and determined to make sure this budding romance had every chance to make it.

Steven had hardly said a word now looked at his employer with gratefulness. "Thank you that would be wonderful."

Evelyn tried to protest, but the kindness of the two people soon quashed any objections. She was hungry. Breakfast was long ago and in all the ensuing excitement she had not realized how desperately hungry she really was.

After the makeshift meal was finished the two sat and talked for hours on end. Steven shared with her in detail his slide into alcoholism and how he lost his job as a horse wrangler. He held nothing back as he told her of his miraculous healing and accepting Jesus as his Savior. He explained how after being forgiven of so much, he dedicated the rest of his life to serving the Lord and how he was seeking a wife that would walk by his side in that endeavor.

So engrossed in the conversation were the two that Steven did not even realize that he was supposed to be working. Elizabeth for her part did nothing to remind him. She allowed them their privacy to just talk.

Evelyn shared with Steven the heartache of growing up in the big city and being teased mercilessly over the mark that marred her appearance. She told of the hurt felt by a young girl who was never invited to the dances or courted by young suitors. Instead she believed that she was going to grow up to be an old spinster.

She was so comfortable with the man seated with her that she pulled her hair back at one point and allowed him to see the mark that had plagued her all of her life. The deep red stain that had caused her to believe all of her life that she was ugly.

It was then that Steven reached across the table and took her hands in his own.

"That is nothing," he began. "My deepest, darkest scars are in here." He tapped his chest with his finger. Reaching back out, he returned to holding her hand. "Miss Evelyn, there is no doubt in my mind that you are the woman that I have been looking for ever since God gave me a second chance at life. I would be honored if you would be my wife."

Evelyn's long pause caused panic to well up inside of Steven causing him to pull his hands away. Afraid he'd moved too fast he was suddenly in fear of losing her.

"I'm sorry," he sputtered. "That was too soon, wasn't it?"

"No," Evelyn smiled, taking his hands in her own. "There is nothing wrong with your timing. I'm sorry I didn't answer right away. I needed to make sure that I was not saying yes simply because of my circumstances." She squeezed his hands. "Steven, I would be honored to be your wife and to share the rest of our lives together. I want to serve the Lord alongside of you for all the remainders of our days."

The commitment was so complete there was no doubt in either of their minds that this was where the Lord was leading them.

* * *

Inga Swensen headed south. She had anticipated escape and even planned for it but had been hoping that by reporting her husband missing she would have misdirected the investigation, but it was obvious the Sheriff began to suspect her. As soon as she ran him out of the barn, she began to put her exit plan into play.

Out on the trail, the real trials began. She found it was difficult to herd all the animals, even with the help of her dog. She needed as much distance between her and Scorpion Wells as possible and found to do that she soon had to leave some of the stragglers behind. She began to push those animal that she had left, far too hard for the climate. The creatures began to experience fatigue, some almost to the point of exhaustion.

She had grown up in a position of privilege and had always had servants to care for her horses. She really knew very little of animal husbandry, for others had always been at her beck and call. After she were married Inga depended upon her husband to care for the horses, cows and pigs while she took care of the house.

When she decided to defy her parents and run off with her beau, she was sure that they could live on nothing but love. Time, along with the difficult life that followed had succeeded in quenching the flames of romance. Inga had not realized the life of privilege that she was leaving behind until it was too late. When she finally recognized what she had left behind, what she no longer had, it made her hard and bitter. Norris was a hardworking man and most pioneer women would have felt lucky to have married him. Hardworking, handsome and loyal, or so she thought until she discovered that he was seeing *that tramp*.

She was no fool. Inga knew very well how long the trip to town should take. And then one day he came home, bruised and battered. Norris would never tell her what happened and this raised her ire. Shortly after that she detected the scent of another woman on his clothing. It was then that she decided to find out what he was really up to. The shunned wife chose to follow him on one of his forays into town to see for herself. Dressed in some of Norris' old clothing that she had tailored to fit her, Inga followed her man to town. What she discovered was enough to put her on the path to vengeance. Now she had exacted her revenge and it was time to find a new life.

Four days into the trip, she made her turn toward the west and her ultimate destination of California. She had heard stories of the fertile valley and miles upon miles of orange groves. Unbeknownst to her thirty miles away, between her and her dream lay the edge of one of the hottest places on earth. Death Valley was aptly named, for anyone who tried to travel without enough water and was not well versed in the ways of the desert, was destined to die. Even with enough water, traveling in the daytime will kill you. Drinking water that has been warmed by the sun will not cool the body and the intense heat can cook a person to death, water or not. The barrels of water that she was carrying had been heating up for the last several days. Inga recognized none of this as she turned the team toward this virtual hell. She was acclimated to the high desert climate, but this portion of the desert was an entirely different beast. So in deadly ignorance, she rode on.

The small caravan began their decent into the inferno while in the deceptive cool of the morning on the sixth day. The chill of the desert made for quick traveling but even with the reduced herd the entourage was not traveling fast enough to suit their master and she was in a frenzy to get them moving. She had no idea that there was no pursuit because the Sheriff was so seriously ill. All she knew was that she needed miles between her and the long arm of the law from Scorpion Wells, so she pushed. She continued her frantic rush down into the valley.

As the sun rose in the sky, so did the temperature, until the scorching orb beat down upon them. The sand reflected the heat up until the thermometer hit 118° degrees and it was still climbing, but Inga didn't notice. It was not because of her intense focus on her escape, but because she was too hot to understand what was happening. Her dark travelling clothes absorbed the heat and even though she drank the heated water from her supply, it didn't help. As the heat sickness over took her she failed to notice the cows dropping off one by one to just stand by the trail, tongues lolling until they collapsed and died. When one of the horses stumbled and went down in a tangle of harness, she could not comprehend what was happening at first. When the problem finally registered in her heat addled brain the exhausted woman succeeded in climbing down from the wagon but moved as if in a trance. Somehow she got the harness cut loose from the dead horse and then cut the other horse out as well but the exertion added to her confusion. She could feel the burning sand through her shoes, her feet were excruciatingly hot, but she had no energy to get up on the horse. It came as a foggy realization that the dog was gone and she did not have any idea where he went or when he had left her.

Dumbfounded by the heat she turned and began walking deeper into the desert. She had passed the point of no return long ago. She did not know it, but she was dying and at this point she was unable to recognize that she had lost the will to keep living.

She stumbled on without motivation. She was simply walking without purpose because she did not know what else to do.

Had she found shade early in the day for herself and the animals and only traveled after the sun went down, she might have survived. But she did not know that then and now she did not care.

She tripped, pitching forward face first in the blistering hot sand which instantly scorched the skin on her face and hands but by now she was beyond feeling pain. Blackness washed over her and death came quickly, finally releasing her from the torture that she endured for the last hours of her life into another kind of torture. It was an eternal torture as her soul was swept away to the very depth of hell just as the sun began to set over the desert.

CHAPTER TWENTY FIVE

Eli had made some progress in finding a solution for Evelyn's current predicament. Mary and Susan were two women who had been Saloon Girls, but they had given their lives to Jesus and had left their old life behind. Now they ran a small dress and milliner shop in town. They lived in an old house where they designed and sewed dresses and made women's hats. They themselves acknowledged that God had blessed them tremendously and their business was busting at the seams. The two women were willing to take on an apprentice in return for room and board.

Unfortunately, it was time for the Preacher's shift at the Saloon, so he did not have time to share his findings with anyone. Instead, still preoccupied with the Evelyn's plight, he donned his apron and began serving food and drinks.

He spied a familiar figure at a table near the wall and walked over to greet "Molasses" Mike.

"How's the steak?" Eli grinned at the gravy stain on the front of his shirt. The man did like his food.

Mike stopped with the fork halfway to his mouth. If there was anything he liked more than eating, it was talking.

"You know Sam makes the best grub in this here town," he replied. "It's worth spending some hard earned money fer."

"Glad you're enjoying it. Can I get you…"his sentence was cut off by a disturbance at the bar.

Eli spun on his heel to see two cowhands squaring off to fight. He was already moving as one cocked his fist back. Grabbing the man by the shoulder, he pulled back which spun him around. The cowboy staggered back, already off balance by the whiskey he'd imbibed causing him to fall to the floor.

The second man held his hands up indicating surrender as he swayed in his intoxicated state.

"Out!" There was no room for arguing.

"Okay, okay," the vaquero slurred. "I juss wana finish my drink."

"No." Eli spoke with finality. "You're done for the night. You can come back again when you're sober."

He took a step toward the man which caused him to turn and flee from the room.

He watched him long enough to make sure he was really on his way out and only then did Eli start to turn toward the aggressor. He expected the man to still be on the floor but as he moved, he caught sight of a raised whiskey bottle out of the corner of his eye. He raised his left arm to shield the blow as he tried to duck out of the way.

The roar of a gunshot along with the sound of glass breaking shattered the air. Instinctively, Eli reached for his own pistol, but there was no need. The confused and drunken cowboy stood there stunned, his hand bleeding from the broken bottle.

Glancing around the room on high alert, Eli spotted the source of the shot. Mike, still seated in his chair was holding a smoking pistol in his right hand while his left hand held a forkful of mashed potatoes, dripping with gravy.

Now that he knew the source of the shot and while the cowboy was still in a daze, Eli grabbed him by the back of the shirt and his belt. Together they hit the batwing doors at nearly a run with the bartender using the cowboy's head as ram. When they crossed the boardwalk, Eli skidded to a halt at the same time launching the other man out into the dirt road. He hit the ground with a thud, too drunk to reach out his hands to stop his face from plowing into the sand. He lay there in the dirt for a minute before staggering to his feet and weaving down the road toward another of the many saloons in town, the incident already a dim memory in his mind.

Eli returned inside and walked to the table where his benefactor was seated.

"Mike, thank you. You saved me from an awful headache," he acknowledged.

"Well, what else could I do?" the old man replied. "I'm still thirsty and who's going to bring me another beer."

Eli returned with a mug full of the frosty beverage.

"Sir," he addressed Mike, "this one is on me."

CHAPTER TWENTY SIX

Matt was seated with Judge Middleton, both men had cups of coffee in front of them as they discussed the business before them.

"How does the boy feel about you adopting him," the judge asked.

Matt shrugged. "We have not brought it up to him," he replied. "We decided to see what the legal issues were before we asked him. I...we don' want to get his hopes up if it were not possible."

The judged nodded his understanding. "As long as he has no relatives who object to the adoption, I think we can make it happen in short order. First things first, we need to see if Joshua wants this."

"Thank you, Judge," the Sheriff answered. "Becky and I will speak to him about it tonight."

They engaged in casual conversation as they finished their coffee. Matt finally drained his cup and stood up. He held up the paper in his hand.

"Thank you for signing the warrant. Miss Elliot has finished up the drawing and it is a fantastic likeness of Mrs. Swensen."

"Good job on the investigation," came the Judges reply. "You will have no problems with the prosecution of this case... that is if we can ever find her."

Matt left the café and Elizabeth came to the Judge's table with the coffee pot. "Can I refill your cup for you?" she asked.

"Thank you," he replied. "If you don't mind, I would love one of those sticky buns in the case."

"Of course." The sticky buns were a favorite in the community so she made an effort to make enough to satisfy the town's collective sweet tooth.

The Judge had just started on the tempting treat when the door opened. He looked up to see the Preacher coming through the door. Eli made his way toward the table and Judge Middleton stood up and reached out his hand.

"Judge, it's a pleasure to see you again." Eli and the Judge both shared a passion of reaching the lost for Jesus. They recognized it was the only way that people were going to change.

"I am so glad to see you again."

"May I join you?" Eli queried.

"Of course," came the reply.

As they drank coffee together they caught up on all the things that had gone on since the last time they had seen each other.

"I hear that congratulations are in order," the Judge smiled. "I understand that you and the Widow Franco are getting married. Let me tell you, she is a magician in the kitchen. You are a lucky man."

"She is at that," Eli laughed. "But I tend to think of myself as a blessed man, not a lucky one and it is for so many more reasons than just her skill in the kitchen. She is an incredible woman who loves the Lord as much or more than I do. She is kind and considerate and almost always thinks of others before herself. In fact, she is one of the reasons that I hunted you down."

In hushed tones, the men conversed so the other patrons could not hear what was being said. When the two men had come to an agreement, the judge pulled out his pocket watch and checked the time.

"Oh my, is it really that late?" he exclaimed. "I need to get going."

He laid a coin on the table and shook hands with the preacher before heading to the door.

By now the café' had emptied out so Eli stepped behind the counter where his bride to be was cleaning. He took her in his arms and wrapped her in a hug.

Without warning the door slammed open and Jeff came running inside. He looked frantically around.

The Preacher was the first to respond to the interruption. "Jeff, what's the matter?"

Out of breath, the boy wheezed, "Steven…where is he?"

Eli turned to Elizabeth with a questioning look.

She answered the boy's inquiry, "He's picking up supplies. Jeff, what's going on?"

"It's my pa!" The young man was in a panic. "He,s hurting ma."

"Stay here," Eli commanded Elizabeth. He grabbed Jeff by the shoulder. "Let's go. Is he at your house?"

Jeff just nodded. Together they took off, but the older man did not wait for the youngster. Eli entered the house a full twenty yards ahead of the boy and the sight that greeted him stopped him in his tracks.

Jeff's mother was seated on an old dilapidated couch. The portion of her face that was visible was bruised and swollen. Her lip was split and blood was running from her nose and one ear. There was also blood streaming from a wound on her scalp underneath the hair, covering much of her face.

Eli was numb with shock. The woman seat in front of him brought back the memory of a prize fight he once witnessed where the two pugilists had fought nineteen rounds and both men were as battered as the lady before him. She was sobbing uncontrollably into a dirty dish towel. Lying face down on the ground near her feet was her husband. Visible on his upturned face was a large gash on his forehead and blood was still pooling around him.

Eli turned and stopped Jeff as he was coming through the door shielding the boy as much as he could from the sight. "Get Doc Mercer right now," he ordered.

Jeff obeyed immediately. In his world, a question would have been answered with a blow to the face, so it did not even register to ask why.

As soon as the young man disappeared out the door, Eli turned back to the still form on the floor. He searched for a pulse in the wrist but none was present. There was no rise or fall of the upper torso and he could not detect any air coming out of the nose or mouth.

He turned to the crying woman. "What happen?" he demanded.

She did not answer. Instead, she held the cloth to her face and let out a shrill scream into it.

The door burst open and Matt rushed in.

"Eli, what in the world? What's going on?"

Eli shook his head, "I don't really know. He's dead." He had seen enough bodies in his career to feel confident in his assessment of the man's condition.

Matt nodded. He trusted Eli so he simply stepped around the body and sat down on the couch. He placed a gentle hand on her shoulder and addressed the still sobbing woman.

"We need to get you calmed down so you can tell us what just happened," he said softly. "I'd like you to take a slow breath and then let it out slowly."

He demonstrated with his own breathing the very thing he was requesting.

She tried to comply but her breath came in and went out as a shudder. She tried again, with the same result. On her third attempt she succeeded in drawing a bit smoother breath. Each successive breath came more easily and less fractured until she accomplished what he requested. His calm demeanor conveyed to her that it was finally going to be alright.

Several minutes went by before the poor woman was able to form words.

"He, he, he felled and hit his head on the table." She stammered.

Eli looked at the indicated furniture and located a piece of skin and a trace of blood on the corner closest to the body. He turned to Matt and nodded.

The Sheriff took the cue and gently prodded. "How did he come to hit the table?" He repeated the words that she had used so she would know he was listening.

The flood gates opened. Still crying, she filled in her visitors. "He done be drinkin' whiskey all mornin'. I gived him an egg fer his breakfast, but he tolt me I didn't cook it proper. He done hit me across the face, agin and agin. I don't know how many times he hit me. When he rared back agin, I moved and he done fell on thet there table."

The words were punctuated by sobs, but Matt was able to get the gist of her story.

Eli heard enough. He exited the door in time to meet Doc Mercer. "I don't think there's anything you can do for him." He spoke quietly so the boy coming up from behind could not hear. He stepped aside and caught the boy before he could follow the doctor inside.

"Jeff, I need you to come with me." Eli was surprised that the boy did not question him, but again, it never went well for the young man when he did. As they headed back toward the café, Jeff kept glancing back over his shoulder, but he did as he was told.

By now, Steven was back from his errands and Eli pulled him aside, quickly explaining what had transpired just down the road.

Steven turned to the boy, who was seated at one of the tables. People were beginning to trickle in for the afternoon rush.

He slid into the chair next to his young co-worker. "Jeff, your pa got hurt and the doctor is there checking him out." His heart went out to the boy. He did not want to tell the kid his father was dead unless he knew for sure. He did not doubt Eli, but he would wait for the doctor's final call on this.

Eli started back, only to meet the Sheriff halfway.

"Eli, doc says he busted his skull and was dead before he hit the floor. He's there with the missus, tending her wounds and praying with her of all things. Who'd of thunk it?" Matt shook his head with wonder. "Would you mind coming with me to talk to Jeff?" he asked.

Soberly, Eli nodded. He was concerned how the boy would take it. "Yeah, he's at the bakery with Steven right now."

The men slid into the remaining two chairs at the table and Jeff looked at both their faces.

"He's dead, ain't he?" Though phrased as a question, the look in the boy's eyes made it more of a statement. He knew the answer before he ever asked the question.

"I'm afraid so." Eli had never found a good way to tell someone that a loved one had died, maybe because there is no good way. He'd discovered that he just needed to be there for them for the aftermath. To listen, to give a hug, to pray or whatever else that person needed in the moment as they processed their grief or disbelief. You never know how someone will react. He simply was not prepared for Jeff's response.

"Good. Now my momma ain't gonna get hurt no more." There was no emotion upon the young man's face. He turned to Steven, "You could be my pa." For the moment there was hope in the boy's eye.

"Jeff, I will always be your friend and I will always be there to listen to you and to help you out, as long as you and your ma live here." He wanted to break the news gently, but he didn't know how. "I'm getting married."

The crestfallen look on the boy's countenance was the first sign of real emotion that he had shown throughout the exchange.

Jeff turned back toward the Sheriff. "Is my ma gonna be okay?" He asked.

Matt nodded. "Yes son. She's hurt pretty bad, but the doctor is caring for her right now."

Steven continued, "Jeff, now you are the man of the house and it is your job to help take care of your mother. I will be around to show you how to do that right. I want to see you grow up into the man that your pa was never able to be."

"You will?" Jeff was suddenly hopeful.

Steven smiled at him, "Of course I will."

Surprisingly, it was Jeff who changed the subject.

"Mr. Bosco, who ya marryin'?"

"I am going to marry a beautiful young lady named Evelyn." Steven replied. "I've been writing to her and she came here so we could be wed."

Eli and Matt glanced at each other over the description of his intended. Matt didn't know what to think. Eli on the other hand, was ecstatic that Steven could see the beauty of the woman and not the blemish that had plagued her all of her life. Eli could not have been more proud of his younger friend, who sought out that which was really important.

Steven turned to his young charge. "Now that you are the man of the house, you call me Steven." He said. "We work together, you and I and we ain't any different from one another."

"Yes sir." Jeff was enthusiastic in his response.

Suddenly the boy pushed back from the table without a word. The three men swiveled their heads as they watched to see what he was going to do.

Elizabeth had given the men their privacy, having a good idea of what was going on. Jeff marched across the room, straight to the proprietor of the café.

"Miss Elizabeth," he began, "Since I'm the man of the house," mimicking the words Steven had used, "I was wonderin' if I could work more fer ya. I need to make money to help out my ma."

Elizabeth gave the bewildered boy a big hug. She squatted down so she was more on his level.

Her eyes glisten as she replied, "Jeff, I will give you as much work as you can handle, on one condition."

"Yes ma'am. What?" he queried.

"You have to go to school every day. You will need to come straight here and do your homework and then and only then will you be allowed to work. Am I being clear?" She tried to give him a stern look, but the boy wasn't fooled. Even though he knew she meant what she said, he had also experienced the abundant kindness that helped shape who she was.

"Yes ma'am. School. Homework. Work. Got it." He responded, then spoke as an afterthought. "I'm gonna take Rock home with me now."

Elizabeth smiled. Her gentle spirit would not allow her remain stern with the boy.

"Yes, I suppose you will."

CHAPTER TWENTY SEVEN

Eli stood at the front of the church. He had Steven up on the raised platform with him along with Judge Middleton.

Gazing out across the congregation, it appeared that everyone in town had showed up. People were stuffed into the pews in such a way that the already stuffy building was almost unbearable. All the doors were open to let the slight breeze through and every window that could be opened was flung wide. Those who were not able to find seats were standing in every conceivable nook and cranny, leaving only the main isle way open.

Other than the occasional traveling show, there was not a lot of entertainment in town and so no one was going to miss this.

Ben and Naomi, holding young Elijah were in the front row. Matt, Becky and Joshua were behind them in the second row. Seated next to Joshua was Michelle while two pews back behind them sat her father and mother.

Eli smiled as he looked down and saw that. It appeared that Wilfred Youngblood had taken their talk to heart and capitulated about the boy. The fact that Matt had not beat the man within an inch of his life could be attributed to the fact that Joshua had never told him what really happened while his soon to be adopted father lay sick in bed. By the time Matt felt well enough to get out of bed, the bruising had all but disappeared and the boy had been able to down play what had occurred.

Eli was encouraged by the maturity the boy had shown in the handling of the situation. He was already quite a young man and with the tutelage of Matt and Becky, he was going to be able to accomplish great things by the time he was old enough to leave home.

Scanning once again as they waited to begin, Steven saw Jeff standing in the back. He was wearing his Sunday best, which were threadbare and worn, with patches sewn on. The boy's hair had been slicked down in an attempt to manage the unruly locks, but even at that there were stray wisps that could not be tamed. When their eyes met, Jeff began waving wildly at his best buddy. Nervous though he was, Steven could not help but smile, in fact the boy's enthusiasm nearly made him laugh. He gave the boy a wink.

All at once, the pianist began to play the wedding march and as if by magic, Elizabeth and Evelyn were standing at the back of the church. Together they began the slow walk toward the front.

Eli could not take his eyes off his bride, dressed in a pale lavender gown made of taffeta that accented her olive complexion and set off her black hair and dark eyes. The bodice hugged her trim figure and the high neck line complemented her long neck. Juliet style sleeves finished off the upper portion of the ensemble. Her skirt gently flared and the hemline barely brushed the ground. He had no way of knowing that she had begun working on the dress shortly after he had saved her on the street that day. Even then, if anyone had thought to ask her, she knew she was going to marry this man.

In the same token, Steven only had eyes for his wife to be. She had on a beautiful white cotton dress that she had sewn in the previous week, with the help of Susan and Mary. Fit for a bride's first trip down the aisle, the modest neckline dipped down slightly and it was outfitted with Bishop styled sleeves. An ample train flowed behind. She wore a small silk hat atop of her head which the veil was attached to. She no longer tried to hide the mark that had plagued her all of her life. Her beau's acceptance of her just as she is gave her a confidence she'd never possessed before.

Everyone stood as the song began to play and all eyes in the church were focused on them as they floated down the aisle together. It had been Elizabeth's idea to have a double wedding and Evelyn was grateful for the suggestion, for she had few acquaintances in town. Through Eli's and Elizabeth's graceful offer, she was able to have the big wedding she'd always dreamed of.

Neither of the brides had a father who was alive to give them away so when they reached the front of the church, the two grooms stepped down to take the arm of their betrothed. Judge Middleton stood nervously alone on the platform. His own wife had arrived on the morning stage and she was seated on the opposite side of the aisle from the Wheaton's. The Judge looked down and smiled at her, feeling encouraged by her presence here today.

He looked out over the sea of faces and cleared his throat.

"For those of you who have the option, please be seated." The Judge began.

"Folks," he continued, "I am not a preacher so don't expect any long sermons out of me, but I do have a word for these two couples who are before us."

"Eli, Steven the main thing that I want to say to you is straight from God's Holy Word. In Ephesians chapter five it says 'Husband, love your wives, even as Christ also loved the church, and gave himself for it.'"

He looked up from the Bible in his hand. "Men, let's consider how Christ loved the church? First and foremost, He put our best interest ahead of His own. He could have stayed up in heaven with God the Father, looked down on earth and said something like, 'Them poor little fools down there. It's a crying shame they had to go and mess things up like they did.' He could have done that and it would have served us right." He set the Bible down on the podium in front of him and continued. "But He didn't. Instead, He left the glory of heaven and became humbled as a man. He lived, breathed and slept alongside of the very men that he created. He taught and demonstrated how God wants us to live, always putting us, mankind, ahead of himself. Then finally, He died in our place, taking our sins upon Himself."

"Gentlemen," now he was addressing all of the men in attendance, "this is how we are to love our wives. Always looking out for their needs before we even think of our own. We are to love them so much that we would be willing to lay our lives down for them. Think of it this way, if your wife was out in the street and a stampede of cattle was rushing toward her, are you willing to push her out of harm's way and be trampled by the herd instead of her? That is basically what you as a husband is called to do."

He switched his attention to the brides.

"Ladies, in the same chapter we are told that you are to 'submit yourself unto your husband, as unto the Lord.' Submitting does not mean that you do not have a say in your household, but that you recognize that your husband has the final say."

He turned back toward the men, "Before you start to gloat about that, remember your role. It will be easy for your wives to submit to you if you are loving her the way you are supposed to. As the leaders of your household, you set the tone for your marriage. Men if you do things right, there will be peace and harmony under your roof. If you are selfish, you can expect plenty of discord. The main burden rests upon your shoulders."

"Eli, Steven, would you turn and take the hands of your bride please," he commanded.

"Elijah Exeter, do you take Elizabeth Franco to be your lawful, wedded wife, to have and to hold, for richer or for poorer, in sickness and in health, till death do you part?" he asked.

Eli looked deeply into the eyes of his loved one and felt a thrill go through his body as he answered, "I do."

The Judge asked Elizabeth the same question.

Her eyes misted with tears of joy as she replied, "I do."

The Judge turned to Steven and repeated the vow.

Steven stared in awe at the woman whom he had fallen so quickly and deeply in love with. "I do." He managed to choke the words out, thoroughly overcome by the moment.

Finally the Judge turned to Evelyn, repeating the vow in a question to which she answered, "I do."

After they exchanged the rings, the judge looked at them and said, "Gentlemen, you may kiss your bride."

Finally, the moment that he had waited so long for had arrived. Eli leaned forward and as he took her in his arms and crushed his lips to her, he felt intoxicated with her scent, her feel…with her.

"Whoop, whoop." One of the cowboys in the back started the shouts which were followed by cheers and whistles. The whole place erupted in pandemonium as everyone joined in the celebration.

When the noise finally died down and the blushing grooms stood there looking kind of foolish, the Judge continued on.

"By the power vested in me by the State of Nevada and in the presence of God and all of these witnesses," he announced, "I now pronounce you husbands and wives."

EPILOGUE

Eli had his arm around the shoulder of Elizabeth, his wife of just five short weeks. He held her close to his side as he choked back the sorrow that well up and nearly overcame him. Together they watched the wagon rumble away holding his son, their daughter-in-law and grandson. Elizabeth was not successful in holding back and tears streamed down her face, for even though they were only a few hundred feet down the road, she already missed her new family. It was painful to watch them leave after all the wonderful time that they had shared in the last couple of months. But by far, the hardest part was not knowing if they would ever have the opportunity to see each other again.

Oregon may be only a couple of hundred miles away, but that distance might just as well be a different country. Danger and uncertainty lay ahead for the young family as they rode toward their destiny. But Eli, of all people, understood the need to follow your calling, for it is only in obedience to God that one can be truly fulfilled.

For now, his own destiny was right here, in Scorpion Wells with his new wife by his side. With one final wave to the retreating wagon, he turned and took Elizabeth in his arms holding her close and comforting her in their shared sorrow. As the sun rose, they looked forward to the next chapter in their life together, a chapter which they had no doubt was ordained by the hand of God.

Thank you to my readers. I am so grateful to all of you and I would like to hear from you. I am including my email address and I would like to hear your comments, good and bad. I will try to respond to them as I can.

Please send your comments to exeterseries@gmail.com.

God bless you and I hope you are looking forward to the next installment as much as I am looking forward to finishing it.

Gary Jon Anderson has been married to his wife, Larena, for over three and a half decades. Together they have three adult children, one granddaughter, two step grandchildren and a step great grandson. Recently retired from full time police work after 33 years, he plans to spend more time writing in this phase of life.

Made in the USA
Middletown, DE
30 June 2019